A Sophie Kimball Mystery

Broad
4 Murder

**Turn on, tune in,
drop dead . . .**

J.C. Eaton

KENSINGTON
U.S. $8.99
CAN $11.99

Don't Miss the Previous
Sophie Kimball Mysteries!

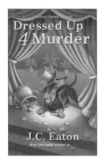

EAN

ISBN-13: 978-1-4967-2456-4
ISBN-10: 1-4967-2456-9

Also by J.C. Eaton

The Sophie Kimball Mysteries
Broadcast 4 Murder
Dressed Up 4 Murder
Molded 4 Murder
Botched 4 Murder
Staged 4 Murder
Ditched 4 Murder
Booked 4 Murder

The Wine Trail Mysteries
Sauvigone for Good
Pinot Red or Dead?
Chardonnayed to Rest
A Riesling to Die

Broadcast
4 Murder

J.C. Eaton

KENSINGTON BOOKS
www.kensingtonbooks.com

KENSINGTON BOOKS are published by

Kensington Publishing Corp.
119 West 40th Street
New York, NY 10018

All Kensington titles, imprints, and distributed lines are available at special quantity discounts for bulk purchases for sales promotion, premiums, fund-raising, educational, or institutional use.

Special book excerpts or customized printings can also be created to fit specific needs. For details, write or phone the office of the Kensington Sales Manager: Attn.: Sales Department. Kensington Publishing Corp., 119 West 40th Street, New York, NY 10018. Phone: 1-800-221-2647.

Kensington and the K logo Reg. U.S. Pat. & TM Off.

First Printing: November 2020
ISBN-13: 978-1-4967-2456-4
ISBN-10: 1-4967-2456-9

ISBN-13: 978-1-4967-2459-5 (ebook)
ISBN-10: 1-4967-2459-3 (ebook)

10 9 8 7 6 5 4 3 2 1

Printed in the United States of America

*For the KSCW-LP 103.1 radio station and the Sun City West Broadcast Club
Keep those tunes and chatter coming!*

ACKNOWLEDGMENTS

We're always on the lookout for new staging grounds for murder, so when KSCW's Keith Fowler suggested using Sun City West's radio station, we were literally "all ears." We thank Keith, along with George Kuchtyak, Jr. and Chuck Mulcahy for giving us a behind-the-scenes look at local broadcasting.

And to Paul Hiler, whose lake fishing photos and late evening anecdotes in the dog park inspired us to create a fictitious fishing aficionado, we are eternally grateful. To the late Brandy Smidt and her little Chiweenie, Johnny, we thank you for helping bring Streetman to life and joy to the four-legged kids in the park.

Of course none of this would be possible without our incredible team of readers and techies. A tremendous thanks to Larry Finkelstein, Pam Grumbles, Gale Leach, Susan Morrow, and Susan Schwartz from "Down Under."

Not a day goes by that we don't appreciate the efforts and dedication of our amazing literary agent, Dawn Dowdle, from Blue Ridge Literary Agency, and our incredible editor, Elizabeth May, from Kensington Publishing. We'll never know how we got so lucky!

Production editor Rebecca Cremonese deserves a big shout out for ensuring our novel is of the highest quality for readers. Along those lines, we thank the staff at Kensington Publishing for the amazing job you do. From the art department to the marketing team, you're top-notch all the way!

Most of all, we extend our heartfelt thanks to you, our readers, for joining the looney world of Phee, Harriet, Streetman, and "the book club ladies" in Sun City West.

CHAPTER 1

Harriet Plunkett's House,
Sun City West, Arizona

Myrna Mittleson, all five-foot-nine of her, charged out of my mother's house and nearly bumped into me on the walkway. "Oops! Sorry, Phee! I'm in a rush to get to the beauty parlor. God bless the state of Iowa!"

It was a Saturday morning in late January, and I was returning a large salad bowl I had borrowed for a neighborhood dish-to-pass party. Before I could utter a word, Myrna blew past me and raced to her car, a nondescript beige sedan. *God bless the state of Iowa?* I knew my mother's Booked 4 Murder book club friends leaned toward the eccentric side, but for the life of me, I had no idea what Myrna was talking about.

The door to the house was still ajar and my mother stepped outside.

"Did you hear that?" I asked. "Iowa? I thought she was from Brooklyn."

My mother ushered me inside. "She is. But right now we're enamored with the state of Iowa."

"Huh? Why? I don't get it."

"Quick! Come in. Close the door behind you before Streetman runs out. I think I heard a bird chirping and he's likely to run after it."

I looked around the room and spied the little Chiweenie sitting on the couch, trying to tear off what looked like a Christmas tree plastered to his back.

"Um, I don't think so. And what's he wearing? Is that supposed to be a Christmas tree with a hoop skirt under it?"

"It's one of Shirley's designs. We're getting an early start for the Christmas in July program."

"Good grief! The holiday event was only a few weeks ago."

"You have to plan early in these retirement communities."

"Your dog is planning early. Look! He pulled off one of those dangling ornaments."

My mother groaned, walked over to Streetman, and removed the costume. "We'll try later," she said to the dog.

I shuddered. "Anyway, here's your salad bowl, and for heaven's sake, please tell me what's this business with Iowa. Not another retirement community you're looking into, I hope."

"Good grief no! I'm not leaving Arizona. I love Sun City West. Best thing I did was get out of those Minnesota winters. Same deal with Myrna, only she's from New York."

I tried not to roll my eyes and nodded as my mother continued.

"Last night Myrna and I got the most wonderful news

about Vernadeen Stibbens. Sit down and I'll tell you all about it. I was going to call you, but I knew you'd be stopping by on your way to work."

I was totally lost but used to the way my mother's conversations circumvented the main idea until boomeranging back to the point. I plopped myself down on a floral chair so as not to disturb the dog's position on the couch. God forbid I upset that neurotic little ball of fur.

My mother put the salad bowl on the coffee table, grabbed the chair next to mine, and leaned toward me. "Vernadeen Stibbens was asked to be one of the judges for the sewing contest for the Iowa State Fair, and she'll be on the homemaking committee as well. She still has her condo in Davenport, so technically she's a resident there. She was one of the judges for that contest back in 1995. Can you imagine? She'll be reprising her role once again."

"And you and Myrna are doing cartwheels because someone you know is going to be on a committee? Or worse yet, judging someone's stitching? I don't get it."

"If you'd let me finish, Phee, I'd explain. Vernadeen Stibbens has her own live radio show on KSCW, the voice of Sun City West, every Tuesday morning. *Sewing Chats with Vernadeen*. Of course, they tape it and run it over and over again during the week."

"I'm still—"

"Shh! I'm not done. Anyway, Vernadeen will be gone most of the spring and summer because of her role at the state fair. That means *Sewing Chats* will no longer be on the local airwaves."

"And that's a cause for celebration?"

My mother shuffled in her chair and the dog immediately jumped down from the couch. "Isn't that adorable? He thinks Mommy is going to give him a treat. I can't disappoint him. Hold on a second."

My mother walked to the kitchen and returned with a dog biscuit. The dog immediately devoured it.

"Now," she said. "Where was I? Oh yes, Vernadeen's show. It was deadly. Topics like nuances of double stitching and harmonious hemming with cross-stitches. Herb Garrett from across the street said he recorded it for nights when he had insomnia. When he found out she had been one of the state fair judges, he asked how many people she put to sleep with her commentary."

"I'm still not sure why you and Myrna are so overjoyed."

My mother patted the dog's head as she grinned from ear to ear. "Myrna and I are rejoicing because we've been asked to take over Vernadeen's slot on the radio with our own show."

My jaw dropped and I had to remind myself to breathe. *Heaven help us.* "Ah-ha! And now the real reason! But what show? What are you and Myrna going to talk about? You don't sew and Myrna wouldn't know a cross-stitch from a straight stitch. Now, if you said Shirley Johnson, I could understand. She's a talented milliner and teddy bear maker, but you and Myrna? Seriously?"

"Oh for goodness' sake, Phee. We're not going to have a sewing program. We're going to have our own murder mystery show! No one knows more about mysteries than our Booked 4 Murder book club. Cozies, forensic, hard-boiled . . . You name it, we'll talk about it. Myrna even has her own little segment planned for elements of suspense."

"The only element of suspense I can think of is when Aunt Ina finds out."

"Oy! Don't remind me. I'd better give my sister a call before she hears about it from the grapevine. You know how people around here can gossip."

Intimately. I know this intimately. "Um, when do you and Myrna get started?"

"Tuesday morning we're going over to the radio station to meet with the station manager to find out what's involved. It can't be all that hard. If I have any questions, I can always ask Herb."

"Herb Garrett?"

"Of course Herb Garrett. How many Herbs do I know? He and his pinochle buddies have their own show on Thursday nights: *Pinochle Pointers.* Once our show gets underway, Myrna and I will have guest speakers from our club. Cecilia and Shirley are already chomping at the bit to do a program about household poisonings as they relate to murder mysteries."

"Gee, I'm surprised Louise Munson doesn't have one planned about parrots that kill. Especially given the one she owns."

"Don't give her any ideas. Those things bite. I suppose Ina will want her own segment, too. I can just see it now. She'll be rattling off about obscure authors from countries none of us have heard of."

"Er, um, yeah. I suppose. Look, Mom, I've got to get going. I'm working from ten to noon this morning and it's already nine twenty. I'll talk to you later. Thanks for the salad bowl."

I made a beeline for the door before she insisted I pet Streetman or, worse yet, give him some "kissies." Besides, he seemed perfectly content back on the couch.

"I'll call you later. On your real phone. I hate when that cell phone of yours goes to voice mail. It always cuts me off."

"Okay, fine. Later. Love you!"

I was out the door and buckled up in my car just as Cecilia Flanagan pulled up. Her old, black Buick was unmistakable. Yep, word did travel fast, especially with my mother at the other end of the phone line. I imagined Cecilia had stopped by to get all the juicy gossip about Sun City West's latest radio show. I beeped the horn and waved as I pulled away from the curb and headed to Williams Investigations in Glendale, where I'm employed. I have my own office and appropriate door sign that reads, "Sophie Kimball, Bookkeeper/Accountant," even though everyone calls me "Phee."

Nate Williams, the owner of the detective agency, was a longtime friend of mine, and like me, had worked for the Mankato Police Department in Minnesota. When he retired as an investigator, he moved out west and convinced me to take a leave of absence from my job in accounts receivable to do his accounting. It was an offer I couldn't refuse, and one that got better the following year, when another detective from the Mankato Police Department, Marshall Gregory, also retired and joined the business.

I'd had a crush on Marshall for years and, unbeknownst to me, he felt the same way. Maybe Nate figured that out all along and pulled the right strings. Now, almost two years later, Marshall and I were sharing a house together and slowly broaching the subject of marriage. *Slowly*, because I was still in shock, following my Aunt Ina's nearly catastrophic wedding ceremony to three-time divorcé Louis Melinsky. Besides, as my friend Lyndy put it, "You're both in your forties and consenting adults. What else do you need?" Even my daughter, Kalese, a teacher in St. Cloud, agreed when I called to tell her about my living arrangements. I figured it was because she wanted me to be as relaxed about her living arrangements if and when the time came for her to drop a bombshell like that.

I chuckled as I watched Cecilia exit her car. Still the same black skirt and white blouse. *Uh-huh. I know a former nun when I see one. Even if my mother says it isn't so.* I figured that by five this evening, the Greater Phoenix community would know that my mother and her book club would be hosting *Murder Mysteries to Die For*, or whatever title they decided to give the show. As long as she didn't invite me to be a guest, I would be in the clear.

Augusta, our secretary, was at her desk, coffee cup in one hand and fingers furiously hitting her computer keyboard with the other, when I breezed into the office.

"I don't know how you can type with one hand," I said.

"Hey, good morning to you, too, Phee. I learned how to do that when I had carpal tunnel surgery a few years ago. I take it Marshall's still on that case in Florence, huh?"

"Oh yeah. He left at an ungodly hour. He got a new lead on the whereabouts of that not-so-deadbeat dad. Can you imagine? The guy absconded with their four-year-old in the middle of the night. The wife thinks they may be with friends of his somewhere near Apache Junction."

"Why didn't she just go to the sheriff's office and have an Amber alert issued?"

"According to Marshall, the woman's madly in love with the guy and thinks he'll eventually return. She didn't want to sully his name. Can you believe it? Still, she wanted him found. That's why she hired us."

Augusta groaned and took a sip of her coffee. "Nate's downtown, by the way, with the office manager at Home Products Plus. I don't expect him to come up for air any time soon."

"Yeesh. That's a snarly case for sure. The manager's convinced someone's got a rogue operation going since their inventory dwindled without explanation."

Just then the phone rang, and Augusta picked up, but not before adjusting her tightly sprayed bouffant hairdo.

"I'll catch up later." I walked to my office. At least my work was clear-cut and reasonable: invoices to send and a few bills to reconcile. Since Marshall was out on a case, I decided to stick around and grab lunch with Augusta, something I did once in a while because our office usually closed at noon on Saturdays.

When I told her about my mother's latest endeavor as we munched on baked subs from the deli around the corner, Augusta grimaced. "A radio show? A murder mystery radio show? Let's hope it turns out better than her last theatrical performance. Last thing you need is another murder."

I let my fork slip back onto the plate. "Bite your tongue. I'm sure they'll just be talking about murders." Too bad I was wrong.

CHAPTER 2

M y mother and Myrna had gotten the grand tour of the radio station on Tuesday, and she wasted no time telling me about it that evening. I kept moving the phone from ear to ear because my neck had started to develop a cramp. Meanwhile, Marshall gave me a funny look and a wink as he grabbed the remote and plunked himself into a chair. I moved to the kitchen, leaned an elbow on the table, and muttered "Uh-huh."

"So, like I was saying, Phee, it's a very easy setup. George Fowler—that's the station manager—was very helpful. And Howard Buell, the programming director, gave us the complete tour. Myrna and I will each have our own mics and all we have to do is talk. The program runs for a full hour. The station door will be open, so we can go directly to the broadcast table. Someone should be around to help us, but if not, we know exactly what to do."

"Um, why wouldn't anyone be around to help you?"

"Normally they would, or I should say Howard Buell, the programming director, *would,* but his pickleball team has a match in the morning. Granted, those courts are only a few yards away, but still, it's not as if he can answer a cell phone or anything if he's whacking around a pickleball. Besides, it's a small setup, and most shows are live but also taped. George said he'd be in and out and not to worry about it. Myrna and I are certainly capable of pushing a few buttons."

Thank God they didn't volunteer for the aviation club. "Sounds good. What's your first show going to be about?"

"Murder in general. We'll mention our favorite authors and go from there. In the future, George or the DJ will show us how to accept callers so we can answer their questions. Oh, before I forget, I called your aunt and told her about the show. She practically shrieked in my ear. Wants to do a segment on Bulgarian mystery authors with a penchant for pistols. Guess we'll cross that bridge when the time comes. Of course, knowing Ina, it will be sooner than we think."

"So, next Tuesday, huh?"

"At ten sharp. Say, you take a break around that time, don't you?"

"I, um, er, it varies."

"Mark it on your calendar and take your break at ten. That way you'll be able to hear the beginning of our show. Maybe Nate and Marshall would like to—"

"No. They won't. They're working cases. They don't have time to listen to murder mystery book club chats."

"Never mind, it will be taped. Oh, I almost forgot to mention the most exciting part about this. Myrna and I will get to attend the Greater Phoenix Broadcast Dinner next month. All the Phoenix radio stations attend. Maybe I'll even be able to chat with Beth from *Beth and Friends* from 99.9 KEZ. It's some sort of an award dinner. Herb went last year, but all he talked about was his porterhouse steak. Oh my gosh, maybe Myrna and I will win an award."

"Uh, I wouldn't get too carried away if I were you. I think those awards are meant for outstanding broadcasting."

"Myrna and I can be outstanding. We can certainly be—I've got to run. Streetman is whining at the door. I'd better hurry. He gets very impatient."

"Okay, catch you later." I hung up and plopped myself onto the couch. "Remind me to thank Streetman or I'd still be on the phone."

"Good timing," Marshall said. *"NCIS: New Orleans* starts in a few minutes. I'll mute the commercials and you can tell me all about KSCW's latest programming."

KSCW's latest programming, as it turned out, was the hot topic of conversation for the week leading up to my mother's radio debut. Without fail, she called me every night to keep me informed about the show. Mostly reiterating odds and ends of gossip she or Myrna heard regarding their show.

"Can you imagine," my mother said a few days before her show was set to air, "that obnoxious Sylvia Strattlemeyer told Myrna we stole the radio slot from her? Now I ask you, who on God's green earth would want to listen to an hour on the intricacies of selecting the appropriate beading needle? Her audience would be lining up to poke her in the arm with it. Sylvia told Myrna that Howard Buell himself promised her the slot. Of course, if you want to know the honest truth, Myrna told me Sylvia and

Howard had been dating, but he broke it off. I suppose that's why she didn't get the slot. I've only met him that once, but I can tell you one thing: He was smart to call it quits with Sylvia."

I tried to be as supportive as I could, but her endless diatribes were getting on my nerves.

The worst was the Monday night before the show. Her call came in like clockwork at eight forty-five. "We may lose the show, Phee! Lose the show! It's awful. I feel as if someone poked a lance through my stomach."

"Lose the show? What are you talking about?"

"I was at the checkout line in the supermarket today, and out of nowhere this balding man with a potbelly tapped me on the shoulder. I'd never seen him before, but apparently he knew who I was because he addressed me by name."

"What did he say?"

"'You must be Harriet Plunkett.'"

I stifled a groan. "Then what?"

"I said yes, and he said, 'Hope your radio show tomorrow doesn't turn out to be your last, because the station is going to do away with all of the live broadcasting if I have anything to say about it.'"

"Then what?"

"Then the cashier asked to see my loyalty card so I could get a discount, and by the time I was done, the man was gone. Anyway, I called George Fowler as soon as I got home and told him what had happened. According to George, the broadcast club that runs the station has been offered a lucrative sum of advertising money by local businesses if the programming was to go more commercial. You know, lots of product pitches every two seconds."

"Did George have any idea who that man was?"

"He sure did: Malcolm Porter. He owns a small variety store in Peoria and lives in Sun City West. Said Malcolm has been duking it out with Howard over the advertising. Even accused Howard of canceling some of the ad contracts."

"Did he? Cancel those contracts?"

"No. Only the station manager can do that. But still, I'm worried, and I can't tell if George supports the live programs or not."

"Well, no sense worrying about it now. I'm sure your show will be a big hit with lots of followers and KSCW will want to keep you on the air indefinitely." *My God! I'll stop at nothing to get off the phone.*

The next morning I made it a point of letting Augusta know that at precisely nine fifty-nine we were to drop everything, take our breaks, and turn on the radio to KSCW, 103.1 FM. Marshall had left at the crack of dawn for Florence, a good two-hour drive, and Nate was conferring with a client, the first of his many appointments. At least those two would be spared.

"The coast is clear," Augusta announced. "Grab a coffee and I'll meet you in the breakroom. If anyone comes in, we'll hear them. I'll leave the breakroom door open."

"Geez. I can't believe I'm actually nervous about this. I hope my mom and Myrna don't get all mucked up or babble on and on without making any salient points about the books they've read."

Augusta turned on the radio to 103.1 and smiled. "I'm sure they'll be fine."

A commercial for Melvin and Sons Plumbing ended and a prerecorded announcement came on. I guess my mother did know how to push the right buttons.

"And now for our next local show. Allow our hosts to introduce themselves."

My mother's voice came across very loud, and I wished there was some way to tell her to tone it down.

Augusta saw me cover my ears and laughed. "Don't worry. Half the listeners probably forgot to put in their hearing aids."

My mother seemed to go on and on, and I wondered when Myrna would get a chance to speak.

Then, like a bullhorn, Myrna's voice came through. "Harriet, do something! Someone's been murdered!"

"That should catch the listeners' attention," Augusta whispered.

Myrna continued, "There's a knife in his chest! And blood. Lots of blood."

"You're right," I whispered back to Augusta. "Myrna's really good. Lots of emotion. I wonder what book she's talking about. It could be anyone's guess."

Myrna's voice got even louder, if that was at all possible. "It's a scissors! Not a knife, Harriet. A pair of scissors is sticking out of his chest!"

Augusta crinkled her nose. "It can't be Agatha Christie. She liked killing with poisons."

Just then, my mother was back on the air. "Don't touch anything. Get away from that closet! My God, Myrna! The killer could be in here with us!"

"Wow," Augusta said. "This is better than I thought."

Myrna let out a scream and the station went dead. Only a robotic hum remained. Augusta and I looked at each other for a few seconds.

"I don't think that dead air is part of their radio show," Augusta said.

I was already out of my seat and at the door. "Do me a

favor, call nine-one-one, tell them what you heard, and I'll head over to Sun City West. The radio station is inside the Men's Club building on Meeker Boulevard. Let Nate know, too. Last I knew, he was with a client in his office."

"Got it. Call me when you know anything."

I don't remember leaving Glendale or making the twenty-five-minute drive to the radio station. Everything was a blur. I tried to tune in to KSCW from the car radio, but all I got was static. *Maybe my mother hit a wrong button and turned everything off. Maybe there's nothing to worry about, and this is really her idea of a murder mystery show.*

No matter how I tried to rationalize the situation, I couldn't shake the thought that Myrna had somehow discovered a dead body in the radio station. But how? I thought she and my mother were supposed to be seated at the broadcast table. It didn't matter. I wasn't about to take any chances.

As I pulled into the parking lot behind the Men's Club, I saw a tall man wearing an Ohio State Buckeyes jersey race to the station door. His long, curly hair bounced up and down on his forehead, and I thought perhaps he was sporting a toupee.

I bolted from my car and was at his heels in seconds. "Hold on," I shouted. "My mother's in there." Off to our left was a sheriff's posse car, so I knew Augusta had placed the call.

Sun City West was a municipality serviced by the Maricopa County Sheriff's Office, unlike the nearby City of Surprise, which had its own police force.

"Which one?" the man asked. "Plunkett or Mittleson?"

"Plunkett, Harriet."

"I'm George Fowler, the station manager. I stopped in

to Dunkin' Donuts for a quick coffee when someone recognized me and asked why there was dead air at the radio station. I figured your mother and her friend ran into some sort of problem."

"Um, you could say that. Myrna just informed the West Valley that there was a dead body in there, along with a possible killer."

"Holy crap! It better be part of their show. If not, we're in deep doo-doo. We'll be forced to cancel our live programming in favor of digital broadcasts. Heck, the station won't even be in Sun City West. It would be in name only. Let's hope it was a mechanical glitch."

Just then, two sheriff's cars pulled into the driveway, both of them with flashers on.

I knew I had to move fast or one of those deputies would prevent me from entering the building. "Sorry, Mr. Fowler. Somehow I don't think this was mechanical."

I charged past him and pulled the door open, praying to the gods that the dead air was due to my mother and Myrna's broadcasting incompetence and not the result of something much worse.

CHAPTER 3

My mother and Myrna, along with a stout male posse member, whose white hair looked as if it had recently been slicked down with gel, stood in front of a large, walk-in closet as if they were stuck to the floor. The three of them turned their heads in my direction as soon as they heard me enter. The man from the posse rubbed his large mustache and motioned for me to stay back.

Meanwhile, George Fowler charged in, but instead of dealing with the obvious situation in front of him, he went straight to the broadcast table and immediately plunked a tape into a large, rectangular machine that resembled an oversize computer tower. "Easy listening music. Can't have dead air."

No sooner had he uttered the word "air" when two other respondents entered the room, and my stomach immediately began to churn. My dumb luck. The county sent the two deputies with whom I had a history, and not a very pleasant one at that. Deputies Bowman and Ranston were the very ones who'd dealt with the other murders in Sun City West and took all the credit for their resolution, when it was Williams Investigations that deserved the kudos.

Deputy Bowman wasted no time barking orders. The man reminded me of a grizzly bear that had just come out of hibernation. "Everyone! Away from the closet! Step back!"

Then Deputy Ranston put in his two cents. "We received a call from the local posse that a deceased person was found in the radio station closet." With his chest puffed out and his chin tucked below his neck, he strode to the spot where my mother and Myrna were still standing.

"Not deceased! Murdered!" Myrna shouted. "See for yourself. There's a large pair of sewing scissors sticking out of his chest."

"You'll have to take a step back." Deputy Bowman motioned for my mother and Myrna to move out of his way.

George Fowler, who was still at the broadcast table, charged over to where the deputies were standing. "Christmas trees in July! We can't have a dead body in here! And what's this about scissors?"

"I'm afraid you'll have to stay back," Deputy Ranston said. "I've placed a call to my office and they're sending a forensics team, along with the coroner. Now, please, step back."

"My God!" my mother shrieked. "Did you get a look at those scissors, Myrna? They're Vernadeen's! Those are her fancy-dancy Gingher scissors. You know, the ones with the golden color on the eye rings. She did an entire show about the five best kinds of sewing scissors to buy, and those were her favorite. Nine-and-a-half-inch shears, if I remember correctly."

Myrna bobbed her head up and down. "I think you're right. She did mention they were extremely sharp and maintained their sharpness even after constant use."

It was unbelievable. I caught a glimpse of the body in the closet and, believe me, scissors would be the last thing I'd recall. Frankly, I was surprised my mother and Myrna had homed in on the weapon instead of the obvious corpse sporting them. I supposed maybe it was the shock of the situation.

The victim appeared to be in his late sixties or early seventies, with short, brown hair and a decent tan. He was wearing dark-blue jogger pants and a nondescript, light-blue sweatshirt, now permanently stained and ripped, thanks to that Gingher, or whatever my mother called those scissors. A pair of Nikes completed the outfit. He was slumped on the floor amid open cartons of old tapes and an endless supply of bottled water, Arrowhead brand to be exact.

"I'll need statements from each of you," Deputy Bowman said while Deputy Ranston appeared to be having his own conversation off to the side of the room with the posse member first to arrive at the scene.

George Fowler elbowed Deputy Bowman and leaned into the closet. "Dear God! That's Howard Buell, our programming director. What's he doing dead on our floor? I thought he was supposed to be playing pickleball. And who on earth would want to kill him?"

The gnarly deputy turned to George. "Sir, we cannot say for sure if he was murdered until our forensics team has completed their part of the investigation and the coroner has rendered a decision."

I thought the veins on George Fowler's head would burst. "Can't say for sure? The guy has a pair of freaking scissors sticking out of his chest. What do *you* think happened? He came in here to grab a bottled water from the closet and, in lieu of returning to the pickleball courts, he committed hara-kari instead?"

"Sir, you're going to need to calm down. In fact, all of you need to calm down. We've got to get statements from everyone and contact information." Then he gave me a look. "Miss Kimball, I believe your contact information is on file, along with Mrs. Plunkett's."

Myrna grabbed my mother by the arm. "Why should your contact information be on file, Harriet?"

"Shh! Yours should be on file, too. Remember? The murder at the Stardust Theater?"

"Oh, *that.*"

Suddenly, it was as if my mother remembered she had a daughter. "Phee! Did you bring Nate or Marshall? And how did you know we'd be standing over a dead body?"

"I didn't. Augusta and I were listening to your show when, out of the blue, there was radio silence. We thought you and Myrna were talking about some novel your book club read."

My mother's face turned ashen. "The book club. Goodness. I can't imagine what they must be thinking."

"I'll tell you what they're thinking," I said. "The same thing Augusta and I were. That you or Myrna accidently hit the wrong button and stopped broadcasting."

My mother shook Myrna's arm. "Oh no. They'll think we're incompetent. Quick, Myrna, start calling them and tell them what happened. I'll take Shirley and Lucinda. You can have Cecilia and Louise. They can call the snow-birds later."

"No one is calling anyone!" Deputy Ranston bellowed, having finished his conversation with the posse member. "This is an active crime scene, and until we get clearance from the sheriff's office, no one is to call anyone or say anything. Now, please, take a seat. I see some folding chairs against the wall. Find one and sit down. We need your statements."

"I don't have a statement," I said to Deputy Ranston. "I drove here and walked in seconds before you arrived."

"Anything could happen in a matter of seconds."

"Oh brother." I tried not to roll my eyes and instead wound up grimacing. "I'll make my statement clear and succinct. 'I thought something might have gone wrong at the radio station when Mother's show went off the air. I drove here from my place of work at Williams Investigations and saw my mother, her friend Myrna, and the posse member standing in front of the closet. End of story.'"

"Not so fast," Deputy Ranston said. "You indicated you saw your mother and her friend standing in front of the closet. What I'd like to know is why they were there to begin with."

"I can answer that," Myrna said. "I was about to talk when I got a frog in my throat. I remembered George Fowler telling us there were cartons of water in the closet if we got thirsty. So, I got up while Harriet was talking and went to get myself a bottle of water. I don't drink tap water. God knows what's in it. Anyway, when I opened the door, that's when I saw the body. And that's when I

said to Harriet, 'Do something! Someone's been murdered.'"

"She's right," my mother added. "Myrna did say that. I
thought she was getting carried away with our broadcast,
but then she opened the closet door wide and stepped
aside. That's when I saw those feet sticking straight out. I
jumped up to get a better look and knocked into the trans-
mitter or whatever they call that thing. I don't know how
long we were staring at the body, but all of sudden, a
posse volunteer came inside. Said someone called nine-
one-one. You don't suppose it was the killer, do you? I've
heard those crazed people do things like that."

*Yep. And equally crazy people announce to the world
that a killer could be inside the local radio station. I'm
surprised this place isn't teeming with curiosity seekers.*

I looked directly at my mother. "Augusta called nine-
one-one and I drove right over here. Frankly, we weren't
about to take any chances."

Just then, Deputy Bowman's phone rang and he shushed
us. All I could hear was his end of the conversation.

"Fifteen or twenty people outside? You've *got* to be
kidding me."

He rubbed his chin and shuddered. "What? No, I don't
need crowd control."

Then he glared at my mother and Myrna. "On second
thought, yes. Send the posse volunteers. And the marked
cars. Don't know what to expect."

At that instant, the forensics crew entered the room,
followed by a pencil-thin woman sporting a jacket that
read "coroner." Deputies Bowman and Ranston spoke
briefly with them before turning their attention back
to us.

"Is there another room around here we can use for questioning?" Deputy Bowman asked.

George Fowler looked at his wrist. "If you hurry, we can use the Stampede room for the next half hour. Then the poker club takes over, and believe me, you don't want to turn them away. It could get ugly."

Deputy Bowman started for the door. "Fine. A half hour. We should be able to wrap things up by then."

We exited the radio station's broadcast room and walked fifteen or so feet down the hall to a large area that was obviously set up for card playing.

"If you don't mind," I said, "I really need to get back to work."

The two deputies eyeballed each other and Deputy Ranston replied, "Fine, we'll be in touch."

"Stop by the house on your way home from work," my mother said. "With your boss or your boyfriend. Better yet, bring both of them. For all we know, the person who killed poor Howard Buell could have it in for all of us."

I was about to respond to her demand but thought better of it. "You'll be fine. I'll call you in a little while."

The fifteen or twenty people Deputy Bowman mentioned had now grown to at least thirty. The crowd practically engulfed the small parking lot in front of the radio station's entrance. Two posse volunteers with bright orange vests stood between the entrance and the curiosity seekers or "road yentas," as my mother would say.

The second the door closed behind me, people began to shout.

"Is it true there's a killer in there?"

"Who was murdered? Someone said something about murder."

"Is this a hostage situation? Where's the SWAT team?"

"Everything's under control," I bellowed into the crowd. "Let the sheriff's office do its job."

I scanned the area for my car, hoping it wasn't blocked in by the melee. That was the second I noticed Cecilia Flanagan and Shirley Johnson from my mother's Booked 4 Murder book club waving their hands in the air.

"Over here, Phee!" one of them shouted, but I couldn't tell which one.

I wove through the crowd until I reached them. Without wasting a second, we skirted to the edge of the building, away from the madness.

Cecilia pulled her black cardigan sweater across her chest and proceeded to button it up. "Are Harriet and Myrna all right? Shirley and I were only a few yards away at the little Buzz coffee shop at the fitness center and everyone was listening to the show."

"They're fine," I said. "Just a bit shaken up."

Then, out of the blue, Shirley took a deep breath and then another. "Scissors. I got a frantic phone call from your mother just as we were on our way here. Said she had to make it quick because they weren't supposed to call anyone. Harriet told me the body was stabbed with a pair of scissors. What kind of scissors? Tell me. I need to know. What kind of scissors?"

What does she mean, what kind of scissors? Scissors are scissors, aren't they? Except for the size, of course. Or does she mean the brand name?

"Um, they looked large, if that's any help; why?"

"Oh Lordy. Please tell me. Were they pinking shears or paper-cutting scissors?"

I bit my lip and shrugged. "I don't think it matters. The guy was dead."

"Tell me one thing: Were the eye rings on the scissors gold?"

"Uh, come to think of it, yeah. In fact, my mother and Myrna had a name for them."

"Gingher. Were they Ginghers?"

I gave her a nod, and next thing I knew, she clutched her chest and all but keeled over. "I'm going to be arrested for murder. Oh Lordy, someone needs to call my lawyer."

CHAPTER 4

Off to my left the crowd had swelled, and so had the number of volunteer posse members.

"Come on," I said, "we'd better not stand here talking. Our voices can carry. Wait here. I'll get my car and we can talk in there. Give me a few seconds to get around the crowd."

I didn't wait for Shirley or Cecilia to respond. I hurried over to where I had parked the vehicle and, miraculously, I was able to maneuver it around the throng of radio listeners who didn't want to miss the latest breaking news.

"Hurry! Get in! I'll pull over to the dog park area and we can chat. It doesn't look too busy right now."

Shirley got in the front seat and Cecilia took the one directly behind me. I parked along the edge of the lot, equidistant from the bocce courts and the dogs. "So, what's this about needing a lawyer? My mother and Myrna were pretty certain those were Vernadeen Stibbens's shears sticking up from the man's gut."

"Vernadeen all but sleeps with those scissors of hers," Cecilia said. "And hers are engraved with a stylized 'VS' on one of the blades. She did a presentation at my church for the ladies' club. That's how I know."

"Those could still be her scissors," I said. "No one has examined them carefully."

Shirley grabbed my wrist and shook it. "They could be. But I don't think so. She wouldn't have gone to Iowa without them."

Believe me, I could think of lots of things I wouldn't travel without, and scissors wouldn't be one of them. Then again, I wasn't a seamstress like Vernadeen.

"Um, so, what makes you think those are your scissors?"

Shirley released my wrist and wrung her hands. "Someone stole my scissors a week ago. I had them in my special Vera Bradley bag, the one with extra inside pouches, and when I got home from the Rip 'n' Sew Club, they were missing."

"Maybe they're still in the club's workroom," I offered.

"That's what I thought, too, but when I went back to check, they weren't there. Oh Lordy, if my fingerprints are found on those scissors, they'll be sending me up the river for sure."

Then she turned her head and faced Cecilia. "You *will* come visit me, won't you? And bring the book club ladies?"

I tried to keep the pitch in my voice to an even tone,

but it didn't work. "No one is visiting anyone in prison. Besides, what possible motive could you have for murdering the programming director for the radio station?"

"Oh my God!" Shirley reached over to grab my wrist again, but I moved it out of her way. "We're heathens. Absolute heathens. We never even bothered to ask who was killed. Oh Lordy, Cecilia, you and I are going to share some little corner in hell that will make Dante's *Inferno* look like Disneyland."

"I'm not sharing that corner with you. A table or booth at Bagels 'N More maybe, but not some steaming pit in hell, if that's what you're thinking. Besides, we don't even know who the programming director is, do we?"

Shirley shook her head. "I doubt it, Cecilia."

"It's someone named Howard Buell," I said, "but I don't think that news is supposed to be released until the sheriff's office contacts the next of kin."

Cecilia leaned forward until her head was directly between mine and Shirley's. "Howard Buell? Howard Maynard Buell?"

"Um, I'm not sure of the middle name. Why? Do you know him?"

Cecilia's voice started to crack. "I think so, but I didn't know he was the programming director for the radio station. If it's who I think it is, I can't imagine why anyone would kill him."

"Who do you think it is?"

"Hattie Buell's husband. Hattie and I were on the refreshment committee for the fortieth anniversary of Sun City West a few years back. She passed away over a year ago. No children."

I glanced at Shirley. "Did you know him?"

She shook her head and began to cry. "Lordy, that poor widowed man, and now I'll be suspect number one."

"Get a hold of yourself. You didn't even know him. Every murder needs a motive, a means, and an opportunity. If, indeed, it turns out that those scissors are yours, you can explain, but if I were you, I wouldn't be offering up any information until I was asked."

"She's right, you know," Cecilia said, "If you go running off to the sheriff's office, they'll get suspicious and think you have something to hide."

"That doesn't make any sense."

"Sure it does. They'll think you made up that story about the lost scissors just to cover your rear."

Shirley moaned. "So what should I do?"

I looked at her and then at Cecilia. "Nothing right now. Let the sheriff's office complete its investigation. If you're contacted, call me. Meanwhile, I'll give Nate and Marshall the heads-up. If need be, I'm sure they'll help you. Listen, I really need to get back to work. I'd drive you to your car, but that crowd's impossible. I'll get you as close as I can."

"Don't get us too close," Cecilia said. "If I'm not mistaken, that's the KPHO News van over by the Men's Club building. I don't want to get on camera. It makes you look ten pounds heavier."

Sure enough, the KPHO van was in front, and it wasn't the only one. Channels 10, 12, and 15 were all lined up as well.

"Remember, don't mention Howard Buell's name to anyone until the news of his death is made public."

"You don't have to worry," Cecilia said. "Our lips are sealed."

Terrific. Their lips are sealed, but their emails are wide open.

"Oh look!" she continued. "That's Louise Munson over there. You can drop us off by her car. We'll be fine. We'll stick around until they let your mother and Myrna out of there. They must be nervous wrecks by now."

Surprisingly, not as nervous as one would think. Then again, it could be a delayed reaction.

"Okay. Try not to get all worked up. I'm sure the sheriff's office will catch the real killer. Nice seeing you again."

Who was I kidding? Since when did the sheriff's office catch the real perpetrators? It was only when Williams Investigations was called in to consult that the killers were apprehended. Anyway, Marshall was stuck chasing after some guy in a custodial interference case and Nate had enough on his plate with Home Products Plus.

I took the back way out of the parking lot after dropping them off, thus avoiding the commotion in front of the Men's Club. A quick glance told me the pickleball players had taken a break in their action to zero in on what was behind door number two.

So much for a leisurely lunch break. I'd have to make up the time eating at my desk. At least my mother and Myrna were all right, and that was all that mattered. Marshall called me later in the day to inform me that he had tracked down the dad in Florence, only to learn the man was now in Benson, staying with friends. It was a long drive and it meant an overnight in Tucson or Sierra Vista before getting on the road again to finalize the case.

I gave him the abbreviated version of the radio station incident, trying not to use the word "murder," but he was a seasoned detective after all, and I should have known better.

"You sure your mom's okay? And what about you?"

"Me? I'm fine. Okay, maybe not exactly fine since I saw the body with the scissors in the gut, but really, I'm fine. As for my mother and Myrna, I don't think it has hit them yet. I'm stopping by the house after work. By then, she should be totally unraveled."

"Unraveled or unglued?"

"Unraveled. Shirley was the one who was unglued, but I'll tell you about that when we have more time. Stay safe. Promise me."

"I will. Talk to you tonight, hon. Miss you."

Augusta thought I had given Shirley good advice about not throwing herself at the mercy of the sheriff's office, but Nate had a slightly different take. It was late in the day and I finally found a few minutes to let him know what had happened in Sun City West.

"I always like to be upfront with these things," he said, "because they have a funny way of coming back to bite you."

"So you think I should call Shirley and have her report the missing scissors?"

"Hell, when you phrase it that way, it sounds like a kindergarten teacher completing a supply loss form. And before you give me one of your quizzical looks, I've had my share of checking into petty pilferings at schools. Frankly, I wouldn't mind doing that again. It beats the heck out of the tangled web I'm dealing with now. The product depletion at Home Products Plus is staggering. I'm positive it's an inside job with lots of tentacles."

"So, about Shirley . . ."

"I've got a decent rapport with Bowman and Ranston.

I'll give one of them a call and see what I can find out. Meanwhile, I'd tell your mother to proceed with caution around that radio station. Unless, of course, they decide to call it quits."

"And miss their opportunity to be on the air? You've *got* to be kidding. They'll show up all right, only it will be with an arsenal of self-defense products beginning with those Screamers Myrna bought a while back. To be honest, it wouldn't surprise me one bit if they came armed with bear spray or something equally heinous. Myrna stocked up on the stuff last year at Cabela's when some-one thought there was a stalker in the neighborhood. It turned out to be some poor man with Alzheimer's who kept getting out of his caregiver's house."

"Oh brother."

"Let me know as soon as you hear anything."

"You've got it, kiddo."

If nothing else, I was right about one thing—the de-layed reaction. Howard Buell's untimely demise hit my mother later that evening when I stopped by after work. I expected to see at least two or three classic Buicks parked in front of her house, but there were no cars belonging to the book club ladies. There was, however, a visitor who'd hoofed it from across the street. Herb Garrett wasn't about to miss out on a firsthand description of a possible murder victim.

"Hey, Cutie!" he announced the minute I set foot in the door. "Your mother told me what she and Myrna discov-ered at KSCW today. I should've listened to their radio show instead of watching *Dr. Phil*."

"That'll be a lesson to you, Herb." My mother mo-tioned for me to sit on the couch across from him. "I even left the radio turned on to the station for Streetman. Oh poor, poor Streetman. No wonder he's under the couch. He's probably still traumatized from hearing Myrna scream. I'm certain he hasn't forgotten about that grim discovery in the Galbraiths' backyard this past fall."

Or that ghastly hoop-shirt Christmas tree outfit you had him try on.

Then, my mother turned to me. "If you must know, Phee, I'm practically beside myself over this morning's nightmare. One minute Myrna was off getting a bottle of water and the next she was face-to-face with a corpse. I don't know how I'm going to sleep tonight. I don't know what was protruding more, the man's stomach or those scissors."

At that instant Herb sucked in his gut. "The man was practically a target for every kook and nut case in this community who fancied themselves the next radio show sensation."

"You knew him?" I asked.

"We have the same dentist. That's how I got to know him, and that's how our *Pinochle Pointers* show got on the air. Say, we've got a good segment coming up this Thursday about scoring tricks. You should tune in."

"No one's interested in that, Herb," my mother said. "Not when there's a murderer running around loose. Good grief, we don't even know if it was premeditated, or one of those awful acts of violence for no apparent reason. If the lips on those sheriff's deputies were sealed any tighter, it would take a complete set of pocket tools to pry them open."

Herb leaned toward me and shook his head. "I think he got into a fight with someone and they lost their temper. Next thing you know, the murderer grabbed the nearest weapon, and the rest is history."

"That would be believable if, say, the nearest weapon was something that was easily accessible in the radio station. But sewing scissors?" I asked.

"Phee's right," my mother added. "Vernadeen's show was the only one with a sewing theme. Thank God!"

Just then the phone rang, and my mother walked to the kitchen counter to get it. I heard her utter four words, and in that instant I knew I had to get out of there and make it fast.

CHAPTER 5

"Seven would be perfect," she said.

What followed was no surprise. My mother informed Herb and me that the book club ladies would be over shortly, and Louise Munson would be picking up fried chicken from one of the supermarkets. Shirley was going to bring dessert, and everyone else was going to bring a salad or side dish. Aunt Ina, of course, would be stopping by AJ's Purveyors of Fine Foods in Peoria to select something one of their chefs prepared. Naturally Herb and I were invited to stay.

"Thanks for the invite, Harriet, but I'm meeting Bill and Wayne at Curley's for a brew. Of course, if you have leftovers . . ."

"Nice try. Streetman will be getting any tidbits of chicken in his kibble, and I plan to freeze the rest."

I almost started to laugh but caught myself. I joined Herb as he walked toward the door. "Tell Bill and Wayne I said hi."

Bill and Wayne were Herb's pinochle buddies, and I got to know them when they volunteered to work the lights at the Stardust Theater for an ill-fated production of Agatha Christie's *The Mousetrap* in which my mother and her friends appeared.

"Yeah, those two are bound to have their own theories," he said, "but I still think someone lost it and went for the scissors. There were lots of people who wanted to have their own shows. All those deputies need to do is find out which one of them was unhinged."

At the mention of the word "unhinged," my mother gasped. "Sylvia! Sylvia Strattlemeyer. She and Howard used to date, according to Myrna. That makes perfect sense. It's always the disgruntled ex-girlfriend or the jealous wife."

I let out a really audible moan. "Since when is it always some romance gone bad? You've got to stop watching so much Telemundo or you'll drive yourself nuts."

"Your daughter's got a point, you know. My money's on someone who was pissed they didn't get their own show."

"Well," my hand was already on the doorknob, "I really need to get a move on. I'll catch up later."

"If I hear anything important tonight from the girls, I'll let you know."

Thirty seconds later Herb and I were out the door, and I raced for my car.

"Whoa, you really must be in a hurry."

"You bet I am. In a matter of minutes one of those book club ladies is going to arrive early and give me an earful of her theories. Have fun at Curley's."

"Tell Marshall he should join us sometime."

Oh, yeah. That's exactly what he'd like to do. It took him weeks to get over the time we sat with your pinochle crew to track a killer.

As I drove home, my stomach churned. Granted, I was hungry, but I attributed the upset to something else. I knew beyond a shadow of a doubt that my mother's friends would have all sorts of wackadoodle theories about Howard Buell's murder. And yes, I *was* calling it a murder, even though the sheriff's office hadn't released their official ruling. I also knew once the shock wore off, my mother would plague me nonstop to "find the killer before the next pair of scissors slices into her intestines instead of a yard of linen fabric."

Like it or not, I'd be cajoled into doing some sleuthing. Most likely with Streetman at the dog park so I could pick up the gossip while everyone else picked up other prizes. Ugh. My mind played out the obvious, beginning with the timeline, as I continued the drive home.

I knew there were pickleball matches taking place at the courts adjacent to the Men's Club building. According to my mother, those started promptly at eight. But what about activities in the Men's Club? Her program didn't begin until ten, so it was quite possible something else could have been going on without her knowledge. A club breakfast? A card game? That Men's Club had lots of rooms for all sorts of meetings, and knowing that most Sun City West residents were early risers, it wouldn't surprise me in the least if Howard Buell's murderer had been in plain sight only hours before.

Then I realized something. I would need to find out the time of death in order to get a better idea of who could have done it. Nate would find out from one of the deputies, but, thankfully, I didn't have to wait.

When the news came on at nine, Channel 15's scroll read "Suspicious Death at Sun City West Radio Station." After listening to breaking news about car crashes in the Greater Phoenix area and an undetermined odor that resulted in an evacuation at one of the terminals at Sky Harbor airport, I finally caught the story about Howard Buell. It was all of ten seconds or less. The man's death was ruled suspicious.

Gee, you think?

The news anchor didn't release the name, pending notification of next of kin, but did say it was someone who worked at the radio station. She also mentioned the time of death was estimated to be three to four hours before the body was discovered. That would make it anytime between six and seven, give or take a half hour.

No wonder Myrna let out that banshee shriek. The guy's blood was probably still fresh. I needed to find out what activities were going on that morning at the Men's Club, and I needed a reliable source. Instead of calling my mother, I turned to the one impartial source I had: Google.

Within minutes I located the Men's Club building schedule from the Sun City West website and learned that only one activity had been scheduled for early this morning: a seven thirty bagel breakfast followed by a game of euchre. It was a regular Tuesday morning event for the Sun City West Men's Euchre Club. Now all I needed to do was find out who the heck was in the club and who might have added murder to their deck of cards.

My God! Why am I doing this?

No sooner had I written the words "Need euchre member list" on a scrap of paper than Marshall called. He had checked into a motel in Benson and, if all went well, was certain he'd find that no-good dad tomorrow.

"We've got to take a drive down here, hon," he said. "Kartchner Caverns State Park is only nine miles from here. Those underground caves are supposed to be phenomenal."

"Sounds good. April maybe? When it's warmer. I know you'll want to do some hiking as well."

"Boy, you've got my number. So, tell me how it went tonight at your mother's house."

"I fled before the book club ladies descended on the place. I only had to contend with my mom and Herb. Listen, I know I should leave this to the sheriff's office, but you know as well as I do I'll never have any peace from my mother. I figured what's the harm in tracking down a few details."

"Uh-huh. Keep going."

"My mother and Myrna weren't the first people in the Men's Club building that morning. The men's euchre club was scheduled to eat bagels and play cards. At least according to the Rec Center calendar."

"Yeesh. You didn't waste any time getting started."

"That's all I did. Get started, I mean. I have to find out who those euchre players are and who was there. I'm sure I'll find the membership list."

"Whatever you do, don't meet with anyone you don't know. We're talking murder, not petty theft."

"I know. And what about George Fowler? The station manager. He had carte blanche to the place. I imagine he's the first person of interest as far as the sheriff's office is concerned. He had means and opportunity. And none of us know about motive, right?"

"Try not to get ahead of yourself, and keep in mind it might not have been anyone connected to the Men's Club. You said yourself the building was wide open, according to your mom and Myrna. Who knows who could've gone in and out."

"Aargh. Wide open and no surveillance. Like with all the other buildings, the club president or designee has a key to their room. Guess that might change in the future, huh?"

"One would think. But someone had to open the building first thing in the morning. Maintenance maybe?"

"Nate's going to have a chat with our favorite deputies as a favor to me. I'll ask him to find out. Oh my gosh! I just thought of something. The pickleball courts are spitting distance from the Men's Club building, and they start practicing at the crack of dawn so they'll be ready for their matches. It would be real easy for someone to slip away during a break, commit the heinous deed, and then lob a ball over the net as if nothing else mattered."

"Um, if you're going to investigate, then remember what Nate always says: 'Don't widen the net of suspects until you have to.' The euchre club would be a good starting point, but don't drive yourself crazy with this. I'm sure those deputies have a good handle on it."

"And if not?"

"Aargh. Then it's business as usual for us if we're asked to consult. Anyway, I hope to get things wrapped up tomorrow. I'll give you a buzz and keep you posted. Make sure you lock up."

"Already done. Love you, too."

It was impossible not to dwell on the suspects who kept popping up in my mind. I'd no sooner start to fall asleep when another name and fuzzy image jolted me awake. It was no use. I was one of those people who had to write everything down and organize it. The clock by my bed read 11:33, and I promised myself that, no matter what, by 11:59 I would turn off the lights for good.

Careful not to accidentally set off the car alarm from the key fob I kept in my nightstand, I rummaged around for a pen and pad. The key fob was my aunt Ina's idea, and a pretty decent one. If an intruder were to break in, I could push the car's siren and hopefully scare the day-lights out of whoever it was. Since Marshall and I moved in together, the key fob was more of an old habit rather than my first line of defense.

With pen and pad in hand, I sat up, leaned against my pillow, and wrote my list, beginning with Vernadeen Stibbens. Granted, she was in Iowa, but did anyone really know that for sure? I moved on to Malcolm Porter, who owned that supply store in Peoria. He was the one who wanted the live broadcasting to go the way of rotary phones and typewriters. Then there was George Fowler himself. I couldn't get past the word "opportunity" when it came to him. Also, he seemed more concerned about dead air than the dead body a few feet away.

Sylvia Strattlemeyer did have a motive if I was to buy

into my mother's theory, and then, of course, there were the unnamed euchre players. Maybe one of them held a grudge. All in all, it wasn't an outrageous list. I'd seen worse. But that was before I got the news from Nate the following morning that Williams Investigations was asked to assist on the case.

CHAPTER 6

Surprisingly, I got a restful night's sleep once I completed my suspect list. I was anxious to share it with Nate the next morning at work, but before I could reach into my bag to pull out the piece of notepaper and knock on his door, he came out of his office and announced in a voice loud enough to be heard in Baltimore, "Marshall won the damn bet! We're on that scissors-stabbing case. I just texted him."

"What damn bet?" I asked. "He didn't mention a bet to me last night."

"That's right. He didn't mention anything to me either." Augusta looked up from her computer screen and reached for her coffee cup.

Nate gave her an odd look and laughed. "We always bet on whether or not the Maricopa County Sheriff's Office is going to ask us to consult on a case. Frankly, I didn't

think it would be this soon. The guy was found dead yesterday and the classification moved from suspicious to
homicide only a few hours ago. Name's been released to
the media as well. It'll probably be on the midday news."

I knew the county was mired in assaults, murders, drug
arrests, kidnappings, hit-and-runs, and all sorts of crimes
that plagued big cities like Phoenix, but Nate and Marshall weren't usually called to consult on Sun City West
cases until the county deputies had completed the initial
legwork.

I took a step toward him. "Did they say why they
pulled you in so early on the case?"

"Oh yeah, and it's a beaut. They got an anonymous
call late yesterday from one of the pickleball players. The
woman insisted she saw someone leave the courts and go
inside the building, but it was too dark for her to give a
description. It was a little before six, the lights on the
pickleball court had gone out, and the sun was just starting to appear on the horizon."

"I thought there was always a monitor there, or someone who officiated the matches."

"This was before the actual competition began. It was
practice time. At dawn, mind you. Those players must
really be fanatic."

"There couldn't have been *that* many players on the
courts, could there?"

"The deputies asked the caller if she could provide an
estimate of players and she guessed around twenty-five.
But wait. It gets better. There were forty-four players
signed up for the match, and because no one knows which
twenty-five were the ones on the court, all forty-four
players need to be questioned. Talk about widening a net
of suspects. That's where we come in."

"Ugh. Sounds worse than when you had to question the archery club that fall." *And Marshall's probably kicking himself in the pants for telling me not to even think about those pickleballers.*

"Needless to say, Deputies Bowman and Ranston need our help interviewing possible witnesses regarding who might have left the court. Keep in mind, one of those would-be witnesses might turn out to be the killer. So, we'll need to be quite savvy with our questioning."

"I don't suppose the anonymous caller saw anyone come back to the courts."

"Of course she did. All the players who weren't there for early practice. God knows how many of them there were. I'm beginning to get a headache already."

"One good thing," Augusta announced.

I walked to the Keurig and popped a K-Cup into the machine. "What's that?"

"You'll have all the inside scoop for your mother."

Nate looked as if he was about to choke. "No inside scoop! All of this is confidential."

"Confidential as in I can't tell my mother you're on the case or confidential as in I can't tell her what you find out?"

"The last part. You can tell her we were called in to consult, and if there's something the sheriff's office feels she needs to know, I'm sure they'll take care of it."

"Oh, she'll need to know all right. In fact, I put together my own list of suspects to get ahead of the game. Here. Take it."

I handed him the note, having made another copy for myself.

"You're becoming a regular Jessica Fletcher, aren't

you? I suppose living with Marshall, it was bound to rub off. So, what've you got?"

I went on to explain about Malcolm Porter's comment and the fact that Sylvia Strattlemeyer got dumped by the victim. Next, I moved on to the euchre players.

"Nice job, kiddo. Right now, all Marshall and I were asked to do was interview the pickleballers. No one knows for sure if Howard actually showed up at the courts and then went into the radio station or skipped the courts altogether. Either way, it got him the same unfortunate result. Yeesh. I'll get a contact list and get started. As far as I know, the sheriff's office is going to speak with the euchre players." Then he turned to Augusta, "You'll need to make some phone calls and set up appointments. Deputy Ranston said we could use the posse station in Sun City West."

"You got it," she replied.

Nate took a breath and gave me a pat on the shoulder. "I guarantee interviewing those players is only the beginning. You should know by now how these things escalate."

Only too well.

"By the way, you didn't mention how your mother and Myrna were dealing with it. It must have sunk in by now."

"I saw her right before the book club ladies converged at her place last night. No doubt she'll call me during my break to insist I do something. I decided not to wait. Hence the list I gave you."

"You don't fool me. You've already figured out a way to have a chitchat with the first name that pops up."

"I, er, um . . ."

"Relax. Chitchatting is fair game. But do it in the open. Just because you're a bookkeeper and an accountant doesn't preclude you from being a terrific sleuth."

"I'm not so sure about that."

"Well, a terrific chitchatter, then. How's that?"

Augusta slammed her elbow onto the table and moaned. "Enough with the chitchatting. I've got forty plus pickleball appointments to make. Someone's got to do the work around here."

"Message loud and clear," was Nate's response as he and I headed back to our respective offices.

True to form, my mother called me at precisely ten fifteen. I was halfway through a granola bar and about to wash it down with coffee when Augusta told me to pick up the office phone.

"I won't keep you, Phee," my mother said. "Shirley and Lucinda are here, and we're on our way to get a bite to eat. The radio station canceled all its live broadcasts this week, but our show will go on as usual next Tuesday morning. They're going to add security in the Men's Club building. Posse members, I imagine. George Fowler called to let me know. Unless those volunteers are packing heat, Myrna and I aren't going to be taking any chances."

"What do you mean?"

"Myrna bought us giant cans of wasp spray."

At least she didn't find an old shotgun from God knows where. "Sounds like a plan. I'm glad you're handling this in a calm and reflective manner."

"Calm and reflective? I barely slept a wink last night, and if Streetman didn't have his fleece blanket, he would have been even more anxious. The dog has gotten quite territorial over that blanket. Won't let anyone go near it. I suppose, in some odd way, it must remind him of his puppyhood. Nevertheless, we cannot go on this way. That's where you come in."

And here it goes. I didn't say a word.

"Myrna and I will be nervous wrecks if the killer isn't caught. And poor Shirley. She thinks her scissors might have been the murder weapon. Why didn't you say anything to me? Oh, never mind. It doesn't matter. What matters is that you need to use your investigative skills to track down that killer before it's too late. You know how pokey that sheriff's office is. Anyway, the book club ladies and I made you a list."

"We've been over this a zillion times. I am not an investigator. But I will tell you something that might put your mind at ease: Williams Investigations was asked to consult. And if you must know, I made my own list." *Oh my God! What was I thinking to tell her that?*

"Hallelujah. I'll email you our list tonight and you can compare them. I've got to go. I can't keep Shirley and Lucinda waiting. Talk to you later."

Can't keep Shirley and Lucinda waiting? What about my lost break time?

I finished my granola bar and washed it down with lukewarm coffee. Then I set about to do the actual work I was paid to do. This morning it was invoice preparation. Clear and exact numbers that left no room for speculation. Unlike everything else going on around me.

I was cautiously optimistic that Marshall would make it back by nightfall, but I wasn't holding my breath. That meant I could do a bit of snooping on my way home from work, even if Peoria wasn't exactly on my route.

The minute we locked up for the day, I headed over to Malcolm's Variety Store. Their website said they were open from nine to eight daily and nine to five on Saturdays. Plenty of time for me to have a conversation with him, *if* he was still there. I took my chances. And enough cash so I'd look the part of a genuine customer.

The store was located on Union Hills Drive, about a mile or so past Sun City and a few yards away from Westbrook Village, another retirement community in the Phoenix's West Valley. It was flanked by an insurance company to the left and a nail salon to the right. *What else is new?* Farther down was a Subway and, on the corner, a Great Clips. The interior of Malcolm's store looked exactly as the website depicted it: a twenty-first-century dry goods store that contained everything from personal health care products to cards and sundries.

When I first entered the place I thought I saw Herb take some towels off a shelf to hand to an elderly lady. It was only when the man turned around that I realized it wasn't Herb. The balding head and potbelly were to blame. Then I remembered the description my mother had given me of Malcolm Porter. It had to be him. At least I had the advantage. What I didn't have was the authority to question the guy. Or any idea what I was about to say. I bit my lower lip and decided to improvise.

"Excuse me, Mr. Porter. Do you carry those small repair kits for eyeglasses? I'm always losing the screws on my sunglasses." *At least it's something I really do need.*

He didn't seem particularly surprised I addressed him by name. It was only later I found out he had ads in all the Sun City newspapers, with his photo plastered in all of them.

"Aisle five near the travel kits. Is this your first time in our store? Most of our customers know this place better than I do."

"Um, yes. I was in the area and took a chance you'd have one of those kits."

"Did you find out about us from the *Sun City Independent*? We always have a dollar-off coupon in there. It's called Malcolm Money."

I shook my head.

"Never mind. I'll give you the dollar off. Most of our customers get the *Independent*, but soon we'll have lots of ads running on the radio."

Oh my God! Did he say what I just thought I heard him say? I've got an opening. I'd better not blow it. "What do you mean?"

"The West Valley Commercial Retailors Association decided to plunk a substantial amount of money into airtime at the local radio stations. That's bound to bring in customers. Nothing like a snappy little jingle that people can't get out of their heads."

"Um, when does your ad start?"

"Not soon enough. We're already on Hometown Radio 108.1 FM and a few others, but it's only a matter of time before you'll hear our ad in the Sun City area. Station 103.1 FM in Sun City West, to be precise. They're poised to move from live broadcasting to prerecorded shows. Once that happens, our ads will be filtered in like fluoride in our water supply."

"I see."

"Say, did you happen to catch the news about their programming director? He was found dead in the station yesterday. And to think that could have been me. I was in there a few days ago to see if we could infuse an ad midway into one of those live broadcasting shows. Howard Buell—that's the guy—said no. Said any kind of interruption throws off the presenters and they get flustered. Good grief! Have you ever listened to one of those shows? A misplaced stapler could send any one of those speakers into a tizzy. Truth be known, I told Howard that, but he wouldn't budge."

"Mr. Porter, it's none of my business, but that could be motive for murder."

"Murder? Over radio ads? Nah. If you ask me, I think it was either a robbery gone sour or something much more personal."

"Robbery? Radio stations don't carry large amounts of cash."

"No, but they do have some pretty expensive equipment. And as far as personal goes, if I were those sheriff's deputies, I'd be having a long conversation with George Fowler."

"The station manager? *That* George Fowler?"

"It's no secret he and Howard were always arguing about something. At least that's what I saw every time I was in the Men's Club building. I play poker there a few times a week. Goodness. Would you just listen to me? Can't believe I'm yammering off at the mouth like this. My wife always says I could talk the finish off a car. Of course, Penelope Porter's no shrinking violet. She could chew anyone's ears off like the best of them. Anyway, nice chatting with you. Take your time and look around. Maybe you'll become a regular around here. Oh, and don't forget to tell the cashier Malcolm said you could have a Malcolm Money dollar."

"Um, thanks. I will. Nice talking with you, too."

I smiled and walked toward aisle five, but not before glancing back to see Malcolm Porter take out his cell phone and make a call. Had I hit a nerve? Or maybe it was only my imagination. I quickly added George Fowler to my list of suspects.

Sure enough, I found the eyeglass repair kit without any trouble. Then I turned to the opposite side of the aisle, where the sewing section stood. A blue and white sign hung directly over it that read, "We Carry Drency and Gingher Scissors."

CHAPTER 7

I knew what Nate would say without even asking. "Just because Malcolm's store sells Gingher scissors doesn't make him complicit in Howard Buell's death." However, it did provide the proprietor with a handy-dandy weapon. *If* indeed the guy had a genuine motive. I jotted down the info on my newly scribed suspect list and popped a Marie Callender's chicken dinner in the microwave. I promised myself I'd do some real cooking once Marshall got back. Or at least make an attempt. Thank goodness the guy wasn't too fussy.

At a little past eight my friend Lyndy called, and I filled her in on everything that had transpired in the last thirty-six hours. Lyndy Ellsworth and I had become fast friends when I moved here a few years ago. She, too, was in her forties, single, and dealing with a wacky relative in Sun City West.

"Yeesh, Phee! It's like these bodies keep landing in your mother's backyard. I'm surprised my aunt didn't mention it. She's all over that kind of gossip."

"Give her time. The details only made the news today. But I got smart this time. Well, not exactly 'smart,' but ahead of the game. Instead of waiting for my mother to nag me to death because she thinks she and her book club ladies are potential victims, I decided to do a little fact checking on my own. Of course, she'll still insist I talk with Cindy Dolton at the dog park."

"The lady with the white dog who knows anyone and everyone?"

"Yep. That's her. The eyes and ears of Sun City West. Unfortunately, I'll get stuck bringing Streetman. He's fine in the car, but once he gets into the park, it's anyone's guess whose dog he's going to shower his attention on. The last time it was a basset hound named LuLu. Poor thing couldn't shake him off her back."

"Maybe you'll get lucky and the sheriff's office will apprehend the killer."

"Not likely. Or not anytime soon. They're mired in interviews and even called Nate and Marshall to assist."

"So, what's your next step?"

"The victim's ex-girlfriend. It's either that or I learn how to play euchre."

"Huh?"

"A group of men were in the building playing euchre around the time of the murder."

"Go with the ex-girlfriend. Those deputies have probably spoken to the euchre players by now. Besides, do they even know the victim had a former girlfriend?"

"Good point. You should be sleuthing with me."

"I'd rather sleuth from the sidelines. And, truth be known, you might be better off leaving the entire deal to the professionals. You don't want to risk putting yourself in jeopardy like you did that night at the Stardust Theater."

I gulped at Lyndy's last statement. Mainly because she was right.

"So," she said, "any interest in an early morning hike on Saturday?"

"For sure. Marshall will be working, and I'll need the stress relief. Talk to you later this week."

"You got it."

I took a hot shower and immediately glanced at the landline to see if the red light was blinking. Nothing. Then I checked my iPhone, in case Marshall had sent a text or left a voice mail. Still nothing. Then, as if he read my mind, the phone rang, and I grabbed it.

"I'll be home in the morning, hon. Got as far as Casa Grande before I conked out. Mission accomplished. Turns out the guy moved in with an old girlfriend and actually registered his daughter at one of the elementary schools in Benson. Didn't even try to change her name or use fake identification. Anyway, I gave all the details to the wife, including the address, the school, photos, you name it. She's well within her rights to have him arrested for abduction, but that's up to her. Williams Investigations fulfilled its contract. I did impress upon her not to act alone and to notify the authorities. I'd feel awful if this thing escalated into one of those ugly scenes where someone shows up brandishing a gun. My gosh. I'm going a mile a minute. I didn't even ask how you are doing."

"I'm fine. Everything's fine."

"Good. Because starting tomorrow, I'll be working much closer to home. I take it Nate filled you in."

"Uh-huh. Frankly, I'm glad the two of you were pulled into this case. Last thing I need is another murder looming over Sun City West. By next week the term 'rational thought' will disappear completely from my mother's vocabulary. Trust me."

"Oh, I do. Believe me. I've seen those women in action. Try not to worry about it. I'll drive right to the office once I get up and get showered. The only thing I've got in my overnight bag is dirty laundry, and it's not going anywhere."

"Want me to pick up something to make for dinner?"

"Nah. We both need a break. Let's grab a pizza or burgers."

The next few minutes were those sweet, cuddly ones in which we said how much we missed each other. Then I crept into bed and didn't get up until the alarm went off the following day. Only it wasn't the alarm I had set. It was my mother. Calling to inform me about some crazy garage sale she and the book club ladies heard about late last night.

"Do you need any home goods? Towels? Sheets? Pots or pans? Microwavable bowls?"

"You're calling me at six in the morning to talk about microwavable bowls? And no, we don't need anything."

"Lucinda's neighbor found out about the sale and called her late last night. I think the seller is some sort of hoarder who buys all this stuff on the cheap and then unloads it at garage sales."

"Um, I don't quite think that's a hoarder. More like an entrepreneur."

"Anyway, I've got to run, Phee. Shirley is picking me up at seven and we're off to the Thursday garage sales. Any news from Nate? Did they catch the scissors-wielding maniac?"

"No, not yet. As far as I know, Edward Scissorhands is alive and well somewhere in the vicinity."

"That's not funny."

"Well, you asked. By the way, how's Shirley doing?"

"She says she jumps every time the phone rings or there's a knock at the door. She's still convinced those were her shears sticking out of Howard Buell's gut."

"Tell her to relax. According to Nate, the forensics lab should have results today."

"I'll bet anything they belong to Sylvia Strattlemeyer. Tell me the second you find out."

"I can't do that. I'm not at liberty to divulge that kind of information."

"Not at liberty to let your mother know if there was a cold-blooded killer lurking around? Myrna and I are going to be in that radio station this coming Tuesday. Even with that flimsy security they plan to provide."

"Maybe by Tuesday the case will be solved." *Who am I kidding?*

"Harrumph. What about dish towels? People always need dish towels."

"Fine. Dish towels. Love you."

Sure enough, I found out whose fingerprints they were the second I stepped into the office.

Augusta was all but chomping at the bit to share the news. "Mr. Williams got a call from Deputy Ranston a few minutes ago. The forensics lab matched up those fingerprints, and it's a doozy."

"Oh no. Please don't tell me they belong to any of my mother's friends."

Augusta clasped her hands together and rested her chin on them. "Maybe you should hear it from Mr. Williams himself. He told me, but that's because I was the only one here."

"Yeah. Sorry about that. My mother called at dawn and wouldn't stop yakking. Apparently, there's a good garage sale going on."

"Don't need other people's junk. Unless it's tools. You can get some good deals on tools. I once bought a log splitter still in its original box. The owner decided to get a gas-burning fireplace instead of spitting wood."

"Um, yeah. Sounds like a good deal."

"What good deal?" Nate stepped out of his office and walked to the coffee maker.

"A log splitter," I said. "Augusta's."

He shook his head, looked directly at Augusta, and then popped a K-Cup into the machine. "I suppose you heard the forensics lab matched up the fingerprints on those scissors. Ranston called me first thing this morning."

"Please don't tell me they belong to Shirley Johnson. Her prints are on file with the state because she volunteers at the elementary schools."

"Nope. Not Shirley. The prints happen to belong to Ursula Grendleson."

I shrugged. "And?"

"And here's where it gets really weird. Ursula Grendleson passed away twenty years ago. At age ninety-seven. She graduated from Arizona State University back when it was Tempe Normal School and taught home economics in the Phoenix area until she retired in the late sixties and moved to Sun City. She was one of their first residents. Never married. No children. Her prints were on file in the state database because she also volunteered in the schools. At least up until 1998. Can you imagine?"

I gasped and Augusta let out a laugh. "Told you you'd better hear it from Mr. Williams."

I looked at both of them. "That doesn't make sense."

"It does if someone stole the scissors from somewhere. I did a little checking. Gingher scissors have been around since 1947. Given the fact that Ursula taught Home Ec, she must've had an entire collection of scissors. God knows where they wound up."

Augusta all but spit. "In old Mr. Buell's gut, if you don't mind me saying."

I shook my head and rubbed my hands together. "This is awful. Absolutely awful. My mother must never get wind that those scissors belonged to a deceased person. She'll be on the phone with Shirley like no one's business, and you know how superstitious Shirley and Cecilia are. I can hear it now: Shirley will be wailing and lamenting that some dead spirit is haunting the radio station. And Cecilia will be worse. No, they must never find out."

Nate removed his coffee cup from the machine and took a sip. "We have no control over what the sheriff's office shares with the press."

"Well, they can't share this! You've got to do something. Call Bowman. Call Ranston. Tell them to keep their mouths shut."

Nate set his coffee cup on Augusta's desk and patted my shoulder. "Relax. They're not about to leak information on an active crime case."

"What's your take on it?" I asked.

"Too early to tell. We've got witnesses to interview, a

timeline to narrow down, and some background checks to complete."

"I thought you and Marshall were simply going to interview the pickleball players. Oh, speaking of which, he'll be in this morning. He closed that case."

"I know. Got his text. Also got one from Bowman. Short and to the point. They need us to do more legwork. The county deputies are stretched to the limit with other cases." Then he turned to Augusta. "What time did you say that first pickleball interview is?"

"At one. In the posse station at Sun City West. That should give you time for your appointment with the Glendale manager of Home Products Plus. You didn't say if he was coming here or you're going there."

"I'm going. It's only five minutes away. Besides, I need to get a look at their setup. It's not only the Phoenix store that's losing inventory."

Augusta moved her fingers across the keyboard and looked at the screen. "I left you plenty of time for lunch, but your pickleball schedule runs until five. Then it starts again at ten thirty tomorrow. I scheduled Mr. Gregory for tomorrow, too, but wasn't sure about today, so I left him alone."

"When he gets caught up around here, send him my way. I should be pulling my hair out by then."

"At least you have hair, Mr. Williams. Most men your age are usually—"

"Thank you for the insight, Augusta. I'll keep that in mind as I watch the gray hairs take over."

The truth of the matter was that Nate Williams was a damn good-looking man, with salt-and-pepper hair and a decent physique. Even though he was in his sixties, he looked more like someone ten years younger. My mother's friends wondered why Nate and I didn't become romantically involved, but I had always thought of him as a friend. Besides, I never got over my crush on Marshall Gregory. Thank goodness he felt the same way about me.

Marshall breezed in at a little past eleven. I had plenty of warning from Augusta, who shouted, "Marshall's at the front door," as if it was the health inspector and I was running a restaurant.

I got up and greeted him with a hug at the door before it even closed. We managed a quick kiss before Augusta cleared her throat at least three times.

"I'll make up for lost time later," he whispered and I squeezed his hand. "It's good to be back," he said. "Got to admit, I had a hunch we'd be taking the lead on the Buell case. Nate texted me about those interviews. I'd better get caught up with my emails so I can be at the posse station by one. Maybe with the two of us working, we'll have a fighting chance of getting out of there at a reasonable time."

I smiled. "From what I understand, it's a much younger crew than the last set of interviews you had. I doubt you'll have to listen to anyone's tales of World War II."

As it turned out, I was right about my impression of the pickleball players. It was a quarter to eight and we had just returned from our favorite pizzeria. Snuggling next to Marshall on the couch, he recounted the entire afternoon.

"I'll say this much: those pickleballers are energetic, enthusiastic, and sharp. They were also insistent I move to Sun City West and join their club. One of the men told me I had a racquetball arm, but insisted it could be remedied. Whatever *that* meant. Another woman gave me the history of pickleball. There was no stopping her. Did you know it started in the state of Washington, where some politician's family improvised badminton with paddle balls? Well, now you do!"

"Ouch. Nate must have pitched a fit."

"You could say that. We divided up the interviews and every time I looked his way, he mouthed 'Save me.'"

"Any luck identifying the person who was seen going into the Men's Club?"

"I wouldn't call it luck. For a bunch of sports enthusiasts who have to home in on a small ball with holes in it, none of them managed to get a good look at the individual who was seen leaving the court and going into the Men's Club. And yes, four people saw someone. Two of those people insisted it was a woman and the other two were positive it was a man. Yikes!"

"But wouldn't the players whose team that person was on notice that he or she disappeared?"

"Maybe not. They do take breaks, you know. And everyone mills around. Plus it was practice time."

For a brief second I thought about the other crew who had a propensity for milling around. And for yelling "Poop alert!" when they weren't chatting up a storm. Like it or not, I knew I had to pay Cindy Dolton a visit.

CHAPTER 8

The following day Nate and Marshall continued their pickleball interviews and conferred with Deputies Bowman and Ranston. According to Marshall, the euchre players didn't hear a thing. Bagels 'N More delivered breakfast to the card players at six and, as far as the men knew, everything in the building was fine.

Their card game was down the hall from the radio station, and as one of the men admitted, "We're so damn loud we could drown out a freight train. That's why we don't play in anyone's house. The women would kill us."

I knew Nate and Marshall would use a systematic approach to the investigation, and that meant they'd be dealing with an entirely different set of suspects than the ones who bounced around in my mind. Sure, there was George Fowler, the station manager, and Malcolm Porter, who'd made it no secret he was unhappy with the live broadcasts. Beyond that were the pickleballers and the euchre players. Nate and Marshall would have to search far and deep for connections that could lead to murder. But what about the Bagels 'N More delivery people? Couldn't one of them harbor a grudge? And what about the Rec Center maintenance person who unlocked the Men's Club building? I'd be sure to toss those tidbits in their direction when they returned to the office.

Meanwhile, I had my own suspects to deal with, even though I wasn't exactly sure how to approach them. As much as I hated to admit it, a jilted ex-girlfriend with a pair of scissors in her hand could very well do the deed. And while my boss and my boyfriend relied on databases such as TLOxp for licensed investigators, I had my own methods. Namely, Facebook.

When ten fifteen rolled around, I made a cup of coffee and helped myself to one of the minicupcakes Augusta had brought in from Quick Stop.

"I'd love to stay and talk," I said to her, "but I'm going to do some snooping on the internet. I need to find out about Howard Buell's ex-girlfriend."

"The one you mentioned the other day?"

"Uh-huh. Sylvia Strattlemeyer. My mother and the book club ladies have all but convicted her of murder."

"Okay, then. Done deal."

"Very funny. I'm going to see what clubs she's in and how I can possibly connect with her."

"Gee, maybe you can even friend her."

"I'm not going that far."

"If you find something really juicy, let me know."

"Believe me, I'll let everyone know."

My mother had mentioned Sylvia hosting some boring radio show about beading, so I hoped her Facebook page would indicate she belonged to the Sun City West Beaders Club. I set my coffee cup on the desk, popped the minicupcake in my mouth, and logged on to Facebook.

Sylvia Strattlemeyer's banner photo showed two hairless cats dressed as rabbits with long, pink-and-blue bunny ears. A small inset photo featured a headshot of a middle-aged woman with bright red hair and equally bright red lipstick. She was wearing round glasses and had an eye-catching red-and-white scarf draped across her neck.

I scrolled farther down and noticed an entire collection of photos featuring the two hairless cats in various outfits, as well as group shots with Sylvia at assorted restaurants. In all those photos, she was surrounded by a tableful of women. Only one photo was different. It was Sylvia, but her hair was no longer red. It was silver, but I recognized the same red-and-white scarf she had worn for her inset shot.

Next to her was a man who appeared to be in his late sixties. Howard Buell perhaps? Same short brown hair and tan, but it was tough to compare a corpse to a Facebook photo.

Then I glanced at Sylvia's list of friends. All unrecognizable names. That meant she didn't travel in the same circle as my mother or her crew. I darted my eyes to the newsfeed, and that was when I hit pay dirt. Photo after photo showed Sylvia posing with all sorts of Sun City West clubs. Their signs and posters shouted out "Rip 'n' Sew," "Creative Stitchers," "Encore Needle and Craft," and "SCW Beaders."

Yep, if anyone had a need for a good pair of scissors, it was Sylvia. And she had a good motive, too. Maybe those Telemundo shows weren't all that far off. I closed the app and opened one that called for my immediate attention. It was an accounting spreadsheet I had been working on. As I tallied the numbers in front of me, I made a mental note to pull up the Sun City West club list during lunch to check their meeting times. Maybe I'd hit the jackpot and one of them would be on next week's schedule.

The rest of the morning was as routine as could be. Me, with my nose stuck to the computer screen, and Augusta in a similar mode. At a little past noon I checked the club meeting times and learned that the Creative Stitchers had a meeting planned for Monday at seven, followed by coffee and desserts. It also said anyone interested could attend. That was all I needed to put it on my calendar and pray Sylvia would make an appearance.

Nate and Marshall returned to the office at a little before five with nothing to show for their day's efforts except detailed sets of notes.

"I wouldn't exactly call it a waste." Marshall poked his head into my office and leaned a hand on the doorjamb. "I got lots of tips about pickleball strategies and one recommendation from a lady to get a copy of *The Art of Pickleball* by Gale H. Leach."

"What about Nate?"

"He fared a lot better. Three women wrote down their phone numbers for him."

I tried not to snicker. "So, not a single lead?"

"Not any viable ones. Not yet. We're still checking background information on the players because, as you know, people have been known to cover things up. At least we can do that from the comfort of our desks tomorrow. I don't know about you, but it's Friday, and I sure could go for the all-you-can-eat fish-and-chips at Rubio's."

"Sounds fantastic. By the way, I'm checking a lead of

my own. Not that this person was near the scene of the crime, but according to Myrna and my mother—"

"I know. I know. Sylvia Strattlemeyer. Funny, but her name came up with some of the pickleballers."

"She used to play?"

"Nope. She made T-shirts with decorative beading for a few of them. The shirts read 'Get Pickled on Our Courts.'"

I rolled my eyes and choked back a laugh. "She's a person of interest, you know."

"Don't tell me. You plan to accidentally run into her and give her the fifth degree without her even knowing what you're up to."

"Um, something like that. Besides, I've always taken an interest in sewing."

"Really? Since when? I'm the one who sews the missing buttons on our clothes."

I walked to the door and planted a kiss on his lips. "That's because you're a natural. Give me a minute. I'll shut down the computer and get ready to head out."

"I really am a sucker for your charms. Might as well meet up at Rubio's because we've got both cars. Tell me, what will you be up to tomorrow while I'm slaving away at background checks?"

"Lyndy and I thought we'd do a bit of hiking. Don't worry, I won't wear myself out in case you and I decide to do the same on Sunday."

Augusta and Nate were already at the front door by the time I shut off the lights to my office.

"Marshall took off already," Augusta said. "Something about getting a good table at Rubio's."

"Yeah," I said. "Between the snowbirds and the regular Friday family crowd, those places fill up fast. You know both of you are welcome to join us."

Augusta shook her head. "Got a thick porterhouse steak waiting for me to throw on the grill, but thanks anyway."

"Nate?"

"Believe it or not, I actually do have a social life. I'm meeting a friend for dinner."

"Not one of the pickleball players?"

"Hmm. Marshall just had to mention that. And no, not one of the pickleball players. A retired police officer I happen to know. Anyway, I'll catch you on Monday, Phee."

"And you'll see me first thing tomorrow, Mr. Williams," Augusta said. "I'm beginning to enjoy these half-day Saturdays."

The weekend came and went like a fast nor'easter blizzard without the snow. Lyndy and I took one of the lower trails at Lake Pleasant and picnicked on cold Raising Cane's Chicken Tenders. Then, on Sunday, Marshall and I took a longer hike at White Tank Mountains, ate terrific subs, and collapsed on the couch to watch a *Psych* marathon. That was when the phone rang. One look at the caller ID and I cringed. My mother!

"I meant to call you yesterday, Phee, but I got caught up at Bagels 'N More. Can you believe it? The ladies and I were there for over two and a half hours. Then I had to make up the time with poor Streetman, who was all alone in the house. Anyway, you're not going to believe what I bought."

"Linens? Towels? More refrigerator magnets with frames for the dog's picture?"

"Honestly, sometimes I think you're actually jealous of him."

Who wouldn't be? The British Royal Family doesn't

dote on the princes and princesses as much. "I'm not jealous."

"Good. Because I bought you Egyptian sheets and towels. Bargain basement prices. And those dish towels you wanted. Stop by anytime to get them."

"Um, maybe tomorrow. After work."

"Any news on the investigation?"

"If you mean has anyone been apprehended, no. But Nate, Marshall, and the deputies are making headway with their interviews."

"A horse can make headway, too, at a race, but it doesn't mean he'll finish. Keep after them. The Booked 4 Murder ladies and I are on edge. In case you haven't noticed."

"If I haven't, I'm sure you'll remind me."

I thanked her for the home goods products and reassured her that the case was moving along. Technically, I wasn't lying. It was moving along, but so did slugs after a good rain.

I was back at work on Monday, and no one was any closer to solving Howard's untimely demise. At least there was the Creative Stitchers meeting to look forward to, on the off chance Sylvia would be in attendance.

"All I'm doing is getting a sense of whether or not this Sylvia Strattlemeyer is capable of murder," I told Nate and Marshall that morning.

Nate was off to meet with another rep from Home Products Plus, and Marshall had an appointment with Deputy Ranston about some possible suspects.

"Not that I would ever discount any prying you do, kiddo, but keep in mind it's more than a gut feeling." Nate glanced at the wall clock and started toward the door. "Was she in the vicinity at the time of the crime?

That would give her opportunity. How angry was she at Howard? There's motive for you. And, finally, what would she be doing with a twenty-year-old pair of scissors that belonged to Ursula Grendleson? Did she know Ursula?"

"My gosh. I'll be lucky if I find the answer to just one of those questions."

"Just one?" He winked and was out the door.

Marshall gave my shoulder a squeeze. "You'll be fine. One answer is one step closer, even if your suspect isn't on anyone's radar."

"Yet," I said. "Yet."

"I'll save you some tuna salad for dinner, okay? It's the only thing I can rig up on short notice. No guarantees on the taste. Anyway, you might not notice the flavor because you'll be starving by the time you get home from your mother's house and that stitchery meeting."

"I love your tuna. I'd never had it with green olives and chives until I met you."

Augusta looked up from her computer. "I've got a great recipe for tuna. Calls for Worcestershire sauce instead of mayo and lots of diced turnips. Or you can substitute with parsnips."

I widened my eyes and shook my head. "We'll stick with mayo and olives."

The next chance I had to speak with Marshall came at four thirty, when he returned from Sun City West. He and Deputy Ranston wound up interviewing the morning maintenance crew who worked the day Howard's body had been discovered. Maybe those sheriff's deputies were on the right track after all.

"Any luck?" I asked Marshall as he rapped on my doorjamb.

"We've got a tight timeline and that helps, but we're still way off from solving this one."

I was about to suggest the Bagels 'N More delivery people when Augusta shouted out, "The bagels those euchre players ate didn't get there by themselves. Maybe the delivery guy did it."

Marshall shouted back, "Isn't that stretching it a bit?"

Next thing I knew, Augusta was also at my door. "It's always the people no one suspects. Just saying."

Marshall shrugged, tossed me a look, and turned to face Augusta. "Oh, what the heck. Might as well throw another fish in the net."

"Do you want me to call Bagels 'N More to find out who was out on delivery that morning, Mr. Gregory?"

"Why not? At this point it can't hurt."

Augusta waited until Marshall returned to his office. Then she approached my desk. "Figured I'd save you the time. You can thank me later."

"Only if the delivery guy turns out to be the killer."

CHAPTER 9

It was a quarter to six when I got to my mother's house. Thankfully, I didn't see the usual lineup of Buicks parked in front. Streetman took one look at me when I opened the door and ran under the couch.

"Good grief! I'm practically that dog's second owner. I take him to the park all the time and what does he do? Hides under the couch when I walk in."

My mother glanced at the living room. "That's because he needs time to process who's here. Give him a minute or two and I'm sure he'll come out. Anyway, let me show you what I picked up at that sale."

For the next fifteen minutes my mother showed me box after box of towels, sheets, comforters, tablecloths, and plastic sink liners. All expensive, brand names.

She was practically beaming. "You can never have too many sink liners. Once you rinse off anything that's had red sauce on it, the sink liner stains and you can't get it out."

"Um, yeah. I suppose. But what about all that other stuff you bought? What on earth do you plan to do with it? Hold your own sale?"

"Holiday gifts for next year. I bought all size linens and towels. Oh, let me show you the ones I have for you."

I had to admit, my mother did get "the deal of the day." I offered to pay her for the bedding and towels, but she insisted it was a housewarming present, even though Marshall and I moved in months ago. I picked up the boxes and walked to the door. "Got to get going, Mom."

She was right about the dog. He came out from his hiding place and furiously licked the bottom of his paws from his new spot: right in front of the door.

My mother held up her hands and blocked me from taking another step. "Don't make any sudden movements when he's cleaning himself. For some reason it unnerves him. Give me a moment."

I stood perfectly still while she went into the kitchen and came back with a piece of ham. She waved it in front of the dog, cooing, "Mommy has a ham yummy for her little man." Then she motioned for me to proceed. "If anything happens to me at that radio station tomorrow, promise me you'll take good care of Streetman."

"Huh? What?"

"You know what I'm saying. That killer is still loose."

"I thought there was going to be security at the station."

"There is. They're sending a posse volunteer. I don't even know if they're armed, but Myrna will bring an arsenal of her home defense products."

"I think you'll be fine. I'll be sure to listen to your

show during break tomorrow. Anyway, I need to get a move on. Thanks again for the towels and stuff."

I gave her a hug and headed straight for my car before it dawned on her to ask if I was going right home. I didn't want to tell her I was on my way to the Beardsley Recreation Center Building for the Creative Stitchers meeting or she'd be on the phone with everyone in that book club of hers, telling them Sylvia Strattlemeyer was going to be arrested.

I knew how my mother's thought processes worked. She could go from point A to points D and E without ever looking back for B and C. And, apparently, that Chiweenie of hers was no different. And why she insisted on entering him in that Christmas in July event was beyond me.

Beardsley Recreation Center was the first of the rec centers to be built in Sun City West. It sat on the corner of Stardust Boulevard and Beardsley Road and housed an aquatic center as well as an activity building for clubs, each with its own large parking lot. Behind the buildings was a huge expanse of lawn for open-air performances and movies. In addition, numerous barbeque areas, each with its own canopy and seating area, dotted the perimeter.

I found a parking space in what could best be described as "the north forty." It was so far away from the building I counted my walk from the car to the club room as part of my weekly exercise routine.

Having been here on a prior occasion involving yet another murder, I knew my way around the club rooms. Each one had its own marquee over the door, and some even had decorative hanging signs. A number of women walked past me, some carrying armloads of fabric, others with plastic bins full of heaven knows what. I spotted a few with artificial flowers, most likely for the floral arrangement club.

Creative Stitchers was situated in a double room adjacent to an interior courtyard. The doors were wide open as I approached, and a hefty woman wearing tan slacks and a patterned top greeted me.

"Welcome, I'm Eunice Moore. We're so happy you could join us this evening. Please take a name tag from the table and help yourself to refreshments. We'll get a chance to chat later, I'm sure, after the business meeting."

She must have noticed the horrified expression on my face. "Don't worry. The meetings are always short. Old minutes, treasurer's report, and new business."

"Uh, thanks. I wasn't really sure what to expect."

"Fun! Lots of fun! Our stitchers enjoy sewing and talking."

Sounds like the Booked 4 Murder book club, but with needles and thread.

The chairs in the room were arranged in a large semi-circle, which gave me a terrific opportunity to see if Sylvia Strattlemeyer showed up. If not, at least I'd had the pleasure of meeting Eunice and eating ginger snaps. Most of the women worked on their projects while the officers gave their reports. Eunice was right: The meeting was short and to the point. The only thing new on the agenda was the March craft fair at the R. H. Johnson Recreation Center. Unfortunately, the business I had hoped to conduct never happened because there was no sign of Sylvia.

The meeting concluded and everyone was invited to

enjoy the assorted cookies and work on their projects. I milled around for a few minutes, and just as I was about to make my escape, in walked the white-haired lady I'd seen in that Facebook photo. No mistaking her. Bright red lipstick, bright red nails, black leggings, and a colorful tunic top. So what if she was no longer a redhead?

The woman plopped a satchel on the table a few spots from where I was sitting and made a beeline for the refreshments. Her voice permeated the room. "Eleanor, good to see you. Myrtle, you look wonderful. I absolutely adore your new hair color. Francine, are you still working on those hand-sewn bags? I've got some ideas about bedazzling them. I got the most wonderful beads from a show in Tucson last month."

Yep, it was Sylvia all right. Now all I needed was to break into a conversation with her. I was inches away, ginger snap number six or seven in my hand, when, all of sudden, Eunice grabbed her by the shoulder. "Awful thing about Howard, but you're so much better off without him. That man would have gambled all your money away. Of course, no one deserves to be murdered. Tsk-tsk. A shame. A darn shame."

I nearly choked on my cookie. Eunice then put a hand on each of Sylvia's shoulders and kept talking. "I'm telling you, it was only a matter of time before all the casinos around here split that inheritance he got. It wasn't any secret how fast he was going through his late aunt's estate."

Oh yes it is. It's a big secret. Because the sheriff's office has no idea.

There were only so many cookies I could eat without looking like a glutton. Still, I remained frozen in front of the pastry trays while Eunice kept babbling on.

Finally, Sylvia spoke. "Foibles or not, I adored that man. His death has left me with a deep hole in my heart."

And an empty pocketbook? Mentally, I rolled my eyes.

"You poor dear," Eunice said. "Do you have any idea who could have murdered him?"

"Not really. It wasn't as if he carried billfolds of money with him. Unless, of course, it was a casino day. And the sheriff's office didn't say it was a robbery. In fact, the news media never even said how he was killed. I do know one thing, though. Howard made prearrangements for his cremation and burial. No family to speak of, so I doubt they'll have his body lingering on too long."

By now, Eunice had removed her hands from Sylvia's shoulders and grabbed her by the wrist. "Surely you must have some idea who did him in."

"Only a hunch. About three months ago George Fowler—that's the radio station manager—approached him about adding more canned programming to the show. Howard was opposed to anything that would take away from the hometown flavor. They argued about it constantly."

"You should go straight to the sheriff's office and tell them."

Before Sylvia could say a word, someone shouted, "Eunice! We need your opinion on a color pattern."

"Later." Eunice took off.

I was now elbow-to-elbow with Sylvia. Our eyes met and I blurted out, "Um, sorry, I overheard a bit of that and I don't think you should tell those sheriff's deputies anything."

"Oh, believe me, I have no intention of doing so. I'm off the radar, so to speak. No one knows Howard was my former boyfriend, and I intend to keep it that way. Last thing I need is to become a murder suspect. They always think it's the ex-wife or the ex-girlfriend. And if I was going to knock him off, I certainly wouldn't do it in a public place like that radio station. I'd probably do what that woman up in Prescott Valley did with her miserable husband. She poisoned him a little bit each day with antifreeze. Guy never noticed until he dropped dead."

"Ew."

"By the way, I'm Sylvia Strattlemeyer. You must be new to the Creative Stitchers. Tell me, who does your work?"

"My work?"

"You know, your face and body sculpting. You look much too young to be with this crowd."

Finally someone noticed! "Oh, I don't live here. I'm, uh, just visiting my mother, and I thought I'd see what some of these clubs are about. I'm Phee."

"Nice to meet you. Creative Stitchers is a fun place. Check out Rip 'n' Sew, too. Much better refreshments. Anyway, I should mingle, seeing as I got here late."

I told her it was nice meeting her as well and then I slipped out of there as fast and as inconspicuously as possible. I wasn't convinced she was the killer, but I wasn't about to let her off the hook either.

That conversation she had with Eunice replayed over and over again in my head on the drive home. Marshall all but got it verbatim when I walked in the door of our house.

"A gambler, huh? I wonder if he blew his aunt's estate and wound up owing the wrong people money. It's certainly a new twist to check out."

I put my bag on the kitchen counter and poured myself a Coke. "It makes no sense for someone to kill a person who owes them money. You can't collect a debt from a corpse."

"Maybe not an intentional act of murder, but quite possibly an argument that got out of hand. Then there's the matter of those scissors. It's a conundrum all right."

"Does that mean you're going to be looking deeper into Howard's background?"

"More like his habits. We've got the timeline narrowed down, but not the days leading up to it. Your choice bit of info might be the break we need. Give me a minute to get the bread and tuna salad on the table and you can give me your take on Sylvia."

"I'll grab the plates and silverware."

Once we sat down and made our sandwiches, I told him my impression of Sylvia.

"Yeesh," he said. "She was perfectly fine with a long poisoning, but not something in a public venue?"

"It was more of a matter-of-fact reflection. I didn't get the impression she was a killer. Then again, I'm not taking her off my list."

"Um, who else is on your list?"

"George Fowler moved to the top. Both Malcolm Porter and Sylvia Strattlemeyer said he and Howard had been arguing. Maybe George wanted Howard out of the way so the canned programming would be used. And maybe, just maybe, there was something in it for him in the form of payola from those sponsors."

"Actually, it's something the sheriff's office is looking at."

I wiped the corner of my mouth with a napkin and nodded. "If any scuttlebutt wafts my way, I'll be sure to share it. Oh, before I forget, my mother bought us a ton of home goods. Linens. Towels. You name it. Some garage sale she and the book club ladies went to. All new stuff in their original boxes. I'll put it in our linen closet after we eat."

"That was really nice of her."

"She can't resist a good deal, but yeah."

"I take it the 'show must go on' tomorrow?"

"Undoubtedly. You think my mother's going to miss out on her newest claim to fame? Besides, she and Myrna are already shopping for outfits to wear to the Greater Phoenix Broadcast Dinner."

"Wish I could catch their show, but I'm tied up with appointments tomorrow morning."

"Don't worry. I'll fill you in."

"At least this one should be a little less dramatic."

As things turned out, he was wrong. Dead wrong.

CHAPTER 10

"All set for the next go-round?" Augusta asked at precisely nine fifty-five. She leaned into my office, coffee cup in hand, and pointed to the breakroom. "This is the high point of my morning. I can't wait to hear today's installment of the Booked 4 Murder radio show. Too bad Mr. Williams and Mr. Gregory are out of the office."

"I think they did that on purpose." I laughed.

"Get moving. Show starts at ten sharp."

There was no one other than us in the office, so I grabbed my coffee and followed Augusta into the breakroom. We kept the door open in case we had walk-ins, but we weren't expecting anyone until the early afternoon.

I turned the radio on to 103.1 FM and took a seat at our worktable. Augusta flung herself in the seat opposite mine and propped her elbows on the table, cupping her hands to her chest. We both waited for the canned music to stop and my mother's program to begin. I held my breath until I heard her voice.

"Good Morning! This is Harriet Plunkett, along with Myrna Mittleson, and we're pleased to welcome you to the *Booked 4 Murder Mystery Hour.* Today we'll be talking about cozy mysteries that will keep you guessing and laughing."

"And eating!" Myrna added. "Some of those books have wonderful recipes. Carol J. Perry's *Grave Errors* has cowboy cookies in them. Oatmeal with chocolate chips. And Stephanie Blackmoore has a wonderful recipe for rosemary cheese straws in her novel *Engaged in Death.* I could eat them all day."

"Enough with the food, Myrna; let's talk about murder. For those listeners who are not familiar with cozies, these delightful whodunits have no violence or—AARGH! AW! WHAT ARE YOU DOING HERE? HOW DID YOU GET IN?"

I shoved my coffee cup to the side and stood up. "My God, Augusta. What if it's Howard's killer? Maybe we should call nine-one-one."

The phone was a few feet from my chair and I reached to grab it. Just then, I heard my aunt Ina's voice. It was unmistakable, like my aunt Ina herself. "You told me I was going to be on the show, Harriet. That's why I'm here. And I got in because the posse volunteer let me. I'm ready for my program."

"That's next week! Don't you ever write anything down? Today Myrna wants to talk about *Aunt Dimity's Death.*"

I don't know how it was possible, but my aunt Ina's

voice got even louder. "Your aunt died, Myrna? I'm sorry to hear that."

"Not Myrna's aunt!" my mother exclaimed. "It's a book, for crying out loud. A wonderful cozy mystery series by Nancy Atherton."

"Oh. Well, that's better than having Myrna inconsolable over her deceased aunt. Anyway, I thought perhaps I could introduce readers to a little-known work by Hostalena von Honigsburg, from eighteenth-century Prussia. Her novel, *Murder in the Family Crypt,* will have readers glued to their seats."

"They'll be glued because they've fallen asleep and their bodies have gone numb. You can talk about something else next week. Myrna is anxious to tell readers about her favorite cozy mysteries."

"Uh-oh," Augusta said. "This could get ugly."

"It's already ugly. I'm praying they don't start a family argument over the air."

Then, out of the blue, the topic of cozy mysteries evaporated with my aunt's next thought. "Is that the closet where the dead programming manager was found last week?"

"That's the closet all right," Myrna said. "Now every time I go to open a closet in my house, I take a step back and steady myself."

"Myrna's right," my mother added. "You don't get over seeing something like that. Those images remain in your brain like maraschino cherries do in your body."

"That's just an old wives' tale," my aunt said. "Maraschino cherries take as long to digest as anything else you eat. Of course, it depends on how well you chew them."

And suddenly the conversation went from murder to

mastication. The tension I originally felt in my neck when the subject of Howard's demise came up, gradually dissipated. I was terrified my mother or Myrna would reveal information that was meant to be confidential. Fortunately, that didn't happen. For the next ten minutes, the *Booked 4 Murder Mystery Hour* covered all sorts of mysteries, none of which had anything to do with the books they were reading.

I bit my lower lip and grimaced. "Ugh. I hate to say it, but after today's debacle, the station manager is going to pull this show off the air faster than the recreation board yanking Streetman's dog park privileges."

"I want to hear the rest of this show," Augusta said, "but I've got to get back to work. What do you say we leave the radio on with the sound turned up?"

"Fine with me."

I went back to my spreadsheets and only caught occasional words or phrases. According to Augusta, who decided to forfeit some lunchtime in order to listen to the rest of the show, my mother and her crew were able to focus and carry on a reasonable conversation about the cozy mystery genre.

"Well, that's good news, isn't it?" I said to Augusta.

"*That* part is, sure."

"What are you *not* telling me?"

"They sort of looped back to Howard's murder."

"Oh God no!"

"That wasn't the worst part."

"You mean there was more?" *I don't want to know. I don't want to know.*

Augusta's eyes moved in the direction of the coffee maker in the outside office. "You may want to refill your coffee."

"Just tell me."

"Fine. Your mother described the scissors sticking into Howard's gut and then told everyone that her daughter, who's with a very prominent investigative firm in the valley, is working the case."

I opened my mouth, but nothing came out except for a small squeak.

"Are you all right, Phee? It could have been worse, you know."

Finally the words came. "How could it possibly have been worse?"

"She didn't mention where you worked. And the Valley of the Sun, aka Phoenix, is awfully big. I wouldn't worry about it if I were you."

"Trust me, I'm worried. She told the whole world what the murder weapon was! I don't know how I can remotely explain that to Nate."

"He knows your mother. He'll understand. So will Marshall."

"I hope so. Um, by any chance, did my mother mention my name?"

"No. Not yours."

"What do you mean 'not yours'? Whose name did she mention?"

"Her dog's. Streetman. She intends to bring him into the radio station for her program next week. Something about canines being very helpful when it comes to solving murder mysteries."

"Maybe in the books they read, but not in real life. What on earth is my mother thinking?"

Before Augusta could say a word, I answered my own question. "Heaven help us. I know what she's planning. She's going to have that dog snoop around the radio station for clues. She's done that kind of thing before, you know, and let's just say it didn't turn out well."

Augusta crinkled her nose and gave it a rub. "A week's a long time off. Howard's murderer could be behind bars by then."

"I'm not counting on it."

Marshall returned to the office at a little before one with some cold subs from Quick Stop. "I figured you and Augusta might not have had lunch yet. Help yourself. Nate's on his way to meet with the regional manager for Home Products Plus. They may have a lead on that case. Meanwhile, I had the pleasure of working with Deputy Bowman on Howard's gambling history. He figured the guy might have been at one of the casinos right before he was murdered."

"Any luck?" I asked.

We followed Marshall into the breakroom, where he put the subs on the table and shrugged. "It's going to be a long process. Bowman and I contacted all the major casinos in the area, and that took all morning. Howard wasn't on any of the buses that take the Sun City area residents to those places. Of course, that doesn't mean anything. He could have driven himself. Those casinos aren't that far away."

"Only been to one of them," Augusta said. "Talking Stick Resort. And that was for the entertainment. Got a good deal on tickets for James Taylor and Bonnie Raitt. I work too damn hard to blow away money." She reached for a ham and cheese sub and grabbed a paper plate from the cupboard.

Marshall thumbed around one of the drawers for some napkins. "If Howard was the gambler Sylvia claimed he was, it might take us forever to figure out which casino he frequented. Too bad his car didn't have one of those Hum devices or we'd have a better idea. The car, by the way, was found parked in the Rec Center lot with a zillion other vehicles. Aargh. Bowman's team got a search warrant, but it didn't yield anything."

"That's too bad," I said.

"We've got another list to work on later today. At least twenty-five smaller places. God knows when I'll get home. Sorry, hon, but I'm afraid you'll have to do dinner on your own. I'll grab a burger tonight."

"No problem. I'll nuke an egg or something."

"Those subs are pretty big, Mr. Gregory," Augusta said. "Maybe you won't be very hungry and Phee can nuke an egg for you when you get home."

"Thanks a heap," I said to Augusta.

Marshall laughed. "I'll take my chances. Oops. It's getting on one thirty and I've got a one forty-five appointment about a missing person. After that, I'll be back at the posse station with Bowman. Oh, I almost forgot: Did you catch Harriet's radio show this morning?"

Augusta and I looked at each other without saying a word.

"Uh-oh," Marshall said. "From the looks on your faces it must have been a doozy."

I winced. "Um, yeah. You might say that. My aunt Ina got the date wrong and showed up. I'll tell you all about it tonight."

And please tell me Nate didn't listen to it either.

"Yikes. I can't wait to hear all the salient details."

"Oh, you'll hear salient all right, Mr. Gregory."

I glared at Augusta and she stifled a laugh.

"Catch you ladies later." Marshall breezed out of the breakroom.

I figured there had to be a better way of finding out where Howard did his gambling without having to track down all the casinos in the valley. Plus, there were tons of casinos up north, as well as the ones in Tucson. And what about Vegas? That was only a five-hour drive away. Surely someone had to know where the guy was the day before he wound up in the radio station's closet with Ursula Grendleson's Gingher scissors sticking out of his gut.

"Oh my God, Augusta! I could kick myself for not thinking of it."

"Of what?"

"Facebook. Maybe Howard had a Facebook page. I checked Sylvia's. I don't know why on earth I didn't think of checking Howard's. Come on. This should only take us a few seconds."

"Us?"

I motioned for her to follow me. "Yes. *Us!*"

We hightailed it to my office and I immediately scouted for the guy's page. Granted, it was a long shot, but it was better than nothing. Sure enough, Howard's profile appeared. Single, and his photo must have been taken while George W. Bush was still in office.

"Would you look at that?" Augusta leaned over my shoulder. "He's got a recent post on the page. Looks like he's drinking coffee near a swimming pool. Looks older than the profile picture, but still the same brown hair and tan."

"I know that place. It's the Buzz coffee shop at the R. H. Johnson pool, adjacent to the fitness center. Great hot dogs. My mother and I went there once so she could check out a water aerobics class. Hmm, they're open until nine. I might as well scope it out after work. If he's a regular, maybe someone will have an idea of where he was the day before his death. Or who he hung around with."

"Hot dogs, huh? So much for the nuked egg."

CHAPTER 11

Granted, it was the beginning of February and most Arizonians wouldn't be going near a pool until the temperature reached ninety-five or better, but the Minnesotans who flocked to the R. H. Johnson swimming and fitness area at the Rec Center were happy with an outdoor temp of sixty-five. Funny, but I used to be one of them until I moved here. I shuddered and pulled my cardigan a tad tighter across my chest as I entered the building. It was five forty, early evening, and I hoped my trip wouldn't be in vain.

The Buzz coffee shop, along with the sign-in area, was located to the left of a newly remodeled lounge area. Directly in front was the swimming pool, complete with water fountains and firepits. A woman who appeared to be in her thirties was behind the counter pouring a soft drink for a short man with bright-red swim trunks and an equally loud magenta towel draped around his shoulders.

When the man returned to the pool, I approached the counter. "Excuse me. I work for Williams Investigations in Glendale and I'd like to know if you recognize this man."

I handed the woman a copy of the photo of Howard that Augusta was able to print off from an old newspaper article she'd dug up about the Sun City West radio station.

"I'm sorry. He doesn't look familiar. Is he missing? I hear some elderly people get confused and go missing."

"Um, not exactly."

"You know, you may want to check with the monitor's desk over there and look at the sign-in sheets."

And this is precisely why I'm not a detective. I seem to miss the obvious and prefer going 'round the bush. "Thanks. I will."

The monitor was closer to my mother's age and apparently shared the same taste in hair color. Hers was an eclectic mixture of red, blond, and brown. All in chin-length streaks. Again, I identified myself and showed her Howard's photo.

She put a hand to her mouth and sighed. "Howard was a regular fixture on one of those lounge chairs by the pool when he wasn't at the radio station. I suppose that's how he kept his tan. Is this about the verbal altercation he had the day before his death? Because it was never reported. People get upset and lose it all the time. The only reason I know about it is because I was on duty. And because both men were so loud."

"Both men? Do you know who Howard was arguing with?"

"No idea. I couldn't really see the other man, but I did hear Howard say he wasn't about to sacrifice the radio station for some business's idea of making a profit."

My mind immediately jumped to Malcolm Porter. Profit was what it was all about for him, and having a radio station that ran his ads all the time was a far cry better than one that hosted community chats like *Crocheting with Dora* or . . . gulp, heaven help me, the *Booked 4 Murder Mystery Hour*.

"It would really help with the investigation," I said, "if I could get a look at the sign-in sheet for that day."

The monitor opened the large binder she had directly in front of her and flipped a few pages. "Here you go. Oh dear. Do you think that was his murderer? Right here in our pool?"

"I'm not sure. My firm and the deputies are checking all leads."

I scanned the sign-in sheet, beginning at seven in the morning. No Malcolm Porter. Nothing even close. I also checked for George Fowler, but his name didn't come up either. Phooey. That meant there was another player out there, and none of us had any idea who it could be.

"Find what you were looking for?" the monitor asked.

"I'm afraid not. Thanks anyway. I really appreciate it."

I felt as if my sleuthing was dead-ended at that point because, number one, I really had no idea how to go about conducting an investigation, and number two, I was lacking reliable witnesses as well as an ironclad motive to commit murder. Maybe Lyndy was right. Maybe I was better off leaving this to the professionals. Then again, Lyndy didn't have to put up with my mother and all her nagging.

The next day I found myself even deeper in the well. No sooner had I gotten to work and booted up my computer for a morning of reconciling invoices when Augusta shouted across the office. Thank goodness we were the only two there.

"Phee! Your mother's on the phone and she's hysterical. You'd better take this call now!"

I immediately picked up the line, and before I could finish saying hello, my mother bellowed in my ear, "There was an attempt on my life, Phee. And on Myrna's. Actually, on all of us in the Booked 4 Murder book club."

It was no secret my mother was prone to exaggeration and, well, as far as her lady friends went, "hyperbole" was the best word to describe all of them. Still, something in her voice told me she wasn't exaggerating.

"What kind of attempt? And where are you?"

"I'm at the Sun City West radio station with Shirley and Myrna. We were on our way to have our nails done, even though it's not our regular day. The salon is running a special with midwinter colors, and Shirley wanted something to offset her ebony skin. Then Myrna thought—"

"Enough with the nails, Mom. What happened?"

"Fine. Shirley and Myrna came to pick me up, and no sooner did they get in the house than I got a phone call from the DJ at the radio station. The morning mail arrived and there was a letter addressed to Harriet and Myrna's book club. The DJ thought it might be fan mail. Naturally, we all decided to go to the radio station to get the letter before heading over to the salon."

"Don't tell me: Someone criticized your show."

"It was a death threat. A real death threat. The kind they pull in Homeland Security to check out. In fact, we notified the posse, and they're sending a real Maricopa County Sheriff's Office deputy to the station. He or she should be here any second."

"Huh? For a threatening letter?"

"The envelope contained a white powder." Then my mother asked, "Would you say it was white or more ecru or cream?"

In the background, Shirley and Myrna both responded, "Whitish yellow."

"Wait a second," my mother said. "The DJ wants to talk to you."

Next thing I knew, someone named Bucky said, "It looks and smells like perfumed talcum powder, and there's a note inside that reads, 'Next time the powder won't be talcum. Quit snooping into Buell's death.'"

"Was the note handwritten or typed on a computer?"

I figured whoever sent it most likely used a computer with a Times New Roman font, making it almost impossible to track down.

"Uh, neither," Bucky said. "Talk about old school. This looks like something out of one of those forties movies. The sender cut out letters from newspapers and taped them onto the paper. But get this: the tape is so old it's yellow."

Next thing I knew, my mother was back on the phone. "What if it's not talcum powder? All of us could have inhaled something toxic. Something deadly."

Then Bucky's voice came in the background: "It's talcum powder, Mrs. Plunkett. I'm positive it's talcum powder."

I took a quick breath and spoke in the most soothing

tone I could muster. "Relax. I'm sure all of you are fine. Let me know who the deputy is who comes for the envelope so I can tell Nate and Marshall. I'm pretty sure someone from the sheriff's office will let them know, but that might take a while. Call me back when they get there. Okay?"

"If we're still breathing, I'll call you."

"We're still breathing, Mrs. Plunkett," Bucky said. "It was talcum powder."

I hung up the phone and walked to Augusta's desk. "Some nutcase sent my mother and that book club a threatening letter with talcum powder in it. At least I think it's talcum powder. The DJ at the radio station where the letter was delivered said he thought it was talcum powder."

"Want me to phone up Mr. Williams and Mr. Gregory to let them know?"

"Just text them. I'll give Marshall a buzz."

"Mr. Williams is getting pretty good at texting. Remember a year ago, he wouldn't even give it a try. Guess the twenty-first century finally caught up with him."

I laughed. "I know. But he's still pretty old school about some things. Hey, speaking of old school, whoever sent that message used letters cut out of newspapers and taped them to a plain white sheet of paper."

"I'll be darned. Whoever sent that letter might not know how to use a computer, but if you want my opinion, they went all old school to throw everyone off the course."

"Yeah, I'm thinking the same thing."

Fortunately, Marshall's phone wasn't on mute and I was able to reach him. He had just finished meeting with a client in Surprise and told me he'd swing by the radio station to see what was going on.

"Call me," I said, "and do whatever you can to make sure my mother and her friends don't blow this out of proportion."

"I'll give you a buzz, but I can't promise I'll be successful with the other half of your request."

By the time I heard back from Marshall it was a little past ten. Nate had phoned the office as well but was tied up in Phoenix. His take was similar to mine and Augusta's. He was also positive about one thing: whoever murdered Howard was still in the area or they wouldn't have bothered to threaten my mother and Myrna. Not much of a consolation, but at least there was a good chance they'd apprehend the person.

It was Deputy Ranston who drew the short straw and had to deal with my mother's hysteria. According to Marshall, who witnessed the interviews with the ladies, my mother was the epitome of decorum when compared to Shirley and Myrna. Shirley wanted the sheriff's office to post a deputy by her house twenty-four hours a day, and Myrna was insistent she be given a bodyguard.

Thankfully, Marshall and the deputy were able to convince the women they weren't in any immediate danger and to go about their day as usual. Deputy Ranston put the envelope in a sealed plastic bag for the Maricopa County Sheriff's Forensic Lab to test and told Bucky and the women they'd be notified of the results. He assured them that if they were exposed to anything harmful, they'd be notified immediately.

"I hope you pulled Ranston aside and told him to put a 'Rush' or 'Urgent' on that envelope. None of us are going to get a good night's sleep unless we know for sure it was talcum powder," I said to Marshall.

"Don't worry. Ranston has every intention of making it a priority. As soon as I hear anything, I'll let you know."

Marshall still had a few straggler interviews with the pickleball players but figured he'd be back at the office in the afternoon. As for my mother, I didn't hear from her until later in the day. *After* she and her friends had had their manicures and eaten at the Olive Garden in Surprise. The women decided to dine outside the compound, as they refer to it, because "there might be a target on our heads."

"I hope you learned your lesson," I said to her. "Don't talk about Howard's murder on the air. Not only could it compromise the investigation, but it could really set off the killer."

"Okay, fine. We won't talk about it during our show, but that doesn't mean you should stop poking around. Speaking of which, George Fowler happened to catch some of our show and left a message for me not to bring Streetman to the radio station. Something about liability if he bites someone."

"Good. Keep him home. That's a good place for him."

"Oh, I fully intend to bring him to the radio station. I simply won't do it when anyone else is around. For all we know, George Fowler could be hiding something."

"The forensics team has been all over that radio station. If there was something to be found, they would have."

"Not necessarily. Listen, at night there's no one there. The system is programmed to play music and prerecorded commercials. We'll get in when no one's around and have a little look-see-smell with the dog."

"We? Did you say 'we'? Because I'm not part of that 'we,' and you shouldn't be either. Besides, the place is locked up."

"The radio station room is locked, but not the Men's Club. They don't lock that up until midnight. Myrna found out from Bucky that they keep a spare key to the station on top of the doorframe. We cannot afford to sit idly by while some lunatic murderer has us in his or her sights. It's either you and me, or I take Myrna."

That did it. A vision of Myrna complete with a duffel bag of home-defense sprays and handheld alarm mechanisms was all I needed to utter, "Fine. I'll do it, but this is the last time. The last time."

So much for that.

CHAPTER 12

My mother might have caught me at a weak moment, but I had my strategies as well. Mainly stall, stall, stall, regarding bringing that dog into the radio station. Let alone breaking and entering.

True to his word, Deputy Ranston put a high priority on finding out exactly what that powdery substance was. Shortly before nine, we had our answer. But not before my mother called Marshall and me at dinner to share Louise Munson's thoughts on the matter.

The only thing I really knew about Louise, other than her being a member of the book club, was the fact that she owned an African grey parrot and doted over the bird worse than my mother with Streetman. I always considered Louise to be one of the more sensible ladies in the group, but after her phone conversation with my mom, I had my doubts.

"Phee! I just got off the phone with Louise. She thinks the powder could be meth. She watched a special on Channel Five last week about meth labs all over the valley. My God! Do you have any idea what that stuff does? Louise told me. My mouth could rot out from the exposure, and I'd lose my teeth. I've had those teeth for over seventy years and I intend to keep it that way. I think Myrna might have some implants, but the rest of her teeth are real, and the same with Shirley. This is a nightmare."

Marshall must have noticed the stunned expression on my face because he mouthed, *What's going on?*

I shook my head and mouthed back, *Crazy land*, before responding to my mother. "I can all but guarantee it wasn't meth. Drug users don't give up that stuff so easily. Relax. You're fine. We'll probably hear from the sheriff's office tomorrow. Meanwhile, don't get Shirley and Myrna in an uproar. That's all we need. I'll catch you later."

"Meth?" Marshall asked. "She thinks it was meth?"

I shared the details of Louise's revelation and all he could say was, "That forensics lab had damn well work overtime on this one."

Thankfully, his wish came true. At a quarter to nine, Deputy Ranston called Marshall and asked him to relay the information to Nate as well. Sure enough, it was talcum powder. Harmless, perfumed talcum powder. But there was more. According to the deputy, the talcum powder was an old formula. And the perfume, which the lab readily identified, was something called Evening in Paris, a fragrance, according to Ranston, that was no longer on the market. Not in its original formula anyway. Ranston went on to tell Marshall that the company that manufactured this perfumed talcum powder had been bought out by Chanel in the early 1970s.

"So, ages-old talcum powder. Imagine that. Somehow it doesn't surprise me," I said. "People have all sorts of stuff tucked away that they completely forgot about. Heck, I bet most of the pantries in Sun City West have outdated food."

"Outdated by a few years, maybe, but decades? Who on earth keeps sixty-year-old talcum powder?"

He had a good point. Especially in light of Ursula Grendleson's old Ginghers, which managed to find their way into Howard's gut. God knows how old those scissors were.

"Did Deputy Ranston mention whether or not the lab was able to isolate any fingerprints?"

"They're still working on that. At least we know your mother and her friends were never in any real danger. Ranston's going to call all of them immediately to let them know the findings."

"He's not going to tell them the old formula talcum powder was discontinued, is he? Their imaginations will go wild."

"No. All he plans on telling them is that it was talcum powder."

"Good. The less they know the better in this case."

Unless Ursula Grendleson had come back from the dead to terrorize the living, whoever masterminded the murder and the letter threat must have known how gullible some of those book club ladies were. And they must have known the Booked 4 Murder radio show would be the first one in that studio, just in time to discover Howard's body. But why Ursula Grendleson?

I had exhausted my conversation with the two possible suspects on my list, namely Sylvia and Malcolm, and I had no idea who Howard's sparring partner at the pool was, so I figured maybe it was time for me to look into the one suspect who was off everyone's radar: Ursula Grendleson herself. True, the woman had been dead for over two decades, but that didn't mean the family tree ended with her, spinster or no spinster. That didn't mean the woman was without relatives.

Starting with her obituary in the *Sun City Independent* archives, I planned to find out exactly who this woman was and what possible connection she or her family might have had to Howard Buell.

"It can't hurt," Marshall said when I shared my idea. "At least you'll be working in a nice, safe library or on your computer, not putting yourself in jeopardy."

I failed to mention my mother's harebrained idea about having the dog uncover evidence at the radio station. Besides, I planned on postponing that catastrophe indefinitely.

Nate was the first one in the office the next day and was practically beaming when Marshall and I walked in, followed by Augusta.

"Got news and then some," he said. "Sylvia wasn't Howard's only love interest. Apparently getting a tan wasn't so much a passion of his as watching Betty Hazelton at the pool. One of the pickleball players, who preferred to remain anonymous, left a voice mail on the office phone. Oh, and Ranston called. You're not going to believe this in a thousand years. They were able to pull some prints from the transparent tape. And guess who they belonged to?"

The three of us looked at one another and shrugged.

"Ursula Grendleson. That's right, folks. If this were a Dean Koontz novel, I'd say we were in business."

Augusta and Marshall chuckled, but I froze. "My God. My mother must never get wind of this. Never, ever! We all know she can't keep her mouth shut. And once Shirley and Cecilia find out, it will be a disaster. They'll be convinced it's Ursula's restless spirit avenging God knows what."

"I don't think you have to worry," Nate said. "Ranston doesn't want to make his life more complicated. For now, all anyone needs to know is that the lab figured out it was talcum powder."

After that tidbit of information I was more than anxious to find out whatever I could about Ursula Grendleson. According to Nate, the sheriff's deputies figured someone came across an old box of her discarded stuff, maybe even at a yard sale. It would be virtually impossible to track down, so they planned to focus their efforts on the timeline, as well as Howard's contacts. That left old Ursula all to me.

Of course I wasn't ruling out the latest entry in the Howard Buell playbook, namely Betty Hazelton, whoever she was. *That* information I could easily obtain from my mother, or worst-case scenario, Cindy Dolton at the dog park.

While Nate continued to pursue leads on the Home Products Plus case, Marshall had a few minor cases to deal with before conferring with Deputies Bowman and Ranston at the posse station in Sun City West. That left me with billing to work on and spreadsheets to review, not to mention tackling my latest research project, aka Ursula, during breaks.

"I'll be at your service for the next fifteen minutes,"

Augusta said when ten thirty rolled around, "so let me know whatever you need."

"I'm all set. I've got my coffee, and I'm already in the *Sun City Independent*'s obituary archives. They cover all the Sun Cities, as well as Peoria and some Glendale listings."

"Let me know what you find."

Grendleson wasn't a common name, and I knew she passed away twenty years ago, so I was able to pull up her obit without any trouble. The information Nate had gleaned from the deputies was the same info on the obituary. Ursula graduated from Arizona State University, or ASU, when it was a normal school, and taught home economics in the Phoenix area. However, unlike the scant version of her life that the state database had on file, her obituary was a virtual gold mine.

"Augusta!" I yelled from my office. "I hit pay dirt! Get in here!"

"What? What? My legs can only move so fast."

"Ursula Grendleson retired from Desert Gardens High School right here in Glendale. It was a brand-new school back in 1963, and she was one of its first teachers. Someone who knew her might still be on staff. Ready for retirement maybe, but still on staff. I'm going to work through my lunch hour and leave early to find out. That school is less than three miles from here."

"Do you plan to inventory their scissors drawer?"

"Very funny."

"What else did her obit say?"

"Um, let me look. Hmm, same as what we knew. Never married, but . . . wait a sec. It says she was survived by a niece, Elizabeth Evans, from Iowa."

"Hmmph. Better stick with the school. Much closer."

I closed the screen and tackled my billing like nobody's business. Thankfully, Augusta picked up a turkey sandwich for me from the deli and I chomped on it as I typed on the computer. When it came to eating and typing I was the queen of multitasking.

By ten minutes to four I was out the door and on my way to Desert Gardens High School. My mind kept doing the math during the entire drive. If Ursula retired in the late sixties, then conceivably, a beginning teacher at that time might remember her.

Desert Gardens High School, located near the downtown area, looked like an old Spanish mission that had recently been repainted in shades of bluish gray. Bougainvillea bushes framed the double-door entry and bicycle racks flanked both sides of the building. To my right was a circular drive with two or three school buses. Late afternoon run maybe?

I parked my car in the area marked "Visitors" and walked to the front doors. Locked. The sign on the door read, "Visitors, please use buzzer to the right." I sighed and pushed the buzzer. Things had certainly changed since my daughter, Kalese, had been in school. Student safety meant the buildings were locked tight and carefully guarded.

A voice on the intercom asked for my identification and I provided it. Within a minute or two a stout man with a goatee opened the door. "Please come in. The office is to your left. You'll need to provide ID." He was wearing a badge that said "Building monitor."

Yep, this was a far cry from 1963, when I imagined those doors were wide open for everyone. The office area consisted of two desks, but only one was occupied. A young, curly-haired woman with big, gold earrings asked how she could help me.

I showed her my ID and told her I was interested in learning about one of their former teachers who had passed away over two decades before. "It's for the *Sun City West Nostalgia Radio Show*," I said. "My mother's book club is doing the show, and I told her I'd help out by getting information about one of this school's teachers who used to live in the Sun Cities."

I hated lying. Or even stretching the truth. But this was one place where I couldn't very well tell them I was looking into a murder and wondering what connection a dead teacher might have with the victim.

"Who's the teacher you're researching?" she asked.

"Ursula Grendleson. Home Economics."

The woman looked as if I'd suddenly grown a third eye. "Ursula Grendleson, you said?"

"Uh-huh. Why? Did you know her?"

"Me? Heck no. I mean, no. She retired long before I was ever hired. Hold on a minute, will you? Our current home economics teacher knew her. Only it's no longer called Home Economics. It's Family and Food Science. Let me see if she's still in her room. Dismissal was forty minutes ago, but many teachers stay late to work."

I stood absolutely still while the secretary dialed the classroom.

"Patty?" she asked. "Do you have a few minutes to meet with someone about Ursula Grendleson?" She paused. "That's right. You heard me correctly." Another pause. "No, it's about some nostalgic radio show for the Sun Cities."

After yet another pause from Patty's end of the line, the secretary said, "Mrs. Kanter said to head right to her room. It's down the green corridor on your left, just past the water fountain. The room number is one eleven."

I thanked her and headed out before anyone had a chance to change their mind.

CHAPTER 13

With the exception of microwave ovens and dishwashers, Mrs. Kanter's classroom looked very similar to the one I remembered thirty years ago. Four separate cooking areas, each with its own sink, stove, and refrigerator, and another area for sewing.

The counter had at least five or six colorful plastic baskets, and when I took a closer look I could see that they were all filled with iPads. On the wall above the counter was a plaque that read, "Mrs. Patricia Kanter, Desert Gardens High School Teacher of the Year."

"Thanks for meeting with me." I walked toward Patty's desk and she motioned for me to pull up a chair.

Patty Kanter appeared to be in her sixties. She had short, curly brown hair with hints of gray.

"I'm Phee Kimball and I'm helping my mother, who's working on a nostalgic radio show for Sun City West."

"And they want to do a program on Ursula Grendle-son?"

"Um, well, she would be part of the program. She was very involved in the sewing clubs in the Sun Cities," *or at least I hoped she was,* "and we found some memorabilia that belonged to her." *If a pair of Gingher scissors that was used to kill someone counts as memorabilia . . .*

"I see."

Patty folded her hands and let out a long, slow breath. "Ursula Grendleson. Of all people."

I nodded. "So, can you tell me anything about her? The office secretary said you knew her."

Patty took one of the paper clips that were in a small box on her desk and proceeded to unroll it. "I knew her all right. You know how some teachers are such incredible role models that their students emulate everything they do?"

"Uh-huh."

"It's the same with master teachers and student teachers. I was Ursula's student teacher. Right here in Desert Gardens High School. Quite a number of years ago. In fact, I'm retiring this year. If it wasn't for Ursula, I wouldn't be the teacher I am today."

"Wow. She must have been a wonderful role model for you."

"Wonderful role model? God no! I vowed that when I had my own classes, I would never teach the way Ursula Grendleson did. Her nickname was Miss Gremlinson, and believe me, she earned it."

A lump began to form in my throat and I swallowed. "That bad?"

"Worse than bad. She terrorized those poor kids. If she were teaching today, they'd have it documented on their cell phones and shared all over the internet, but we're talking decades ago. I still cringe when I remember how caustic and miserable she was. And that was only how she verbally harangued her students."

Patty leaned closer to me and whispered, "This can't go any further than this room, but I watched her literally push a student into an open oven in order to get the poor girl to light the pilot light. Back then, gas ovens had pilot lights in the back, and they needed to be lit. I'm sure that girl must have suffered some psychological trauma."

The thought of anyone doing anything like that to my daughter would have prompted a visit to the principal and on to the school board. I bit my lower lip and grimaced. "Yikes. Who would have imagined?"

"I know. I know. That's why I was so shocked when the office called to tell me someone was doing a radio program about her."

"Why didn't the parents complain?"

"We're talking about a different generation. Back then, it was the teacher's word above all else. Besides, those poor students probably never told them for fear that if they complained, Ursula would find a way to retaliate."

"Whoa."

"I know. Pretty awful, huh?"

"You wouldn't happen to know if she had any friends on staff who might still be alive, would you? Surprisingly, there are many people living in the Sun Cities who are in their late nineties and even early hundreds."

"Not that I'm aware of. Whenever we went into the faculty room for a break, everyone left as if we were carrying the plague."

"Yikes. That *is* really awful. No wonder the woman never married."

"Ursula scared off men. And for good reason. In fact, there was an unsettling rumor going around when I started my student teaching. You know how rumors are: one smidgeon of truth mixed in with gallons of hearsay. In her case, the math was backward."

She put down the paper clip and began to tidy her desk, as if the conversation had ended.

"What rumor? You can't stop now. I promise I won't say a word." *Dear Lord! I'm beginning to sound like my mother.*

"Okay. Rumor had it she put a curse on a special pair of scissors she had and told students that if they dared use her scissors instead of the ones that had been purchased for school use, they would end up six feet under. Seriously. I'd heard of master chefs not wanting anyone to use their knives, but Gingher scissors? Give me a break. Anyway, I doubt any of her students went near her precious scissors."

My God! The scissors. A slight tremor started in my hands and I absently tapped one of my feet. "Whoa. That's rather chilling."

"If you knew Ursula, you'd say it was par for the course."

"Uh, yeah. I suppose. Um, about those scissors . . . I don't suppose they're still around?"

"Oh heavens no. They were her personal scissors. They left when she did."

If Shirley, Cecilia, or my mother got wind of what Patty had just told me, they'd be convinced it was an evil spirit that had dealt Howard the final blow. Especially if they found out Ursula's prints were the ones on the scissors. And forget the tape. That would be the crowning touch.

"Are you all right, Miss Kimball? You look a little stunned. It's just a ridiculous rumor."

"Oh, I'm fine. And call me Phee. Listen, I've taken up so much of your time, I really should get going. Again, thank you so much."

"Sure. I doubt I was much help, but if you think of anything else you want to know, you know where to find me."

I wished Patty Kanter much success with her students and her retirement. Then I bolted for the door and my car. Marshall was certainly going to get an earful tonight.

So much for trusting what you read in obituaries. Ursula wasn't the model teacher I had envisioned. In fact, if it was her body that was found in the radio station's studio, there'd be a lineup of suspects, including, but not limited to, her students, her fellow teachers, and anyone on staff at Desert Gardens High School. Unfortunately, it wasn't Ursula's body. It was Howard's and, for the life of me, I couldn't come up with a single connection.

Then again, I really hadn't looked much past Howard's Facebook page. Much as I hated the grunt work, I knew exactly what I had to do. Thankfully, I was familiar with the process, having done this once before. Oddly enough, while checking on another curse.

I had to find out if Howard had been one of Ursula's former students, and the only way I knew how to go about it was to pour through old yearbooks. Old Desert Gardens High School yearbooks that most likely were stashed away in the archives of the Glendale Public Library, the oldest of the Glendale libraries.

It was too late in the day for me to tackle that project, so I put it off until I had more time and headed home.

"A scissors curse, huh?" Marshall laughed when I told him about my encounter with Patty. "Well, one thing's for sure: The woman didn't come back from the dead to do in Howard."

"No, but there might be some bizarre connection." I grabbed the container of chopped veggies we had made and began to toss a salad while Marshall reheated some leftover pieces of chicken. "I need to dig into some old yearbooks. Maybe I can coax Lyndy into helping me while you're at work on Saturday."

"Sounds like a safe plan to me. Meanwhile, our investigation is stalling, but it hasn't come to a complete stop. Nate's meeting with Betty Hazelton tomorrow to see if she can tell us anything."

"The love interest?"

"The *possible* love interest. Remember, that name was secondhand knowledge from an undisclosed source. Still, it's better than nothing."

As things turned out, it was worse than nothing. When Betty Hazelton left our office at a little past four the following day, Nate shook his head and muttered something about needing a stronger drink than our coffee. "That was a total bust. She claimed she didn't even know the guy."

Marshall and I were in the outer office when Betty left because Augusta has alerted us that "the love triangle woman is gone."

"So, how about that," Augusta said. "Maybe the victim enjoyed ogling women in bathing suits."

"What if she was lying?" I asked.

Nate shook his head. "Don't think so."

"Guess we're back to Sylvia. And those euchre players. You know, it could be like *Murder on the Orient Express*, where they were all in cahoots and did it together."

This time it was Marshall who shook his head. "Then there'd be at least five pairs of scissors in the guy's chest."

I knew from past experience that when an investigation dragged, it was back to the timeline and motive. Not to mention digging deeper and probing into all the possible players. Maybe I was being naïve, but I thought if I could uncover some link between Howard and Ursula, the puzzle might solve itself.

Too bad I never got the chance.

CHAPTER 14

My mother called a few minutes after Betty left our office. "Tomorrow's the perfect time for us to bring Streetman to the radio station. It's a Saturday, and the only one in there is going to be Bucky. I already checked it out. Maintenance is going to unlock the building so he can get in. He has no way to relock it. It's one of those keyed dead bolts on both sides."

"How do you know all this?"

"Believe it or not, Herb told me. He got it from one of the euchre players he knows because they do the same thing from time to time. All Bucky's going to be doing is babysitting. He'll be running a three-hour canned program from five in the morning until eight."

I rubbed my temples. "Five in the morning? Have you lost your mind? I'm not getting up at four so the dog can waste our time sniffing around."

"Fine. We'll make it five thirty, but we'll have to be quick. The posse volunteer arrives at six fifteen. Meet me there. That should give us plenty of time. You'll need to be the decoy to get Bucky out of the room."

"Oh brother. This has disaster written all over it." I was practically moaning.

"I can always call Myrna, if need be."

"No, not Myrna, or your plan will jump from disastrous to catastrophic."

"Fine. Five thirty. Love you, sweetheart."

"Wait. Hold on. What do you mean by *decoy*?"

While I was on the phone trying to talk some sense into my mother, Nate and Marshall were doing some fancy footwork of their own. Well, it was actually Augusta, but they were the ones who had her set things up.

The euchre players agreed to meet with them at Putters Paradise for the early dawn breakfast at five. *Don't these people sleep?* And, at five forty, two of the pickleball players who were unable to be interviewed prior said they would be there as well. Augusta also relayed the information to Deputies Bowman and Ranston.

"My mother plans to be at the radio station tomorrow morning and wants me to join her," I told Marshall when he shared the news about his impromptu Putters Paradise plans.

"Huh? I thought their show was on Tuesday."

"It is, but she had some lamebrain idea about poking around discreetly while the DJ runs the canned program."

"I've learned there's no such thing as discreet when it comes to your mother."

"That's why I figured I should go. Just in case . . ."

Thankfully, he didn't ask about the dog, and I certainly didn't bring up the subject. After work we went to Mimi's

Café in Peoria and enjoyed a relaxing dinner. Something we'd been meaning to do for quite a while. Too bad it was the last quiet dinner we'd have for the next few days.

When the alarm went off at four the next day it might as well have been midnight. I stumbled into the shower while Marshall shaved and both of us mumbled about how sleep-deprived we were. Two fast cups of coffee and we were out the door.

"At least you'll be eating bacon and eggs at Putters Paradise," I said. "I'll be lucky if we manage a bagel."

He gave me a hug and a sweet kiss on the lips. "Harriet's lucky. You're a good daughter, Phee. And an even better . . . well, you know."

I did know, only there weren't really any words that sounded right. "Partner" was too businesslike, "girlfriend" was too sophomoric, and "lover" was . . . frankly, too darn over-the-top. Of course, "significant other" made sense, but that, too, sounded so sterile. I kissed him back and returned the hug before we went our separate ways.

I thought Sun City West might be like a ghost town at that hour of the morning, but nothing could have been further from the truth. Joggers and bicyclists were everywhere, along with dog walkers and the early morning Sun City West PRIDES, cleaning up the streets.

My mother's car was adjacent to the pickleball courts and I pulled up beside her. At least she'd had the good sense not to park right in front of the Men's Club, which housed the radio station. The sun was slightly under the horizon, but the sky appeared to be getting lighter. Thankfully, we were the only ones there.

"The pickleballers will be arriving any minute," my mother said, "so we'd better get a move on." She was clutching what appeared to be a large, dark satchel under her arm and there was no sign of Streetman. *Maybe she came to her senses after all.*

Then, all of sudden, I heard a dry, coughing sound and realized it wasn't a satchel at all, but the dog.

"What on earth is he wearing?" I asked.

My mother lifted him up for me to see. "It's a Thunder-Shirt. For anxiety."

His or mine? "My God! He looks like a Snausage. One of those overstuffed doggie treats. He must be really uncomfortable."

"He's not." Then she began to kiss him and mutter, "Mommy's brave little man. Mommy's gladiator."

I thought I'd heave.

"The ThunderShirt isn't just for storms. It's meant to target the dog's pressure points, kind of like swaddling a baby."

"If you ask me, I think he'd prefer that hooped-skirt, Christmas tree getup you stuffed him into."

We walked to the Men's Club entrance.

"Well, the ThunderShirt seems to work. He's not panting, pooping, or whimpering."

"That's because he's tucked into your arms. He couldn't do any of those things if he wanted to."

"Shh. We're here."

The Men's Club door was unlocked, but the hallway lights were off. We crept in quietly and my mother pointed to the frame above the radio station door. "The key is overhead. Open the door without making a sound."

I reached for the key and unlocked the door. My movements were slow and deliberate and my hands were shaking. I turned the doorknob, returned the key to the ledge above the frame, and stepped inside. My mother and Streetman were so close behind me, I swore I could smell that dog's breath.

The lights were on, but they were low. I hadn't realized the room had a dimmer switch. Bucky was asleep at the table, his head resting over his arms and his earphones affixed to his head. Whatever program was playing obviously didn't require much action on his part.

My mother stepped in front of me. "Shh. We'll tiptoe into the closet so Streetman can have a look-see-smell."

I followed her and closed the closet door behind me. It was a huge, walk-in closet that housed scads of equipment, in addition to office supplies, bottled water, and lots of odds and ends. A pull curtain hung from the far end, but I never thought to look behind it.

My mother put the dog on the floor and stood still. "Give him time. He needs to get acclimated before he can scope things out."

I scanned the boxes on the shelves as we waited for the dog to do something. "Someone needs a grammar lesson. Those boxes are marked 'Betty and Nellies' Bargains.' The apostrophe is in the wrong place."

My mother furrowed her brow. "Huh? Someone misplaced an apostrophe on some boxes? That's the trouble these days. Schools no longer teach the important things. They're too busy with social skills and self-esteem building. How can anyone build self-esteem if they can't write a decent sentence?"

Just then, the dog lifted his head and sniffed. He took a few steps toward a pile of old clothing in a box marked "Lost and Found." Next thing I knew, he dumped the box over, pawed at the clothing until he made himself a nest of sorts, and curled up in it. Eyes shut and all.

"That was productive," I said. "Now can we go?"

"It won't be that easy. Streetman doesn't like to be touched when he's sleeping. I usually make cooing sounds to wake him up, but I'm afraid we might wake up Bucky."

I opened the closet door a hair and looked at the table. "Bucky's still sleeping. Coo softly."

The dog had the right idea. It was an ungodly hour of the day, and all of us should have remained in bed. Finally, my mother was able to rouse him by offering him a liver doggy treat and tuck him back under her arm.

"These are organic liver treats made with chicken livers and olive oil. I always keep a few in my pocketbook just in case."

I grimaced and tossed the clothing in the box.

"Ouch! Something pricked me!" I tried to keep my voice low. "It's an old hatpin. What the heck? Guess someone lost it and it was put into this box. You'd think they'd at least use an envelope. Good thing it fell away from that pile of clothes the dog buried himself in. Who wears hatpins anymore? Pretty little thing with a blue stone on it."

"Let me see." My mother picked it up by the stone and took a closer look. "Hmm, I think I've seen that hatpin before. The question is where. Where did I see it . . . It'll come to me. Maybe one of the book club ladies had it."

"All those old hatpins look alike. Other than Myrna and Aunt Ina, I don't think the other book club ladies set foot in here, so it couldn't have belonged to any of them. Forget the hatpin. We'd better get out of this place before the security person arrives. In fact, we were lucky the maintenance people didn't spot us."

Gingerly, so as not to prick myself again, I took the pin from her and put it back in the lost-and-found box. "Too bad we don't have an envelope or something. I'm afraid someone else may get pricked."

My mother pulled out something from her pocket. "Here. It's part of an old napkin. I hate wasting things. Hurry up and wrap it around the pin."

I did as she said. It was now complete with dog hair and a used napkin. I returned the box to the lower shelf in the closet and was about to get out of there when I thought I detected some movement from behind the curtains in the back. I held still for a second and then relaxed. It had to be the airflow in the room.

Next, I opened the closet door, allowing enough light to seep in so we could turn off the lights in there. Then I tiptoed past Bucky, who was still asleep at the desk. Only he wasn't asleep.

In the early dawn light I could make out a small trickle of blood seeping down his neck and onto the desk. Had I looked closer I would have seen more blood. "Don't scream, Mom. Whatever you do."

"Why would I scream?"

"Just take Streetman and go to your car. I'll be right there."

"What's the matter with you?"

"If you must know, I don't think Bucky's sleeping. I think he might be . . . um, er, dead."

"DEAD???" My mother's voice was deafening. "DEAD? Are you sure? Check his pulse. Shake his head. Do something."

"I am doing something. I'm calling nine-one-one, and whatever you do, don't go near the body."

I tapped the three numbers into my cell phone and waited.

"What makes you think he's dead? Some people are

heavy sleepers. Take a mirror out of your purse and put it over his mouth. You'll know if he's breathing."

"He's not. There's an ominous trickle of blood oozing from his neck."

Just then, the dispatcher responded. "Nine-one-one. What's the nature of your emergency?"

I gave her the address and the information.

"Did you check for a pulse?" she asked.

"Um, not exactly, but I'm sure he's dead."

"We're sending an emergency team to your address. They're close by. I'll stay on the line. Please check for a pulse."

One of Bucky's arms was a few inches from his head and I lifted it by the wrist. It was dead weight. "There is no pulse. I'm sure he's dead."

"What's your relationship to the victim?" the dispatcher asked.

"Um, none. He's a . . . or was the DJ at the radio station."

Just then I heard sirens getting louder by the second. "I think the response team is here. Thank you for your help."

I hung up before I had the chance to incriminate myself by saying something I'd regret. Those emergency calls were recorded, and in some instances played over and over again by TV anchors. Just what I needed.

My next call was to Marshall, but with my mother bellowing in the background, I wasn't sure if he could hear me. "I'm at the Men's Club. You need to get over here. Bucky, the DJ, is dead, and I don't think it was a heart attack."

"What? A heart attack? All I can hear is your mother shrieking. Did you call nine-one-one?"

"Yes." Then, to my mother, "Stop screaming. Marshall can't hear me."

At that precise moment I heard the thud of the studio door being flung open and a crew of emergency responders charged into the room.

"Over there! On the table!" my mother yelled. "The radio station killer struck again."

CHAPTER 15

Funny how a little expression like "radio station killer" could stick to an investigation like ants on a glue trap, but somehow it did. In the chaos that followed the initial response, someone must have heard my mother's moniker for the murderer and passed it along. Unfortunately, it wound up on every TV news station from here to Albuquerque.

I was right about Bucky. He was dead. His body was removed from the radio station and placed in the coroner's van while my mother shielded Streetman's eyes from the scene.

"The trauma will be too overwhelming for him."

For him? I'm not doing too well with the situation myself.

Thankfully, Marshall arrived less than ten minutes later because Putters Paradise was only a mile or so away from the Men's Club. "A sheriff's deputy should be here any second. At least the posse volunteers are out in full force. You can see them from the window. Where's your mother? Is she all right?"

"Take a closer look out the window. I'm surprised you didn't notice her on your way in. That's her on the bench by the pickleball courts and that's not her bag, it's the dog. Long story."

"Geez. I hope she doesn't say anything to anyone. Look around. There are more spectators than at an Arizona Cardinals game."

My stomach churned. At this hour of the morning the Rec Center filled up with fitness buffs, bowlers, ping-pongers, swimmers, and tennis players. Not to mention the pickleballers and minigolf aficionados. Oh, and lest I forget, the multitude of dog owners who frequented the park.

"I told her not to say anything to anyone until she gave a statement to one of the deputies."

"Does that count for Myrna and Shirley? Because if I'm not mistaken, they just joined her on the bench."

"Oh crap."

Sure enough, my mother was gesturing with one hand as she clutched Streetman with the other. Shirley kept shaking her head, and at one point put a palm to her cheek. Myrna, who was seated between the two of them, moved her head like an owl, presumably to focus in on whoever was talking.

"This isn't good," Marshall said. "I plan to snag the first deputy who walks into this room and send him or her to your mother for a statement before we all wind up reading it on Twitter."

"You don't have to worry about social media. She

doesn't use it. She prefers yenta media. It's faster and commands a larger audience."

Just then I heard a familiar, if not irritating, voice. It was Deputy Bowman, who sounded like a sea otter. I should know. When my daughter was little, she had a CD of baby animal voices she insisted on playing over and over again. The sea otter's sounds were the most annoying of all.

"Mr. Gregory. Miss Kimball. Sorry for the delay. I was in Peoria when I got the call. Ranston's on another case but should be here any minute." He looked around the room and furrowed his brow. "Where's the victim? I don't see a body."

"Coroner's crew removed it a few minutes ago," Marshall said.

"Who the hell authorized that?"

"Maybe they thought it was natural causes," I ventured, "and didn't consider this room a crime scene."

"They can't make inconclusive assumptions. Not without a complete autopsy report and a toxicology screen. This is the second dead body in less than two weeks that's shown up in this room. And unless the coroner tells me it was due to old age and natural causes, everything should be treated like a crime scene." Then he turned to the three or four posse volunteers who were standing motionless against the wall. "I'll need statements from all of you. Don't go anywhere. Oh hell. Without the exact area cordoned off, I have no idea where to begin."

Marshall waved a hand in front of Deputy Bowman's face. "Miss Kimball's mother, Harriet Plunkett, along with Miss Kimball, were the ones who discovered the body. Far be it from me to tell you how to conduct your investigation, but if I were you, I'd speak to Mrs. Plunkett first. She's seated outside on a bench by the pickleball courts."

I swore the color drained from Deputy Bowman's face. "I remember Mrs. Plunkett from prior investigations. Is that dog of hers with her?"

"He'll be fine," I said. "She's got him in a Thunder-Shirt."

The deputy shuddered and gave us a nod. "Stay put, if you don't mind. I'll be right back. If Ranston shows, he can interview the posse volunteers." Then he looked at Marshall. "No matter what my take on the matter is, there are too many ifs right now. We can't say for sure if this was a suspicious death or one from natural causes. And if it was suspicious, we can't say for sure if it was related to the Buell murder. Otherwise I'd ask you to do the interviewing."

With that, Deputy Bowman left the room, and Marshall and I watched as he thundered his way across the parking lot and over to the bench where my mother and her friends were seated.

"Boy, was he flustered. I don't envy him," I said. "Especially if Shirley and Myrna add their two cents to the investigation."

"Nah. He'll have them wait in their cars or, better yet, go home."

"Like that's going to happen. Shirley and Myrna are going to join that growing crowd of spectators out there. I'd bet money on it. At least the news vans haven't shown up yet. They usually get their info from a dispatch channel. Let's hope they have other, more exciting breaking news."

Before Marshall could answer, the second half of the deputy tag team arrived. "Where's the forensics unit?" Ranston bellowed. "I expected a forensics unit to be here."

"I don't think this investigation is going as planned," I whispered.

Deputy Ranston took a step back to the doorframe, removed a cell phone from his pocket, and turned his face to the corridor. I could hear bits and pieces of his end of the conversation. "That's right. Forensics. On whose authority? Yes. Possible murder scene. Now."

He pocketed his phone and walked toward us. "What can either of you tell me?"

I proceeded to give him a detailed description of everything my mother and I had seen when we entered the studio and when we left. Everything except our reason for being here in the first place. Then I thought better of it and added, "As you know, my mother has a radio show in this studio, and that's what prompted her visit."

"At the crack of dawn?"

I shrugged.

"Did you know the deceased?"

"I only knew of him. Bucky something. The station's only DJ."

"So you wouldn't know if he had any medical conditions?"

"Uh, no. I wouldn't."

Deputy Bowman entered the room a few seconds later. "I told Mrs. Plunkett she was free to go. If we have any more questions for her, we'll send someone to the house. Damn dog snapped at me."

I tried not to laugh, but Marshall wasn't as discreet.

"Central dispatch sent the coroner but not forensics," Ranston announced. "That team's on its way over. Might as well get statements from the posse so they can go about their business. I already spoke with everyone else in the room."

The everyone else was Marshall and me. Marshall explained that he had gotten a call from me once my mother and I had discovered the DJ was no longer breathing.

"Did you touch anything on or around the deceased?" Deputy Ranston asked me.

"Um, well . . . sort of. I tried to take his pulse but gave up."

I thought I heard him groan, but I might have been mistaken.

"Okay. Okay. No sense for the two of you to hang around here. Marshall, we'll be on the horn with you if the coroner suspects foul play. Let Nate know, will you?"

"Sure thing," he said.

When we left the radio station room and exited the Men's Club building, the crowd had swelled to the point that a number of posse volunteers were called to the scene. Marshall and I could hear people shouting as we walked toward my car.

"Was it another murder?"

"Is there a killer running loose?"

"Keep our Second Amendment rights!"

I rolled my eyes and kept walking. Unfortunately, I only managed a few yards when a woman I recognized from the early evening news on KPHO approached us: Kristine Dill. Tall, blond, and absolutely stunning.

She held a microphone so close to my lips I could almost feel the metal. "Can you tell our viewers anything about the latest unexpected death inside the radio station? We already know a body was removed."

I bent my head down as if I was a common criminal

and covered my eyes. "We're not at liberty to talk. The MCSO deputies are on the scene. You'll have to speak with them."

Marshall hustled me into my car and leaned over the driver's side door. "Ten to one your mother's house is filling up with the other half of the crowd that isn't in this parking lot. We'd better get over there to deal with damage control."

"Damage control?"

"Only the verbal kind, hon. The rumors. See you over there. I'll give Nate a buzz at Putters Paradise to let him know what's going on."

As I pulled out of the parking area, I caught a glimpse of a woman in the corner of the now-empty pickleball courts. In her long pants and sweater top, she wasn't dressed for playing pickleball. A second later and she had moved behind the blue plastic windbreakers, completely out of my sight. At the time I dismissed her as another onlooker, but in retrospect, it should have set off a red flag.

When I pulled onto my mother's block my first thought was that someone was having an estate sale. It was prime time for it: early Saturday morning in midwinter. Cars were lined up everywhere, including the entrance to her driveway. That was when I realized it wasn't a sale; it was that book club of hers and its "extended family."

I found a spot at the end of the block and hoped Marshall wouldn't find himself in the next county. As I walked toward my mother's house, someone shouted from behind. "Can you tell me which house is holding the garage sale? I don't see any signs."

I spun around and found myself face-to-face with a pencil-thin brunette in jogging shorts and a tank top.

"I was out for my morning jog and noticed all the cars. I hate missing a good estate or garage sale."

"You're not missing anything. Um, I think my mother invited a few friends over."

"Oh." She sounded disappointed. "Not many people do that anymore. Have people over for breakfast or brunch. Much easier to go to Bagels 'N More. Have you heard of the place?"

Like a second home. "Uh-huh. Good sandwiches."

"I was hoping it was an estate sale. I love a good bargain. You're probably too young to remember Betty and Nellie's Bargains, but she and her cousin used to hold the best darn estate sales in Sun City West. At least I think it was her cousin."

Talk about being a pack rat. There are boxes in the radio station closet from those sales. Yeesh!

By now, the jogger and I were walking side by side as I got closer to my mother's house. I muttered an "Uh-huh" and the woman kept talking. "Sure, there are lots of companies out there that hold estate sales, but those women were able to procure the most interesting items. I once bought a Russian samovar for next to nothing because everyone thought it was a spittoon. Can you imagine?"

"Uh, er . . ."

"Betty Hazelton used to buy up the inventories from houses that were willed to relatives who wanted nothing to do with them. And Nellie—I can't recall her last name—did all the paperwork. They may have had another woman working for them, too. Lots of estates out there with priceless memories, but the only thing the relatives wanted was the money. Betty and Nellie would sell the furniture, the keepsakes, the artwork, you name it. Estate liquidations. Betty was the savvy one. She knew which items to hold on to until they increased in value and demand. Sometimes for years. The woman was a regular dynamo. I heard she got tired of it, though, and went into some other related business. Not sure where the cousin wound up. Too bad."

"Betty Hazelton you said?"

"That's right. She still lives in Sun City West, but forget looking for her sales."

I wondered if it was the same Betty Hazelton who caught Howard's eye at the pool. Only one way to find out. I took a quick breath and the words rolled out of my mouth. "Well, now that she's no longer in the estate liquidation business, she'll have more time for all the amenities here. Like swimming. Wonderful time of year for swimming. Not too hot."

I hoped the jogger would take the bait, but I was wrong. Instead, she gave me a funny look. "I wouldn't know. Of course, if I had a figure like hers, I wouldn't have to go out jogging. And you know what else?"

"Uh, no."

"She's a woman of a certain age and has absolutely no batwings whatsoever."

"Batwings? I'm not sure I understand." *Or even want to.*

"You know. Flabby triceps. Loose skin under the arms. It's a regular epidemic here."

We were now only a few yards from my mother's house.

"It was nice chatting with you," I said. "I hope next time you'll come across a genuine estate sale and not one of my mother's get-togethers."

"Me too."

As I walked to my mom's door, two thoughts crossed my mind: *How many Betty Hazeltons without batwings are there?* and *Do they make a fitness video for that sort of thing?*

CHAPTER 16

"Shirley called the restaurant for me," my mother said when I opened the door and walked in.

My mother's living room looked like a wake. In the fifteen or twenty minutes since she'd left the radio station, she'd somehow managed to procure refreshments. Then I remembered the catering van from Bagels 'N More I had seen when I turned onto her street. It was heading out of her neighborhood. I could kick myself for not making the connection.

"We've got all sorts of bagels and shmears," my mother went on. "Help yourself. Cecilia's on her way over with some pies from the Homey Hut."

I looked around the living room and couldn't believe my eyes. I expected the Booked 4 Murder crew to be here, but what I didn't expect was Herb piling enough cream cheese on his bagel to cover the dough completely.

"What's Herb doing here?"

My mother turned her head and glanced at the long counter that separated the living room from the kitchen. "He's like a homing pigeon. He probably looked out his window, saw the delivery van from Bagels 'N More, and made a beeline for my kitchen."

"What about the men? Isn't that his pinochle gang with him? It *is*. That's Kevin, Kenny, Bill, and Wayne. Good grief!"

Then, as if on cue, I heard Bill's voice from across the room. Loud as ever. "This is better than the lousy spread at your place, Herb. At least Harriet had the common sense to get shmears for the bagels. And they're fresh. Not the frozen kind in those little plastic bags you get at Costco. We ought to start holding our morning pinochle over here."

My mother shouted back, "Not on your life." Then she grabbed my arm and ushered me out of the entranceway and into the foyer. "Poor Bucky. It looked as if he had a cerebral hemorrhage. Did you see the blood trickling down his neck?"

"A cerebral hemorrhage? Back at the studio you were screaming about a radio station killer."

"I might have overreacted."

"Really? You think? You were yelling 'radio station killer' when you and the dog left the building."

"It was the shock, that's all. My mind didn't have time to process what I saw, the stream of blood coming from his ear. Louise Munson told me that massive hemorrhages can cause blood to trickle out of the nose or ears. And he was so young. He couldn't have been a day older than seventy-five."

"I didn't think you looked that closely at him."

"After finding Howard's body with the scissors in it? I had to make sure there was no cutlery or whatever you call it sticking out of Bucky. Which reminds me, was the sheriff's office ever able to find fingerprints on those scissors? Your office must know by now."

"Um, er . . . I don't think—"

"Harriet!" A voice exploded out of nowhere. It was my aunt Ina's, and she charged toward us like a linebacker. "I was on the patio when I got the details from Myrna. About the blood you saw. It had to be a hemorrhage. I think everyone should have a complete brain scan after the age of sixty. CT or MRI. Fully paid for by Medicare. They make a big deal about colonoscopies and mammograms, not to mention those bone densities they keep shoving down our throats, but what about our brains? I bet more people die of strokes than broken bones."

Before my mother could respond Marshall walked in. I immediately rushed over to him, leaving my aunt and my mother to speculate about hemorrhages and medical insurance.

"Make yourself at home," I said, "if you can find a seat. You can relax. I don't think my mother's as freaked out about Bucky's demise as she was about Howard's. Of course, she's under the impression Bucky succumbed to a stroke or something similar."

"Good. Let's keep it that way for now and hope she's right."

"If we act quickly, we might be able to salvage the rest of the day."

Unfortunately, I spoke too soon. Within seconds the book club ladies spied Marshall and converged on him like seagulls at a picnic. I thought their bantering would never end.

"What have you heard about Howard's death?"

"Was it that snippy little tart? You know who I mean. Sylvia."

"What about the station manager? Has anyone questioned him?"

If that wasn't torturous enough, Bill and Kenny, from Herb's pinochle crew, joined the melee. Only they didn't have questions. They had theories. Bill was one step away from my mother's usual go-to spot, insisting Howard was murdered by a love interest gone wrong. And as for Kenny, well, he was convinced it was the station manager, George, someone who was still on my radar.

"I heard Howard get into it with George about a week or so before he cashed it in. They were arguing at Dunkin' Donuts. Great way to start a morning, huh?"

"Do you recall what they were arguing about?" Marshall asked.

"The radio station. What else? George kept saying it was the advertising that kept them alive, but Howard called him a damn fool for not realizing it was the live radio shows."

Malcolm Porter pretty much told me the same thing, only his money was on the advertisers.

I was about to say something when my mother exclaimed, "No! Don't feed him the cream cheese and lox. It's too salty. Give him the plain shmear."

I grabbed Marshall by the arm. "Now would be a good time to make a getaway."

"Done!"

"Wait for me by the door." I wove in and out of the crowd until I reached my mother.

She was at the sink rinsing off the paper plates. "They're the good kind. I can use these again."

"Uh-huh. Listen, Marshall and I are heading home. I'll call you later. Try not to dwell on what happened this morning."

"It was horrible, but natural causes are natural causes. Oh, I meant to tell you, but I forgot. Remember that hatpin you found in the lost-and-found box? I know where I've seen it. I'm positive. Sylvia was wearing one just like it at the Victorian tea fundraiser for the library. It matched the cloche she had on. Goodness. That was last month. The beginning of January."

"Are you sure?"

"Yes, I'm sure. You can ask Shirley. No one knows hats like a former milliner. It does make sense, though."

"What does?"

"The hatpin winding up in the radio station studio. Sylvia was probably there to see Howard sometime between the Victorian tea and his murder."

"Well, he wasn't killed with a hatpin unless Ginghers has a new model going for it."

"Don't be snippy. The hatpin didn't walk over there by itself. It probably came loose from Sylvia's hat, and when someone found it they stuck it in the lost and found."

I rolled my eyes. "It doesn't matter. It wasn't as if it was found at the actual crime scene. Anyway, I'll talk to you later."

I gave her a hug and made a mad dash for the front door.

"Nate's finishing up at Putters Paradise," Marshall said when he closed the door behind us. "It took longer than expected. He just sent me a text. I texted back that there was no need for him to drive over here."

"Thanks. This crowd is the last thing he needs right now. Between all these Sun City West interviews and that

Home Products Plus case he's working on, it's a wonder the guy can even get through the day."

"He's a trooper all right, but that Home Products Plus investigation is really stressing him out. In fact, he mentioned bringing you into the case."

"Me? Now you're sounding like my mother, thinking I'm an investigator of sorts."

"You are. Accounting and bookkeeping sorts. Nate needs someone to scrutinize their inventory records to match it up to their sales documentation. That means delving deep into what they paid for inventory to see if it coincides with what they had on the shelves for sale. He doesn't trust anyone working for the company and neither do the managers at the Phoenix and Glendale stores. He'll talk to you about it later. Oh, and you'll be fully compensated for all the extra time."

"I'm not a forensic accountant, but I'm pretty sure I can handle what he has in mind. Besides, I need something to get my mind off this murder case. It's all I've been thinking about."

Marshall gave my wrist a squeeze. "Come on, let's get something to eat, preferably in a quiet restaurant. Then, as much as I hate to even suggest it, we really need to go food shopping. We're down to one can of Coke, three slices of bread, and a few cereal crumbs."

"Dibs on the cereal!"

The next few days were business as usual, with one new addition to my workload. I was now prying into Home Products Plus's records. The investigation into Howard's murder wasn't slow, it was glacial. Then, everything changed.

It was Wednesday, midmorning, and Augusta rapped on my doorframe. "Your mother's on the line and she sounds agitated."

"What's new?" I thanked her and picked up the phone.

Agitated didn't even come close to the voice at the other end. "When did you plan on telling me, Phee? Shirley's beside herself and Cecilia's on the way to her church to see if she can sneak out a bottle of holy water when no one's looking."

"Church? Holy water? What on earth are you talking about?"

"I'll tell you what I'm talking about. Shirley called me from the Rip 'n' Sew meeting a few minutes ago. They were supposed to have a program on eighteenth-century needlepoint, but instead, that deputy with the thick jowls showed up."

"Deputy Ranston?"

"Yes, yes. Deputy Ranston. He began questioning the women about a former member who died twenty years ago. Someone named Ursula Grendleson. Apparently she used to belong to a number of sewing clubs."

Oh no. The proverbial you-know-what is headed for the fan.

My mother kept talking. "What on earth does that man think? Twenty years ago! No one in the Rip 'n' Sew would have known her. The women in that club may be seniors, but they're not Methuselahs. And that's not the worst part. Do you want to hear the worst part? The fingerprints they found on the scissors belonged to this Ursula woman. A dead woman! You know what that means, don't you? She was the last person to use those scissors. And what did she use them for? To commit murder!"

"Whoa. Calm down. Stop and think. Stop and breathe.

A dead woman did not commit a murder. Most likely the murderer wore gloves or had a cloth held over the scissors so his or her prints wouldn't be uncovered."

"You tell that to Shirley and Cecilia. You know how they are."

Oh, I knew all right. And I knew we were headed for trouble.

CHAPTER 17

My mother kept going like a steamroller. "Shirley is already convinced it was an evil spirit out to seek revenge and Cecilia isn't far behind. She intends to have us douse ourselves with the holy water before we go back into the radio station studio. They canceled our show for yesterday. Something about revisiting the protocol. Anyway, Cecilia took two plastic water bottles with her."

"Is it allowed? I mean, does her church sanction that sort of thing?"

"She didn't check with her church, according to Shirley. She looked it up on the internet and found some writings by a Spanish saint who said you can douse it on your head."

"Terrific. And what did you mean by back into the radio station? You don't really intend to continue with your show, do you?"

"What do *you* mean? Of course I do. I'm not about to miss out on the Greater Phoenix Broadcast Dinner. Opportunities like that don't come every day. *I* didn't know Ursula Grendleson. She died before your father and I even moved to Sun City West."

"Ursula isn't the killer. She died twenty years ago. At age ninety-seven." *Oh no. I can't believe that slip of the tongue.*

"Ah-ha! So you did know about Ursula after all. What else are you hiding, Phee? What else should I be worried about?"

"Nothing. Absolutely nothing."

"So, what *do* you know about this Ursula woman? Did she have relatives here? Maybe it was a longtime family grudge that resulted in Howard's murder. I've read about those things. Some families simply cannot put things behind them. If I held a grudge over every single thing your aunt Ina did, we'd never be able to live in the same state, let alone the same country."

Oh no. Is she going to start talking about Aunt Ina? "I've been on the phone too long, Mom. I've got to get back to work. Tell Shirley and Cecilia not to worry about Ursula. I'll catch you later."

Deputy Ranston had no idea of the hornet's nest he'd uncovered by questioning the members of the Rip 'n' Sew Club. Then again, maybe he did. Those women were bound to talk, and as a result, one of them might know whose hands Ursula's scissors wound up in. And if not the Rip 'n' Sew Club, there was always the Creative Stitchers Club.

If I thought Wednesday's enlightening little tidbit from my mother was jarring enough, it was nothing compared to the earful I got the next day. Talk about the other shoe dropping! This was like combat boots landing on soft ground.

Thankfully, I wasn't at work when she called. I had just gotten home and had started to prepare a medley of salads for dinner: egg, chicken, and tuna. Marshall was still at the office finishing up work on his caseload.

When the phone rang I picked it up automatically. Big mistake. I thought my eardrum would burst from my mother's verbal assault.

"Did you turn on the six o'clock news? It was murder! They said it was murder. Okay, not the 'M' word, but they called it a suspicious death. Foul play suspected. That's murder in my book. Bucky didn't die of a brain hemorrhage. He was killed. That's why they canceled our live broadcast. Protocol my patootie! It's the crime scene revisited."

I immediately walked to the TV, phone in hand, and turned on KPHO on channel five. It was a commercial for car insurance. "Um, I missed the report. They'll have it on again at six thirty. What exactly did they say?"

"You won't believe this in a million years, but you may have been holding the murder weapon. *I* may have been holding the murder weapon."

"What? What murder weapon?"

"The hatpin! The hatpin with the pretty blue stone. The one that was in the lost-and-found box."

"Huh?"

"The news anchor said Bucky—who, by the way, is Bertrand Zebbler—was killed with a large pin. Someone stabbed him in the jugular veins. Did you know there were *two* jugular veins? That's what the anchor said. Internal and external. Didn't matter. They killed him."

"Hold on. Slow down. I get the part about the pin, but how do you know it was the one we saw?"

"You mean the one you touched and then gave to me?"

"I didn't give it to you; you took it for a closer look. And I didn't exactly touch it, I got jabbed with it."

"Next time keep murder weapons away from me. According to the autopsy, they attribute Bucky's death to a pin that someone drove straight into his neck."

"I know, but that doesn't mean it was the one in the lost and found. What kind of deranged killer is going to take the time to hide his or her murder weapon in the lost and found?"

"Someone who knew there was a lost-and-found box. It had to be an inside job."

"Mom, it makes more sense for the killer to take the weapon home with them. It's a tiny hatpin, for crying out loud, not an Uzi."

"I don't know about that."

"Well, I do. I'm sure the pin we saw wasn't the murder weapon. Coincidental maybe, given the fact that it was a pin that killed Bucky, but it had to be a different pin."

"If you say so."

"Look, if it will make you feel any better, I'll let Nate and Marshall know and we'll have one of the deputies retrieve the hatpin from the lost and found and have the lab check it out. Okay?"

"Of course not! What if they find Bucky's blood on that thing? One of us could be locked away for murder. Who's going to take care of Streetman if something, God forbid, happens to me and you're not around?"

A pounding, stabbing pain began on the side of my right eye. Yep, nothing like the start of a tension headache. "Nothing is going to happen to me or to you. Street-man can rest easy."

At that second I heard the key in the door. "Marshall's home. I'm making dinner. I'll keep you posted."

"Make sure you watch the news."

"Don't worry. I fully intend to do so."

"What do you intend to do?" Marshall asked. "Couldn't help but overhear your conversation." He leaned over my shoulder and gave me a kiss on the neck.

"Find the nearest bail bondsman because, according to my mother, I may be arrested for murder."

"Should I sit down for this one?"

"Nope. You can peel the hard-boiled eggs and I'll give you the sixty-second rundown."

"Good grief! The cause of Bucky's death was on the news? I read the text from Bowman less than an hour ago. He was going to send Nate and me a copy of the autopsy report. He didn't say anything about a pin or murder in his text, but he did tell us the estimated time of death. About an hour before you called me that morning. The body was still warm."

"Oh my God! Bucky's killer might still have been in the building. I could have sworn I saw those curtains in the back of the closet sway a bit, but I thought it was from the airflow. And come to think of it, there was a very suspicious-looking woman hiding behind the pickle-ball courts when I left the building to drive to my mom's. She could've been the killer. There are lots of exits in that Men's Club building. To think, my mother and I could have been standing four or five feet from a murderess. Oh good Lord. I'm sounding more and more like my mother every day."

"Relax. You've had a lot to deal with."

"I can't imagine how that info about Bucky's death got leaked to the TV stations."

"Most likely someone overheard something and the authorities had no choice but to verify it. For all we know, Ranston himself could have placed the call. So, what's with the bail bondsman deal?"

I told him about the lost-and-found box and he agreed with me. No one in their right mind would commit murder with a hatpin and then put the pin in a lost-and-found box. Still, he sent text messages to both deputies about the pin in the box. *And* the fact that I had discovered it via getting pricked with the darn thing.

"When you mentioned poking around with your mother, I thought you meant talking with the DJ and maybe snooping about the outer room, not prying into that closet. I hate to say this, but with an hour window for the time of death, it does put you and your mother in a precarious situation."

"You *are* kidding, aren't you?"

"I wish I was." He took my wrist, gave it a squeeze, and then pulled me close. "Don't worry. I know lots of good bail bondsmen."

At that point I gave his ankle a kick and he returned it with another hug.

I don't know who came up with the saying that bad luck came in threes, but they were right on the money as far as I was concerned. I never should have told Marshall about the hatpin in the lost and found because it was tantamount to signing my own death certificate. Of course, it might have been discovered anyway, because the radio station was now deemed a crime scene and was cordoned off until further notice. That meant a continuous loop of classic sixties music ad nauseam and no live broadcasts.

My mother pitched a fit when she got the news from George on Friday morning. He told her to "hang tight" because he was certain the station would be reopened on Tuesday, in time for her show. He also told her the Rec Center would be providing temporary private security, not posse volunteers.

There was no funeral for Bucky, aka Bertrand Zebbler, because his body was being cryogenically frozen. His only daughter belonged to some wackadoodle cult in Oregon, according to Herb, who found that out from who-knew-where, but the information was substantiated by the sheriff's office and passed along to Williams Investigations. I thought Augusta's eyes would pop out when Nate shared that revelation with us.

"The whole body?" she asked. "They're freezing the whole body? I thought they only freeze the heads. I've seen pictures of the heads sticking out of stainless-steel tanks. Are you sure it's the whole body?"

Nate rubbed his temples. "I'm sure."

It was Friday afternoon and no one was any closer to solving the murders. Nate and Marshall were hoping to attend memorial services for Howard and Bucky, but they were out of luck. One speedy cremation and one flash-freezing were the only arrangements that had been made.

"Maybe we could hold our own memorial," I ventured. "It would be a nice gesture, but more importantly, it would be the perfect venue for information gathering. That *is* what you had in mind, isn't it? I wouldn't be at all surprised if their killer showed up. And I say killer, not killers, because I think it's the same person."

Marshall and Nate exchanged glances and Augusta took a giant gulp of her coffee. For a few very long seconds no one said a word.

Finally, Marshall spoke. "You're definitely Harriet Plunkett's daughter."

"So, you like the idea?"

"It may turn out to be the very thing we need to give this investigation a push. Good thinking, kiddo." Nate gave me a wink. "So, does anyone have any idea how to pull one of these events together?"

All eyes were on me.

"Unfortunately I do. The book club ladies. If they can pull together a bagel brunch in fifteen minutes, think what they can do for an afterlife celebration. Heaven help me. I can't believe I just offered up my mother's loony book club."

"Is that a yes?"

"Yes, Nate. It's a yes."

I swear, the next book I buy better be titled How to Say No.

CHAPTER 18

There was one bit of good news and sanity in all this murder mess, and that was the result of the forensic accounting I had been asked to conduct by my boss. I started early on Saturday morning, relieved I didn't have to make up an excuse to avoid brunch with the book club ladies. The task was grueling and I didn't come up for air until the late afternoon. Grueling and puzzling. Not to mention frustrating. The numbers did *not* add up. Outgoing payments were accounted for, but the merchandise that wound up in the inventory didn't match the expenditures.

It had taken me the better part of the day to uncover one of the devious ways in which the Home Products Plus thief or thieves was robbing that business blind, but I was positive there were more. In addition, I had no way of knowing who it was or how many people were involved.

"The goods have to wind up somewhere," Nate said when he and Marshall got back to the office shortly before three.

They were both fielding other cases and making use of every available bit of time.

"Is there any way to narrow it down by date?"

I bit my lip and shook my head. "Inventory arrives whenever it arrives. No real schedule. Bulk orders of bathroom scales on a Monday, linens on a Thursday, shower curtains whenever . . . that part of it is impossible to determine. And the company is dealing with more than one manufacturer. Talk about a mess."

At least it was a paper mess, unlike the sticky little situation I agreed to oversee regarding a touching yet revealing memorial service for Howard and Bucky. My mother was ecstatic when I called her last night to tell her what Nate and Marshall had in mind.

"You're not Paul Newman and Robert Redford." I groaned. "All we need is a nice memorial service in a quiet location so Nate and Marshall can home in on the conversations and watch how the attendees are conducting themselves. Body language can be very telling."

"So can poking and prying. Too bad you have to work tomorrow. The ladies and I will get the planning started when we meet for brunch at ten thirty. I'll let you know what we come up with."

"Nothing too extreme, please. And whatever you do, don't put Aunt Ina in charge of anything." *My famous last words*.

She immediately got off the phone to "inform the ladies they would be organizing a sting operation."

While I was at the office pouring over the Home Products Plus accounts I pictured my mother and the book club ladies shmearing assorted cream cheeses on their bagels and bialys at Bagels 'N More, their usual Saturday hangout. I didn't expect to hear from my mother until later in the day, and I definitely didn't expect a call from my aunt, which was why I nearly jumped out of my chair when Augusta shouted, "Your aunt Ina's on the phone. She wants to know if you prefer Grecian dirges or medieval chants. Something about booking the singers."

"Oh hell no! Put the call through to my office."

"Phee!" My aunt's voice stung my ear. "Your mother is being absolutely obstinate about everything. I'm in the ladies' room at the restaurant. The women still can't decide on a location, but I thought we should book the professional mourners before their schedules fill up."

"Professional mourners? I thought that was only in the Old Testament, and maybe Ancient Rome."

"Oh no. It's a highly coveted profession."

"Coveted or not, the answer is no. This is a memorial service, not a funeral."

"Tell that to your mother's friend Cecilia. She wants Eula Fabrizio from her church to sing 'Ave Maria.'"

Oh God help us. "Aunt Ina, go back to the table and have the group focus on a location. We can fill in the details later. Okay?"

"If that's what you want."

"It is. Trust me, it is."

I leaned back in my chair and used both hands to push myself away from my desk. Then I clenched my fists and silently screamed. It was cathartic, if nothing else. At that point I figured I deserved a break, so I walked to the outer office and told Augusta how the memorial service was shaping up.

She looked up from her desk and gave one of her ears a scratch. "I had an uncle who once held a memorial service for a Brown Swiss cow. Not a common cow in Wisconsin, mind you. He bought it from Shelburne Farms in Vermont. Cow lived a long and happy life. Better than most people. And most people didn't get twenty-minute eulogies."

"Uh, I suppose not. Anyway, I'd better get back to that accounting mess I'm trying to figure out. So much for working a half day."

"Tell me about it. Nate asked me to design new business cards, and it's taking me way longer than I expected. Too many choices. Matte finish. Gloss finish. I'm sticking with plain white."

"Works for me. Hey, want to split a pizza or something? You make the call and I'll pick it up. Faster than delivery."

"The usual?"

"Yep—meat lovers all the way."

"I'd better make it an extra-large pizza. That's Nate's car across the street. Oh, and would you look at that? Marshall's parallel parking his vehicle as we speak. Talk about timing."

"Quick! Phone it in before one of them opts for a healthier topping."

That was midafternoon, and Nate and I finally got to commiserate over the accounting mess.

"Don't worry," I said. "I'll keep at it. Our own office accounting is up to date and reconciled."

"Hallelujah for that."

Less than an hour later the four of us gathered around the breakroom table and stuffed ourselves with a thick-crust pizza that was weighted down by pepperoni, sausage, meatballs, ham, and bacon. I promised myself I'd either jog around the neighborhood or swim laps in the pool, even though it was winter.

Marshall reached for a napkin and looked directly at Augusta and me. "I suppose you're wondering if the sheriff's office is making any movement on the murders."

Augusta bit off a piece of her crust and swallowed it in one gulp. "I wasn't going to say anything, but I've seen cold cases move faster than this."

Nate chuckled. "Thanks for the vote of confidence. At this juncture the deputies believe the murders were committed by one of the advertisers and they may be on to something. That's why we're viewing the ad contracts and meeting with the reps from those companies. Talk about a widening web . . ."

"I don't get it," I said. "KSCW is a small-time radio station. It's not like those businesses were advertising on major stations."

Nate put another slice of pizza on his plate and leaned in, propping an elbow on the table. "You'd be surprised at the listener reach KSCW has. Think about it. It's smack dab in the middle of retirement world: five Del Webb Sun City communities, Westbrook Village, Sun Village, Trilogy, and Robson Ranch communities, not to mention the smaller ones. KSCW plays the music that those retirees want to hear. For advertisers it's a cash cow. According to feedback the station manager got from surveys, most of the advertisers want the station to do away with those live broadcasts."

"I don't understand why they can't stick an ad into the live broadcast. It can't be *that* difficult," Augusta said.

I thought about my mother and her crew. "Are you kidding? In my mother's case it would throw them off. Especially if it meant they actually had to do something with the equipment. Or keep quiet for two or three minutes."

Nate and Marshall looked at each other and they both started laughing. Not chuckles, but full-blown, riotous laughter.

Finally, Marshall spoke. "According to George, they tried it with the *Lake Fishing with Paul* show. One short ad for dinner specials at Kitty's Garden Café. Unfortunately, the ad was wedged into Paul's staggeringly long discourse on bait. Worms, slugs, smelt, you name it. According to the owner of the café, they had the worst turnout in history that week."

"Ew, no wonder the advertisers preferred music. But those local shows are popular. I know for a fact Herb listens to that fishing show," I said. "According to my mother, he even wanted the station to give Paul more airtime."

Marshall finished his last bite of pizza. "That only makes sense. I mean, after all, they can't just cater to the knitters and needlepointers." Then he gave me a smile. "Or mystery readers."

Marshall had gotten us tickets for the Arizona Broadway Theater's production of *Jersey Boys* that night. An early Valentine's present. It was the only time that weekend when we weren't talking about the murders. The subject seemed to consume us, and even though I kept telling myself I was only the bookkeeper/accountant, I was beginning to feel like a young Miss Marple.

Usually I got dragged into these investigations by my mother, who happened to be the most demanding and dramatic orchestrator of all these scenarios, but this time was different, and I wasn't exactly sure why. All I knew was that I was taking the lead and it actually felt good.

Sunday was catch-up day at our house, with Marshall and me going full speed with laundry, linen changes, cleaning, and car washing. It was like running a marathon without someone handing us water and a participation T-shirt. We literally fell into bed that night, too tired to move a muscle. Even the ones we wanted to move.

Then, in the middle of the night, I woke up, remembering something I had fully intended to do but had completely forgotten about because, well, I don't know . . . another murder, a forensic accounting nightmare, and memorial planning for two men I didn't even know . . . I was juggling a zillion things and spinning in circles. What I fully intended to do, in no uncertain terms, was to pore over the old yearbooks from Desert Gardens High School to see if Howard could have possibly crossed paths with Ursula.

I got out of bed, walked to the living room, and used my iPhone to check the hours the Glendale Public Library would be open. Most libraries had at least one or two late nights and, as it turned out, the main library in Glendale was no exception. Mondays and Fridays they were open until eight.

I wasted no time calling Lyndy the next day when I got into the office. She was at work, too, doing medical billing for an insurance company, but, like me, kept her cell phone handy.

"Let me get this straight," she said. "You want me to meet you at the Glendale Public Library after work tonight so we can go over old yearbooks?"

"In a manner of speaking, yes. Look, I know it's last minute, but, face it, what do you really have planned for tonight?"

"Old sweatpants and a rerun of *Psych*."

"This will be better. Hey, I really need you to help because I can't sift through all those books in such a short period of time by myself. I need to look up Howard Buell. The murder victim."

"Uh, hate to burst your bubble, but isn't that something the sheriff's office should be doing? Or the guys in your office?"

"It's not on their radar yet. Come on, Lyndy. We can go to Haus Murphy's afterward. Home of the big pretzel. My treat."

"What about Marshall?"

"He'll be fine. He knows his way around the kitchen and has DoorDash on speed dial."

"The big pretzel, huh?"

"I'll take that as a yes."

CHAPTER 19

Lyndy was already at the Glendale Public Library when I walked in at twenty past five. She was perusing the new arrivals table and jumped when I tapped her shoulder.

"Sorry," I whispered. "I thought my voice might be too loud in here. It's terrible, but I keep getting louder and louder to be heard by my mother and her friends when they talk."

"Don't worry about it," she whispered back. "My aunt is practically deaf and refuses to get a hearing aid. I literally have to scream like a banshee so she'll hear me."

Then she stopped speaking for a second and eyed me. "More ash-blond highlights? Your hair looks phenomenal."

"Thanks. Once I decided to do it, I couldn't stop. Besides, to tell the truth, I'm frightened of what my natural color really looks like."

"Probably brownish. You're in your forties, not your eighties. Relax. So, what are we doing and where do we begin?"

"I need to ask one of the librarians to show us where they keep the archives of old Glendale high school yearbooks. Then we need to find Desert Gardens High, go back fifty-five years to play it safe, and look under the Bs for Howard Buell. We'll need to keep going up a year until we find him. *If* we find his name at all. That's why I needed both of us to do this. That's a lot of yearbooks."

"And if we do? Find the name, I mean?"

"Then the fun begins. We'll have to scour that yearbook and the ones before and after to see if he was in Ursula Grendleson's class. I doubt there'll be a photo, but you never know."

Lyndy shook her head. "I still don't get how this relates to anything. It would make sense if he was the one who killed her, but not the other way around. Especially because she's . . . well, you know, dead."

"Not her. Howard might have been responsible for doing something heinous to her in his youth and someone thought it was payback time. Anyway, we'd better get moving. We've only got two hours or so."

The archive room was adjacent to the main library, and Lyndy and I were the only ones who occupied it. It took the librarian over fifteen minutes to deliver the entire stack of Desert High School yearbooks to us, and I don't think he was at all pleased.

"We really, really appreciate your time," I said as he moved the cart of yearbooks to our table.

"No problem. It's part of my job." He adjusted his round, wire-rim glasses and sighed. I guessed his age to be anywhere between forty and fifty. "It's either carting these old yearbooks or fiddling around with that ancient microfiche machine in the storeroom. We never got the funding to have someone convert those files to disk. I'm just thankful you didn't request yearbooks from the nineteen twenties or earlier. Then we'd have to follow a long, tedious process that involves white gloves. And paperwork. It's always paperwork. Let me know when you're done so I can start putting the yearbooks away. When you're through with a batch give a holler." Then he paused. "Not literally."

"Now there's a man who truly enjoys his job," Lyndy said under her breath.

"Almost as much as the late Ursula Grendleson."

I took out a small pad and two pens from my bag. "Here, we'd better write down which books we've read so we don't wind up doing extra work."

"Good idea."

The yearbooks didn't arrive in chronological order, and neither Lyndy nor I felt like arranging them. Instead, we each grabbed a book at a time and plowed in. It wasn't a problem rummaging through the senior class pictures. Those were easy. All in alphabetical order. Not the case for the candid shots we needed to check out. Those were all over the place.

Occasionally one or both of us would stand up, stretch, and moan. An hour into the process and we were still getting nowhere.

"That big pretzel from Haus Murphy's is sounding better and better," Lyndy said. "I'm starving already."

I handed her a blue Jolly Rancher that had been in my

bag since Prohibition, but she didn't seem to mind. We kept on poring over the yearbooks. It was an hour or so before closing and still no luck. Worse yet, there were four more books to go through.

I flipped open 1968 and glanced over the professional photos. All black and white. Girls with straight hair parted down the middle and guys with neck-length hair sporting ties. *Wait another two years and everyone's hair length will be the same.*

The photos were mesmerizing, or maybe I was getting tired, but I seemed to lose my focus.

Just then Lyndy shoved a yearbook at me. "Will you take a look at this? No Howard Buell, but some girl won the Future Homemakers of America sewing award and she's standing next to the infamous Ursula Grendleson."

I picked up the book. "Let me take a look." The photo was somewhat hazy, but decent enough to make out the deadpan expression on Ursula's face as she and the girl held up the award.

"That poor girl looks terrified," Lyndy said.

"You would be, too, if Ursula was your Home Ec teacher."

I took a closer look. "Oh my gosh, the award! Check out the award!"

I shoved the book back to Lyndy.

"Yeesh. Of all things. It looks like someone went to a lot of trouble to cut out some soft padding so those scissors would fit perfectly in the padding and the frame."

"Scissors! Her award was a framed pair of scissors! What does the caption say? The print is so small."

"Um, remember when I told you that you were in your forties . . . well, I hate to burst your bubble, but that's bifocal time."

"Bite your tongue. These store-bought reading glasses are fine. Perfectly fine. Give me a second."

"Never mind. I'll read it. It says, 'Sylvia Alton proudly receives the Future Homemakers of America Sewing Award from her teacher, Miss Ursula Grendleson.'"

"Sylvia Alton? It can't be! My God, Lyndy, we have to find her yearbook photo. We need a better photo of Sylvia Alton."

"Huh? Why?"

"Because if it's who I think it is, her married name is Strattlemeyer, and she might be the killer."

Lyndy quickly turned the pages to the senior portraits. "No Sylvia Alton. She must've been a junior or even a sophomore when she won that award. Hey, wait a sec. Yearbooks usually list the awards in the back."

I held my breath while Lyndy turned more pages. "Uh-huh. Here it is under 'Local Awards.' It says junior Sylvia Alton received a framed pair of Gingher scissors belonging to her teacher, as well as a sewing kit and a gift certificate from F. W. Woolworth Company."

"It's her! It has to be her! Good Lord! My mother was right all along—the jilted ex-girlfriend."

"Then how do you explain the other murder? That DJ? How many ex-boyfriends did she have?"

"Maybe Bucky knew she killed Howard and was blackmailing her."

"Or maybe it wasn't her."

"Oh, it *was* all right. That would explain the fingerprints on the scissors. Sylvia put on gloves and took them out of the frame. Then *kaboom*!"

"Kaboom? That's your answer?"

"I couldn't think of anything else. Seriously, it *does* make sense, doesn't it? Sylvia's in all those sewing clubs in Sun City West. Too bad this snapshot of her is so small. We need the 1969 yearbook. It's right there, next to your bag."

Lyndy picked up the old yearbook and immediately thumbed her way to the A section of senior photos. "Got it! Sylvia Alton. Check out that hairstyle. It's kind of adorable in a retro sort of way."

"It *is* retro."

It was hard to determine the color because everything looked the same in black and white, but the Sylvia Alton in the photo had her hair parted down the middle into a chin-length bob. "Geez, I can't tell if it's her. That photo was taken over fifty years ago." Then I thought of something. "Oh my gosh! Alton. She was Sylvia Alton from Glendale. Right here. What if she married someone with the Strattlemeyer last name? Hurry, Lyndy! We've got forty-seven minutes. We need to check the Ss in those yearbooks."

So much for finding a Desert Gardens High School graduate whose last name was Strattlemeyer. If the Sylvia Alton in the yearbook was the Sylvia from Sun City West, I'd need to get my hands on a wedding announcement. That was, of course, if it was in the local papers.

"The librarian is going to have a conniption," I said, "but I need to check the old local papers for wedding announcements from 1968 to 1978. Most women married young back then."

Lyndy looked at her phone. "You've got thirty-eight minutes."

"Then we'd better work fast."

I hated it when I was right. The librarian acted as if I'd asked him to walk barefoot across hot coals. Still, he pulled out the microfiche machine and the films for Lyndy and me to scroll. It was a painful process made worse by Lyndy announcing the time every few minutes.

Finally, we found it: July 18, 1974. Miss Sylvia Alton, a recent graduate from the University of Arizona with a degree in education, home economics, was engaged to Fred Strattlemeyer, another U of A grad but with a degree in business administration. A September wedding was planned.

"This probably won't work," I said, "but I'm going to use my phone to take a picture of the screen."

I tried to remain calm, but I felt like cheering. It wasn't until we left the building that I shook Lyndy's arm and shouted, "Eat my dust, Ranston and Bowman! I found your killer!"

Lyndy gave me a jab in my elbow. "Uh, isn't your boyfriend working that case, too? And what about your boss?"

"Don't worry. I'll make sure they get all the credit. Holy cow! I can't believe we did it! No wonder Ursula Grendleson's were the only fingerprints on those scissors. Back from the dead, my you know what. Sylvia was clever all right. Nothing like a tasty dish of cold revenge."

Thankfully, Haus Murphy's wasn't too packed on a Monday night and we were able to get a good table near the front door. A large bar encompassed most of the room, and Bavarian flags seemed to be draped everywhere. The aroma of hot sausages and sauerkraut hit my nostrils the moment we set foot in the place.

"I'm ordering bratwurst *and* the big pretzel," I announced. "And an O'Doul's."

Lyndy looked at the wine and beer list, then put it

down. "Ditto for me. Too bad they don't make a nonalcoholic wine."

"They do. It's called juice."

We ate like savages, bites of pretzel mixed in with chunks of sausage.

"I don't know if it's the hunger," I said, "or the fact that we may have cracked the case."

I was so elated with my discovery that I hadn't stopped to think about how anyone was going to prove it. Because if I had, I would have realized that timeline and viable witnesses trumped circumstantial evidence. Still, it was more than anyone else had going, and I really needed my high-five moment that night.

CHAPTER 20

"I brought you a present," I said to Marshall when I got home. "A giant pretzel from Haus Murphy's."

"Thank goodness. I didn't feel like ordering out so all I ate was some wilted broccoli I smothered with dressing and the last three slices of ham."

I handed him the pretzel. "Then you really deserve this, as well as the earth-shattering news I'm about to share."

Marshall took a can of Coke from the fridge, bit into the pretzel, and sat down at the kitchen table.

I immediately plunked myself across from him and smiled. "I have undeniable proof Sylvia killed Howard. And probably Bucky as well."

"Define 'undeniable.'"

Marshall listened intensely between chomps of pretzel

and gulps of Coke as I made the connection between Sylvia and Ursula.

"So you see," I said, "it practically screams 'murderess.' Sylvia was in possession of Ursula's scissors and knew she had the perfect weapon. Only Ursula's prints would be on them."

Marshall didn't say a word and it wasn't because he was still eating. He had taken the last bite of his pretzel and wiped his mouth. I widened my eyes and waited for his response, expecting utter and complete jubilation.

"Um, uh, don't know how to put this, hon, but Ursula was probably in possession of more than one pair of scissors. She taught sewing, for crying out loud, and she probably sewed for pleasure, too."

"What are you getting at?"

"The scissors Sylvia won fifty plus years ago may or may not have been the ones used to kill Howard. We need a solid motive, not speculation, and something that links her to time and place."

"Can't Bowman or Ranston simply bring her in and grill her?" *Oh my God! I sound worse than my mother.*

"I'm afraid a fifty-year-old yearbook connection isn't a strong enough reason."

"What if they pretend to do a little information gathering about Howard? Kind of like what I did with Sylvia, only in this case they'd have the intimidation factor working for them. Wait! There's more. Have them ask her about her hatpin. The one she wore at the Victorian tea fundraiser for the library. According to my mother and Shirley, it matched the cloche she had on. Have them insist she show it to them. I bet she won't be able to find it because it was the one that jabbed me in the lost-and-found box."

"Hmm . . . you might be on to something. I'm not making any promises, but I'll see what I can do. And thanks, hon."

"For the discovery Lyndy and I made?"

"No, for making it in a library. During regular hours. I've got to admit, the poking around you do with your mother really scares the hell out of me."

"Out of you? It doesn't do much for me either."

I was positive Sylvia was going to break under pressure, especially when confronted by Bowman and Ranston about the hatpin. Surprisingly, it wasn't Sylvia they had their sights set on. It was my mother and me.

It was late morning the following day when Nate walked into my office. Marshall was making the rounds interviewing the radio station advertisers, leaving Nate to contend with the office business.

"Hey, kiddo, I just got off the phone with Ranston. Of all the wacky things. Marshall told them about the hatpin you and your mother found at the radio station, and even though it wasn't technically within the perimeter of the crime scene, they had it tested anyway for remnants of blood."

"Ew. In that dim closet, I didn't notice any blood. Don't tell me. It was Bucky's blood. I'm right, aren't I?"

"Afraid so. They believe that hatpin was the one used to kill him, but Bucky's blood wasn't the only thing they found on the pin."

"I know. I already told everyone. I got pricked by the pin, so my blood must be on there as well."

"Nothing to compare it with and not enough to provide conclusive evidence. It must have been a quick jab, unlike the stab Bucky received. Bits of dried blood were found all the way up the pin. Bucky's dried blood. Whoever wiped the pin didn't do such a great job. But that wasn't what caught Bowman and Ranston's attention. It was the oily substance that was on the stone."

"What oily substance?"

"The lab is running further tests, but it's showing some sort of liver oil."

"Oh no. The liver treats. The organic chicken liver and olive oil treats. My mother gave one to Streetman right before we discovered the hatpin. The oily residue must have been on her fingertips."

"I'll let Bowman and Ranston know before they go all hog wild over this. And don't be surprised if they insist on speaking with you and your mother. It still doesn't add up. Stashing a teeny, tiny murder weapon in a lost-and-found box."

"Unless the killer—and I'm positive it's Sylvia—had to. Because she rushed into the closet when she heard my mother and me in the corridor. She had to dump the evidence in a hurry."

"Boy, do I hate to say this, but that cockamamie theory is starting to add up."

Miraculously, Bowman and Ranston didn't bother to contact my mother or me. I'd like to think it was because they believed Nate about the liver treats, but deep down I knew the real reason: no one wanted to deal with my mother.

I, unfortunately, had no choice. While I was out grabbing lunch and running some errands, Augusta took a message from my mother and used a giant Post-it to attach it to my computer screen. It read, "Quail Room or the Meditation Garden—Call your mother."

Anyone else would have been stymied, but I knew what it meant. The women had narrowed down the location for Howard and Bucky's memorial service and needed me to render the final decision. I picked up the phone and dialed.

"Phee! It's about time you got back from lunch. It took at least half a dozen phone calls, but we finally narrowed the memorial location to two places. It's either the Quail Room at the Foundation Building or the Meditation Garden at the Beardsley Rec Center. Either way, your boss will have to cough up the forty-five dollars for rental. And another seventy or eighty for refreshments. Cecilia is going to do the program and will run it off at her church. They have lovely parchment paper. All you need to do is reimburse them for it. Shirley and Myrna are handling the refreshments, and Louise is in charge of the setup. And before you say anything, I suggest the Beardsley Meditation Garden. We won't be all jammed in there like we would in the Quail Room. And if the killer decides to show up, he or she is more likely to attend a ceremony that's outdoors so they can make a quick exit."

"Fine. The Meditation Garden. Give them the dates in mind and see if you can get us an afternoon the end of next week. Not too late in the afternoon. We don't want it to get dark."

"That wouldn't matter. Everything is lit up here like 'The Star Spangled Banner.' Even those tot lots at Beardsley. A waste of money, if you ask me. Who's going to bring their grandchild to a playground after dark?"

"Uh-huh. Anyway, don't book the memorial until the

end of next week. We need time to get the notices in the papers, on the Sun City West website, and on KSCW."

"Have you talked to Cindy Dolton yet?"

I knew it. I knew it. It was only a matter of time. "Um, no. I didn't think I needed to."

"What do you mean? Cindy could be sitting on a wealth of information with all her contacts."

"Yeah, but it's too bad she sits on it at six in the morning when no one feels like going to a dog park."

"Streetman feels like going. Pick him up any morning."

"I'll let you know."

"Don't pick Thursday. I'm going to another garage sale with Shirley and Lucinda. This one's in Sun City, and it's the same deal as the last one. Lots of new household items still in their original boxes. No wonder people can't fit their cars in their garages. They've got the space filled up with cartons and cartons of stuff."

"Yeah, well, you'll be doing the same if you keep up the garage sale hunting."

"I intent to donate my old things to charity and make room for new ones. I heard this sale is going to have lots of small appliances, like coffee makers and toasters."

"You already have those."

"Well, for your information, maybe I need an upgrade. Is there anything you and Marshall want? Lucinda's hoping to find a crepe maker."

"Why? She doesn't cook." *Let alone make crepes.*

"How should I know? Maybe she plans to take one of those Explore programs on French cooking. Last year they offered Greek and Italian."

"Okay, then. Garage sale. French cooking. Meditation

Garden. I think we've covered it. I've got to get back to work. Catch you later."

"Tell Nate and Marshall to come armed to the memorial service. And when you get up to speak about Howard and Bucky, use enough innuendo to make whoever it is nervous. I'll be darned if I have to wait one more week until that maniac is behind bars."

My mother had rattled off her latest thoughts so quickly I didn't fully grasp what she had said until I was off the phone. That meant I had to call back.

"Mom! What did you mean by *when you get up to speak*?"

"Someone has to eulogize those two. It might as well be you."

"No, it might as well be someone who actually knew them. Call George Fowler. Bye."

Aragh! Cindy Dolton and the dog park. I couldn't think of a worse way to start my day. No matter what day it was. It wasn't the yippy dogs that bothered me, or even the messes I had to avoid, sidestepping my every move on the grass, it was the frantic way in which some of the owners behaved when a dog that wasn't theirs did its business. I still had nightmares over the one guy screaming "Poop alert!" so loud I could have sworn it was code for an incoming missile attack.

Still, my mother was right. No one knew more about the people in Sun City West than Cindy. And if Cindy knew about the people, Herb Garrett knew about everything else. No wonder the folks in my mother's community didn't rely on the internet for their info. Instead of Googling something, they'd simply Herb or Cindy it.

Like it or not, I'd have to take that darn dog to the

park. Not willing to get into another conversation with my mother—two in one day was more than sufficient—I sent her an email. Short and sweet.

"I'll be picking up Streetman at five fifty on the nose tomorrow. Please have him ready at the door."

CHAPTER 21

I finished the final sip of my caramel coffee, compliments of Dunkin' Donuts, as I turned onto my mother's street. Five fifty-five and people were jogging, bicycling, and walking dogs. Didn't anyone tell them it was still dark out? Granted, they were wearing reflective clothing and, in some cases, carrying flashlights, but still, dark was dark. At any rate, it was a regular testimonial to the Del Web premise of "active senior community."

Streetman was at the ready by the front door when I stepped inside the house. His leash was on and he paced everywhere.

My mother bent down, snatched the leash, and thrust it into my hand. "You'd better get going before he changes his mind. He's apt to run under the couch. That's why I put on his leash."

"We won't be long. I'll see what Cindy knows about the radio station crew and their contacts."

"Good. And don't forget to tell her we're holding a memorial for Howard and Bucky."

"Okay."

Streetman jumped into the passenger seat, circled around once, and curled himself into a ball before closing his eyes. *I get it, buddy; six in the morning isn't my favorite time of day either.*

Thankfully, the dog sprang to life the minute I pulled into the parking lot by the dog park. No sooner did I open the driver's side door when he bounced out of the car and all but pulled me across the lot and into the park. Thank goodness the streetlights were all on.

If I hadn't known what day it was, the scene in the dog park was a surefire reminder. Most of the dogs were dressed in cutesy pink and red frou-frou skirts or were sporting red bows around their necks. One dog had a sequined pink jacket with jewels that spelled out, "Lover Girl." Either my mother had forgotten it was Valentine's Day or she'd spared Streetman the humiliation of dressing him in some ridiculous outfit for the occasion.

Bundles, Cindy's little white dog, was wearing a pink collar and sniffing around the fence with Cindy only a few feet away. I entered through the gate, unleashed Streetman, who darted for the nearest tree, and waved.

Cindy raced toward me. "Hi, Phee! I was wondering when you'd make it over here. I've been expecting you."

"Really?"

"Hey, it's been over two weeks with two murders in Sun City West. I knew you'd show up sooner or later. I suppose you're clamoring to find out what I know about that radio station, and I can tell you, not a whole lot, but enough."

"What do you mean?"

"Well, I don't know the ins and outs, but I do know some of the players, so to speak."

"Um, the ones who are still alive or the dead ones?"

"Both. Bucky was a really nice guy and a good DJ. He used to live on my street but sold his house and bought a condo. Said he got tired of yard work and wanted to spend his time doing the things he enjoyed. I ran across him not too long ago at the supermarket. What a bummer, huh?"

"Yeah. It's terrible. What about the other victim? Howard Buell? Did you know him?"

"Only by reputation. He was the one responsible for getting all those local talk shows on the air. Too bad he didn't have one on gambling tips. From what I heard he could have used it. Instead, we've got things like *Stir Frying with Gloria*, and that boring *Lake Fishing with Paul* show."

"Ugh. Believe it or not, that show has a following. Say, I heard Howard was dating a woman by the name of Sylvia Strattlemeyer. Does that name ring a bell?"

"Like the Westminster Chimes. Yeah, I know her. She's one of the few people who actually grew up in Arizona. Most of us are transplants. I don't know if her husband passed away or they got divorced, but she's been single for as long as I've been here, and that's a while. She and Howard were an item for at least a year, but then he broke it off. From what I heard Sylvia didn't take it too well."

"Didn't take it too well as in bawling her eyes out or didn't take it too well as in stabbing him to death?"

Cindy recoiled at my last comment. "Sylvia always had a flair for the dramatic, but I don't see her as the knife-wielding type. Now, if he was poisoned to death, that might be a different story."

Suddenly I remembered my conversation with Sylvia. Something about using antifreeze. "Was she the jealous type?"

"And then some. But I still don't think she's your killer."

She had motive, means, and opportunity. That's the big three in my book.

I continued going down my list of people associated with KSCW and Cindy responded. It was like a game of who's who, with Cindy answering every question. I was astonished at the people she knew, the people she knew about, and the people who knew other people.

No earth-shattering revelations, but at least I felt as if I had covered all my bases should my mother get even more persistent about the investigation. "Thanks, Cindy. This case is really baffling, so every little insight helps."

"Aren't you going to ask me about Cornelia Lynch?"

"Who?"

"Cornelia Lynch. She was the advertising manager for the radio station. One of the few paid positions. Until she got canned a few months ago."

"What? No one mentioned an advertising manager, let alone someone who was fired."

"Not fired, let go. There's a difference. I used to see Cornelia all the time when her four pugs were still alive.

We called them 'The Lynch Mob.' Anyway, Cornelia was in charge of getting ads for the radio station, and it was getting more and more difficult juggling advertisers because there were only so many slots available. Keep in mind, they didn't have commercials running during the live broadcasts."

"Uh-oh. Don't tell me she had run-ins with Howard over that."

"Run-ins? I had the misfortune of overhearing them in front of the post office once. It was like watching a chicken fight. Cornelia was furious with Howard because the station was losing advertising money and she was afraid she'd be let go. Ha! Turns out she was right."

"Um, did Cornelia sew? Not professionally, but, you know, for fun?"

Cindy shook her head. "I doubt she can even thread a needle. Why?"

"It's not a secret. The murder weapon used to kill Howard was a pair of scissors. Sewing scissors. It's been in all the papers and on the news." *Thanks to my mother's big mouth.*

"If it was a pair of regular, old scissors that someone had on their desk, I could picture Cornelia grabbing them in a fit of rage. But sewing scissors? I doubt she evens knows what they are."

Okay, Cornelia may have motive and opportunity . . . and as for means? Who knows?

"Wow, Cindy. I'm really surprised no one mentioned Cornelia. Especially George Fowler, the station manager."

"Yeah, well, it doesn't surprise me, considering he was

the one who let her go. Now he's handling the advertising from what I've heard. Hey, does this make her a person of interest?"

I shrugged. "At this point everyone's a person of interest."

I thanked Cindy profusely and darted out the gate before I realized I had forgotten Streetman. *My God! I really am losing it!* Fortunately, no one noticed, and I immediately raced back to put him on the leash. He had a mouthful of grass and no intention of leaving the park. It took me five full minutes to cajole him. And only because my mother had insisted on throwing a few liver treats in my pocket.

I attributed my momentary lapse about the dog to the fact that Cindy had offered up an entirely new suspect who definitely deserved a look. I was so intent on sharing my newfound intel with Nate and Marshall that Streetman was the last thing on my mind. *And my mother will never find out.*

The second the dog jumped into the car I phoned Marshall.

"Don't make coffee for yourself at home. Meet me at the Java Joint near our office. It's early and I've got a lead you won't believe. They had an advertising manager. Cornelia Lynch. They let her go a few months ago. Revenge is a motive, isn't it? I'll explain when I see you."

"I'll need my first cup of coffee so I won't be comatose driving to get my second. Holy cow! I can't wait to hear more."

Not wanting to get into any details with my mother, all I told her when I dropped off the dog was that Cindy went down the list of suspects with me and nothing stood out.

My mother bent down to pet the dog. "I give it two days. Cindy's on the alert now. If she hears anything, I'm sure she'll let one of us know. Better than those two deputies. They move slower than molasses. Don't they know how terrified we are to think there's a raving lunatic killer around here? At least Nate and Marshall move faster." Then she turned to Streetman. "You were Mommy's good little man, weren't you? Later today you can try on more Christmas outfits your aunt Shirley made. Won't that be fun?"

The dog immediately dove under the couch as if he understood every word she said.

"The dog still has issues, you realize," I said.

"He may be a bit food territorial, but we're working on it. Did you want to stay for coffee? I can reheat the pot from yesterday."

Then it was as if she had been hit with a thunderbolt. "Oh my gosh! I completely forgot to put Streetman in his Valentine's costume when you took him to the park. Shirley got the idea from the New Jersey Devils. Oh no. You don't suppose—"

"Absolutely not! I'm not waiting while you dress him up so I can take him to the park again. Besides, I get the idea he's not overly thrilled playing dress up. He'll get over it." *I know I will.* "Besides, I told Marshall I'd meet him at the Java Joint in Glendale and I don't want to be late. Catch you later."

"Call me if you hear anything. I want that murderer caught and hanged before I go on the air next Tuesday. Oh, by the way, your aunt Ina won't be doing Tuesday's show after all that fuss. She and Louis will be in Tucson for the gem festival. Like your aunt needs more baubles around her neck or on her fingers. Anyway, Shirley and Lucinda will be doing the show with Myrna and me. Sewing-themed cozies."

"Sewing-themed cozies? How coincidental is that? Don't tell me you've got some devious little plan to somehow enable you to talk about the murders, because if you do, you'll be compromising a murder investigation."

"Honestly, Phee. I wasn't born yesterday, but there's nothing wrong with discussing cozy sewing mysteries."

"Well, the ones you discuss had better not have scissors and hatpins as the murder weapons."

My mother groaned and I was out the door. As far as I knew, Streetman was still under the couch, keeping a good distance from those costumes.

Marshall had grabbed a corner table at the Java Joint and told me there was a hot mocha latte on its way for me. In addition, a small basket of minicroissants, jam, and butter was at the table.

I sat down, tore off a piece of a croissant, and took a bite. "This is absolutely unbelievable. The investigation has been going on for over two weeks and no one mentioned Cornelia Lynch. I don't know how the scissors would come into play, let alone the hatpin used to murder poor Bucky, but Cornelia might have sought revenge for losing her job and an income she probably counted on. Lots of retirees can't make it on meager pensions and social security."

"Whoa. All of that without coffee?"

Does the caramel coffee from Dunkin' Donuts count?

At that second my mocha latte arrived and I took a long sip. "I still think it was Sylvia, but Cornelia Lynch is definitely worth checking out."

I then proceeded to tell Marshall everything Cindy told me.

He crinkled his nose and rested his head on a closed fist from his propped elbow. "I gave Bowman the heads-up as soon as I got your call. He went ballistic. Muttered something about KSCW withholding evidence from law enforcement and told me he was on his way to have a little chat with George. I'm supposed to meet him at the radio station in forty minutes."

"What about Ranston?"

"He had fasting blood work this morning and will give Bowman a call when he gets done. Hope you're not upset I called the sheriff's office, but we can't afford to stall on this one."

"No, not at all. I was flabbergasted when Cindy mentioned an advertising manager. I just figured it was something George did."

"Yeah, he's on our radar, too. Verbal spats with Howard over the programming. We've got a few people who could attest to that. And as for Bucky? Zilch so far."

"If Bowman doesn't get anywhere with George, I may have an idea. I need to speak with George about doing the eulogies for the murder victims at the memorial service. If he says no, I'm afraid my mother will stick me with it. Needless to say I've got to be very persuasive. Maybe I can add 'cunning' to the list and see what I can get out of him regarding Cornelia."

"You're really getting into this investigative business, aren't you?"

I grinned. "It's the company I keep." I pulled my cell phone from my bag and looked at the time. "I need to get going, too. I wanted an early start on that forensic accounting for Nate. Whoever's siphoning the goods, they really know how to cover their tracks."

"Yeah, well, they haven't met Sophie Kimball."

CHAPTER 22

I plopped a small bag of minicroissants on Augusta's desk and turned on the coffee maker and printer before heading into my office. I also left a giant apricot Danish on Nate's desk.

It was eight twenty and that allowed me a good forty-five minutes to aggravate myself over those spreadsheets from Home Products Plus before starting on invoices that needed to be in the mail. The inventory losses seemed to come in waves, but nothing I could pin down or predict. This much I knew without hesitation: Someone was cooking the books in such a subtle way as to avoid immediate detection. Too bad the information wasn't encrypted. Then we could wave an IKEA credit card at our cybersleuth, Rolo Barnes, and throw ourselves at his feet. As long as I didn't have to issue him any paychecks like I did when he worked for the police department in Mankato, I'd be okay. Rolo didn't like odd numbers. Or certain number combinations on his checks. Now self-employed, Rolo could fend for himself.

"Thanks for the croissants," Augusta shouted out. "How was your early dog park venture?"

I stepped out of my office and filled her in on Cornelia Lynch.

"She's got a strong motive for murder," Augusta said, "if she thinks this Buell guy was responsible for her losing the job. But that doesn't explain how the other guy's neck became a pincushion."

Suddenly I froze. What if we were looking at two different murderers? Granted, Howard and Bucky worked at the same radio station, but that didn't mean they were killed by the same person.

"What's the matter, Phee? You look as if you've seen a ghost."

"Uh, no. Just thinking. That's all. This entire time everyone's been operating on the premise there was one murderer, but what if there were two?"

"One, two . . . it doesn't matter. Solve the first one and go from there. If there's a link, it'll be uncovered. If not, then Sun City West has two assassins in the neighborhood."

"Shh! I'm taking that thought to the grave."

After a brief phone call George agreed to chat with me about the memorial service for Howard and Bucky. He made no mention of meeting with Deputy Bowman—or Marshall, for that matter—and I didn't bring it up. I told him I'd stop by the radio station after work tomorrow and he seemed amenable.

Marshall, along with Bowman and Ranston, spent the day scrambling to find out more about Cornelia, who happened to be "out for the day" and not returning phone calls.

"It was like undergoing a root canal," Marshall said when he finally got back to the office in the afternoon. "All George could tell us was there were a limited number of advertisers and there was no need to encumber the station with more expenses by keeping an advertising manager on staff."

I thought about what he had just told me. "Wow. That was kind of callous. Given his attitude, I'm surprised he wasn't the victim instead of Howard. I mean, if Cornelia turns out to be the killer."

Marshall walked to the coffee maker and put a K-Cup into the slot. "George's actions were strictly business, but it was Howard who insisted on the live programming. That meant fewer commercials. Anyway, until we get a chance to question Cornelia on her whereabouts the morning of the murders, we can't link her to the crimes. We did, however, add her name to the suspect list."

"Maybe I'll have better luck talking with George after work tomorrow. I'm not sure how I can segue from eulogies to dishing the dirt about Cornelia, but I'll give it a try."

"At least we've got tonight to ourselves. I'm glad we decided to celebrate Valentine's Day at home. This will be my first attempt at broiling Australian lobster tails. The guy at Costco's fish counter said it was a breeze. Olive oil and lemon pepper. He'd better be right."

I gave his hand a squeeze. "It'll be wonderful. I've got the risotto down to a science and I put a bottle of Riesling in the fridge."

"Hey, you two," Augusta said, "I'm trying to get some work done around here, not watch a sappy soap opera."

Marshall gave me a wink. "That's our cue to get out of here."

A bouquet of irises and lilies awaited me at the door when I got home. Marshall arrived a few minutes later with the customary box of chocolates, which we sampled prior to cooking our meal. Sleep was the last thing on our minds that night, and I crossed my fingers we wouldn't be interrupted by any phone calls. We put our cell phones on mute and I lowered the volume on the landline.

"We should be fine." I turned down the covers on the bed. "My mother and the book club ladies are having dinner at the Homey Hut and then they're going back to her house to watch a movie that's older than the hills: *The Shop Around the Corner.* It was that or a showing of *Sleepless in Seattle* at the Stardust Theater. Guess Jimmy Stewart beat out Tom Hanks on that one. Besides, it was a freebie from the library."

Our heavenly night was followed by a hectic and harried morning. With a head full of shampoo, I strained to hear Marshall as I hurried with my shower.

"Your mother's on the phone. She wants to know if you'd like her to get us a SodaStream. She's at another one of those garage sales or whatever you call it."

"Tell her yes so we can get going. Otherwise she'll convince you we need one. It must be a heck of a bargain."

I proceeded to rinse off my hair, hoping it was the end of it.

A few seconds later Marshall was back. "We may be getting a rotisserie as well. It was impossible to hear her with all that commotion. Surprisingly, I did recognize Myrna's voice in the background. It was unmistakable. She kept yelling, 'I saw the Krups waffle maker first.' Then

I heard Shirley yelling that there was another full box of Krups waffle makers."

"Good God! These women buy the frozen kind and plunk them into the toaster."

I continued rinsing my hair. Suddenly I had the strangest thought. *SodaStream . . . Krups . . . It can't be.* I toweled off, shouted to Marshall that the shower was all his, and raced for my cell phone.

"Mom! Are you still at that garage sale in Sun City?"

"Yes. Why? Is there something you want?"

"Look around and tell me what brands you see."

"It's mostly kitchen appliances at this sale, not like the last time. Proctor Silex, some Cuisinart, Krups, oh and a few George Foremans. What do you need?"

"Can you get me the name of the person holding the sale and the address?"

"What on earth for?"

"I'll tell you later. Just do it, okay?"

"You're way too cranky in the morning, Phee. But yes, I'll ask around."

"Good. Thanks. Catch you later!"

I didn't say anything to Marshall because I was probably way off base and needed to make sure of my suspicions. I felt as if I was becoming like my mother more and more every day, especially when it came to jumping to conclusions. This time I needed to temper my actions.

Marshall was going to be tied up most of the day in Phoenix to testify on a case he had undertaken last year.

When I got into work I wanted to delve further into the Home Products Plus accounts but focused on payroll, billing, and insurance, the real reason I was hired. Meanwhile, Nate told Augusta and me he had some interviews to conduct downtown regarding the Home Products Plus situation and didn't expect to be back until after three. It was a little past eleven when I came up for air.

"You looked so intent on what you were doing, I didn't want to bother you," Augusta said. "I peered into your office an hour ago and figured I'd better leave you alone."

"Yeah, well, I finished what I needed to. Now I'm going to grab some coffee and open up that inventory spreadsheet I was working on yesterday. It's funny, but that company is huge and none of the stores in Chandler, Gilbert, Scottsdale, and Mesa have had an inventory loss like the ones in Glendale and Phoenix. Nate also checked with the branches in Tucson, Payson, and Prescott. No problems there either."

"You're thinking a local-yokel bandit?"

"I'm thinking a local-yokel scheme that's gone virtually undetected until now, but I need to be sure. I have the craziest hunch."

"Let me get a cup of coffee. I want to hear this."

I told Augusta the wacky idea that was brewing in the back of my head and, surprisingly, she didn't think it was so off base.

"I need to close in on a few brand names and make some comparisons with normal losses."

"Then what?" she asked.

"Then I hope I'm wrong. It would mean I am in possession of stolen goods, along with my mother and all her book club friends."

"Yeesh."

Yeesh was right. I traced the accounts back six months to look for a trend, and while the gradual leeching of products seemed minimal at first, it grew exponentially. At a little after two my mother called with the information I had requested.

"I found out what you needed. The woman whose house it was at isn't exactly the person holding the sale."

"Huh? What? You lost me."

"The woman was just *hosting* the sale. She got paid by the person who brought in all the inventory."

"Who's that?"

"The woman didn't know. Some delivery guys showed up with the merchandise. It's kind of like one of those parties where they sell Gold Canyon Candles or Pampered Chef. People buy products, but they also sign up to host parties themselves for a cut in the profits. It was done over the internet and she got paid directly into her checking account. She asked if I was interested and I said no. Can you imagine what that would do to poor Streetman? He's only recently gotten used to the book club ladies and Herb. Now, granted, I would be selling the stuff in the garage, but dogs are very perceptive, and Streetman is no exception. He'd know immediately there were strangers on the premises."

"Perception? That's because he would hear them. That's not perception. That's good hearing."

"I'm not going to argue with you, Phee. All I'm saying is I declined to host a home goods sale because it would be too stressful for the dog."

"Good. Good thinking, because those products you bought might be stolen."

"What?"

"Look, I'm not really sure at this point, and I haven't spoken to Nate, so don't say anything to anyone. Um, I'd also keep them unopened for the time being."

"This is horrible. I could be arrested for possession of stolen goods while some maniacal killer armed with a pair of scissors and a hatpin is free to wander loose in our neighborhood."

"You're not being arrested, and it's not as if some lunatic is wandering around murdering people willy-nilly. The murders took place at the radio station, and most likely they were related."

"Oh, *that* makes me feel a whole lot better."

"Well, I'm sorry, Mom, but I don't want you to blow things out of proportion. And if you're so worried, why are you continuing with your show?"

"We've been through this before. I don't want to miss my opportunity to attend that banquet and rub noses with all those radio celebrities."

"Aargh."

I was still muttering to myself when Nate walked into the office an hour later. I heard his voice and all but accosted him at the door. "I think the Home Products Plus case is closer to us than we realize. And I think the evidence is sitting in lots of kitchens and bathrooms in Sun City West and Sun City."

"Hold on, kiddo. Let me catch a breath and you can fill me in."

Twenty minutes later I showed him what I had uncovered on the spreadsheets and told him about what I believed to be a clever and clandestine operation that involved the unwitting "hostesses" for a stolen goods business.

I expected him to pooh-pooh it, but this time it was different. This time he thought I was really on to something. "Okay, that narrows down *process*, but not perpetrators. The surveillance that both stores have didn't yield a whole heck of a lot. The goods are all coming from different manufacturing companies, so it's not likely the drivers were paid off. More than likely the goods got whisked away as they were being unloaded. Both stores have now set up wider-angle surveillance outdoors. It's funny, but the stores concentrate on theft inside their buildings, not outside."

"As soon as I'm done chatting with George after work, I intend to look at the linens and towels my mother bought us a few weeks ago. Maybe the box has some sort of sticker indicating it came from Home Products Plus."

Nate shook his head. "Doubtful. Those stickers are affixed by the receiver, not the manufacturer. You can still give it a look. Hey, don't get your hopes up regarding any info from George." Then he paused for a second and smiled. "Still, if anyone can move a conversation seamlessly from memorial eulogies to a murder investigation, I've got my money on you."

"Don't bet too much. And if you must know, I'm afraid to ask how the investigation is going."

"Still trying to reach Cornelia. I can't believe she managed to stay out of the picture as long as she did."

"Do you think someone was trying to protect her?"

"It's a possibility. Anything is at this point."

CHAPTER 23

George tapped his fingers on his desk, quickening the pulse each time. We were seated in the radio station's small studio with a canned music program running. If the finger tapping wasn't enough, he looked at his watch every few seconds. "I haven't eaten dinner yet, so this better not take too long."

"I understand. I haven't eaten either." *Oh dear God! Please don't take this as a hint that I want to go out to eat with you.* "I'll try to make it fast."

"Good."

I squirmed in my chair and tapped my teeth. "Um, as you know, because neither of the station employees have relatives or friends in the area, a number of us thought it would be a good thing, I mean, a *proper thing* to hold a memorial service. The Booked 4 Murder book club made arrangements for it to take place at the Beardsley Rec Center's Meditation Garden."

"Meditation Garden, huh? This isn't going to be one of those wacky New Age things, is it?"

Only if we put my aunt Ina in charge. "No, very normal and dignified. We thought perhaps because you're the station manager and you knew them best, you should be the one to deliver the eulogies."

George's groan was probably audible in New Mexico. "Don't think so. Howard and I weren't on the best terms, and all I could possibly say about Bucky was that he knew how to run the equipment without screwing up."

"Um, maybe you could mention that."

"Nope. Don't think so."

"I'm sorry to hear about your relationship with Howard. I imagine it was about his passion for the live broadcasting and community outreach. Hmm, come to think of it, Cornelia lost her job over that, didn't she?"

"People are let go for all sorts of reasons. I can't talk about personnel."

"So, it wasn't over the programming and lack of space for more advertisers?"

"I already explained all that to the deputy and the gumshoe who was with him."

"Can you tell me the last time you saw Cornelia?"

"Hell no. I can't even remember what I ate for lunch. It was a few months ago. Damn. I need to call her. She still has the key to the station. Never returned it."

Holy cow! That's opportunity with a capital O. And I can't believe he let it slip. Better change the subject fast. "I know you declined our request about the eulogies, but will you please give it some thought?"

"I'll give it thought, but the answer will still be no."

I got up from the uncomfortable chair and thanked George for his time. Then I made a beeline for home, hoping Marshall was back from downtown so I could tell him what Cornelia still had in her possession.

My eyes teared as soon as I opened the door to our house. Onions! And lots of them.

"Hi, hon! I'm chopping peppers and onions to fry up with a steak I bought on the way home. Hope you're hungry."

"Famished."

I walked into the kitchen and threw my arms around his waist as he was chopping the veggies. "Cornelia has a key to the radio station. I don't think George even realized what he told me."

"Whoa. That kind of changes things regarding the hierarchy of suspects. Still no luck contacting her, though. Her neighbor thinks she might be on one of those bus tours to California, but she isn't sure. We're still monitoring Cornelia's place."

"You don't suppose her dead, decaying body is in there, do you? I'm not saying foul play, but that kind of thing is pretty common in senior communities. Ugh. I hate to think about it."

"Relax. That thought crossed my mind, too, but not natural causes. Bowman had one of the posse volunteers do a welfare check. Cornelia's got one of those Sun City West Fire Department lockboxes on the side of the house with her key in it."

"And?"

"No sign of her, but according to the posse volunteer, the place was spotless. She also has one of those vacation mailboxes so no one can tell if anything is piling up. Interesting. I never heard of them until I moved here. Clever idea, huh? The mail drops into a long cylinder from the box."

"Uh-huh. My mom's got one, too, but I doubt she'll go anywhere unless she can take the dog. She had a hard time boarding him when we attended my aunt's wedding. Anyway, give me a minute to change into something comfortable and I'll set the table."

"Take your time. I'm not done with the veggies."

While Marshall played Gourmet Detective in the kitchen, I threw on a pair of jeans and a T-shirt. Then I opened the hall closet and pulled out the linens and towels my mother had given us. Everything was in the original boxes. Wamsutta Cool Touch Percale and Abyss Habidecor. Nate was right. There was nothing on the packaging that indicated Home Products Plus. Product labeling apparently happened after the merchandise was received and ready to be stocked. I took a deep breath, returned the boxes to the closet, and joined Marshall for dinner.

The next few days were static and routine. Cornelia hadn't returned from wherever the heck she was, and there were no further developments in the case. Or cases, to be more precise. Poor Bucky. Even in my mind, his murder was relegated to second place. Then Tuesday rolled around, and it was as if the world turned upside down. It started with my mother's radio show. Or disaster, as it became known. At least Marshall was out for most of the day, so he was spared the calamity that permeated the airwaves. Not so for Nate, Augusta, and me.

Augusta came to work an hour early that morning because she planned to take a longer morning break in order not to miss Sun City West's version of the *George Burns and Gracie Allen Show*. Her words, not mine. For some odd reason my boss decided to tune in as well because he was stuck at his desk catching up on paperwork.

At nine fifty-three, Augusta turned on the radio in our breakroom and I joined her at the table, coffee cup in hand.

"Our next appointment isn't due for an hour and I can grab the phone in here," she said.

Canned music was playing on KSCW and I glanced at the wall clock. Five more minutes to go. Suddenly, there was a piercing sound and I heard a man's voice.

"Harriet! What are you and those women doing here? I'm supposed to be going on the air in five minutes."

"Oh my gosh, Augusta, I don't think they realize they're on the air. Someone must have hit the wrong switch and cut off the music."

Augusta opened her mouth to say something but couldn't compete with my mother's radio voice.

"What the heck are you talking about? This is the *Booked 4 Murder Mystery Show* and today's guests are Shirley Johnson and Lucinda Espinoza. They'll be chatting about sewing-themed cozies."

"Like hell they will! The schedule got changed. Don't you read your email? This is *Lake Fishing with Paul,* and today we're going to talk about lake trout."

"Oh no we're not! You go ahead Shirley, practice your introduction for the show. We go on in a minute."

There was a slight pause and then, "I'm Shirley Johnson, and with me today is Lucinda Espinoza. We're joining Harriet Plunkett and Myrna Mittleson to talk about—"

"The Arizona lakes that hold state records for brook and brown trout. Beginning with Sunrise Lake . . ."

"Get out of the way, Paul. Today we'll introduce three wonderful authors, Cate Price with *Deadly Notions* . . . Is that a good introduction, Harriet?"

"—cutthroat trout from Luna Lake . . ."

"Melissa Bourbon with *A Seamless Murder* . . ."

"Rainbow trout from Tempe Town Lake, and . . ."

"I mean it, Paul. No one wants to hear about trout. Unless they're served on a plate with plenty of almonds and sauce."

Nate burst into the breakroom, doubled over with a hand on his stomach. "This is hilarious. They don't realize they're on the air."

"That's a great introduction. Try to speak slower," my mother said.

Then Paul's voice: "Try not to speak at all. Oh, for God's sake! We've been on the air all this time. Sorry, listeners, this is Paul Schmidt, and today I'm going to introduce . . ."

"Cozy mysteries with wonderful sewing themes. I'm Shirley Johnson and with me today are . . ."

"The other not-so-familiar names for lake trout: mackinaw and lake char. That's right, we're talking trout fishing today because . . ."

"There's nothing quite as satisfying as holding one of them in your hand and turning the . . ."

"Twenty-two-pound winner from . . ."

"Lucinda Espinoza, along with—Hey! You can't yank the mic from me!"

"I just did. Sorry, listeners. Today we're talking trout and—"

"Oh no we're not!"

By now Nate wasn't the only one doubled over. Augusta laughed so hard she lost her breath on two occasions. "It's like watching a train wreck. You want to turn the other way, but you can't."

Meanwhile I was frozen at the table, unable to move. And then, if the unwelcome show introductions weren't enough, the next segment was worse. Far worse. I think my mother started it, but I wasn't sure. Nate and Augusta were laughing so loud I missed part of the broadcast. When I was finally able to hear it, Myrna's voice was on the air.

"Listeners are much more interested in murder mysteries than fish, isn't that so, Lucinda?"

"Absolutely. Especially because we've had two murders in this radio station, and with a scissors and a hatpin . . . or a very large pin really. Things cozy mystery seamstresses are well acquainted with."

Oh God no! Oh hell no! Am I hearing what I think I'm hearing?

Paul's voice all but exploded. "I suggest if you don't want the next murders to take place with fishhooks, you'd better get off the air now."

"Lordy," Shirley said. "Are you threatening to kill us with a fishhook?"

"I'm tempted. I'm really tempted. But I don't see any J hooks or circle hooks around here. Come to think of it, I don't see any sewing scissors either. Killer must've brought his or her own."

"Or stashed them here ahead of time," my mother added, unaware it would be the one thing that got Paul to stop talking about fish.

"Premeditated, huh?"

"I'm thinking a love interest gone wrong," Lucinda said.

I clapped my hands, making Nate and Augusta jump. "That beats the cake, doesn't it?"

"Show's not over yet," Augusta whispered.

I began to grind my teeth, stopping only when I heard Myrna's voice. "If you want my opinion—"

I don't. I don't. No one does. Keep your opinions to yourself.

"Whoever killed Howard Buell and Bucky Zebbler went to a lot of trouble to set up someone else."

Paul's voice got even louder, if that was humanly possible. "What makes you say that?"

"Because—"

And then dead air.

CHAPTER 24

The radio silence was deafening. I pushed myself back from the table and stood. "Maybe I should—"

"I'm on my way now," Nate said.

Before Nate could stand up, the book club ladies and the fishing guy were back on the air, as if nothing had happened.

"You hit the Off button, Myrna," Paul said. "Watch it."

"Oh, is that what it is? Good. Because I'll hit it again if you start to talk about trout."

"Fine. You're the murder experts around here; maybe we should talk about that. I heard both men were killed by a woman who was already dead."

"Where did you hear that?" This time it was my mother's voice, followed by Lucinda's.

"Yes. Who told you about Ursula Grendleson?"

My jaw dropped, and so did Augusta's. Only Nate remained stoic, and that didn't last long.

"Stay calm. Nothing any of us can do at the moment. If we're lucky, Bowman and Ranston aren't listening to 103.1 on their radios."

"Let's hope my mother and her friends don't get arrested for interfering with a crime investigation."

Augusta gave me a nudge and smiled. "Let's hope you and Marshall stock up on lots of dog food."

"Not funny," I whispered.

At that moment another voice came on the air: George Fowler's. "And that concludes this morning's live radio broadcast featuring local news and activities. And now, a selection of Barry Manilow favorites."

Nate didn't budge from his seat. "Barry Manilow may be ready to take a chance again, but I'm not. I'd better make some calls and do some damage control."

"Um, is there anything I can do?" I asked.

Nate shook his head. "I don't know if there's anything any of us can do. With luck, it'll blow over."

Famous last words. It didn't blow over. In fact, it became a regular windstorm, starting with a frantic call to my house the next day at seven in the morning.

"Phee, it's Lucinda. Please tell me I didn't wake you, but I just got a death threat."

Hearing that one of your mother's friends was the recipient of a death threat wasn't the best way to start the day.

"My God! Hang up and dial nine-one-one."

"They can't do anything. I need an investigator. Before I'm memorialized along with Howard and Bucky. My God, Phee! A death threat. On my front door!"

"Okay. Slow down and tell me what happened."

"I get the *Daily News Sun* delivered to my door every morning. When I went out to pick it up something was hanging from the knob of the security door. It was a clear plastic bag with something stuffed in it. I couldn't tell what from the way it was jammed in there, but I figured it had to be one of those promotional things. Last week someone gave us refrigerator magnets for Cool and Comfort. And the week before that, these cute little red combs from The Cut and Curl."

"I'm listening." *Losing patience, but listening.* "Go on." *Get to the point. I haven't had my coffee yet.*

"The bag was heavier than the other ones, but I thought maybe the promotional gift was a box of food. They do that sometimes. Not in the summer, but now, when the weather is cooler."

Oh, for heaven's sake! Get to the point. "Uh-huh."

"I brought the bag into the house and removed the . . . the . . . Oh, Phee! It was horrible! Horrible! It was a cloth doll with a note pinned to the chest. And I don't mean pinned horizontally. The pin was sticking straight in like a dagger."

"What did the note say?"

"'Keep.'"

"Keep what?"

"That's all it said. 'Keep.'"

"Um, maybe they meant for you to keep the doll. Maybe one of your neighbors made it."

"I don't think so. They also included photocopies of

Howard and Bucky's obituaries. It was a death threat all right."

"Don't touch it. Take it over to the posse station. I'll let Marshall and Nate know. Meanwhile make sure you keep your door locked. If I find out anything, I'll call you."

The phone was barely back in the cradle when the next call came in.

"Phee! It's your mother!"

I rolled my eyeballs. "I know. Trust me, by now I recognize your voice. What's going on?"

"Shirley called me a few minutes ago. Woke Streetman up from a sound sleep. She thinks someone put a voodoo curse on her."

"Let me guess. They sent a doll to her house with a pin in it."

"How did you know?"

"And there was a note attached, right?"

"Did she call you?"

"No. Did the note say 'Keep'?"

"No. It said, 'Shut.' Who sends a note like that? Shirley is beside herself. Said she was going to call your aunt about incantations to remove voodoo curses."

"Terrific. That'll keep Aunt Ina out of our hair for a while. Mom, do me a favor and go look at your front door. See if there's a plastic bag hanging on it."

"A plastic bag? That's what happened to Shirley. Someone put the doll in the bag and hung the whole thing over the doorknob. She found it when she stepped out to get the paper."

"Go check your door. I'll stay on the line. If there's

anything there, don't open it unless you put on gloves. I know you've got a zillion pairs of those plastic cleaning gloves."

"Hold on. I have to put Streetman on his leash. I might as well take him outside for a minute."

"Call me back, then. I can't be on hold while the dog pokes around for a good spot to pee."

Marshall had just stepped out of the shower and overheard part of the call. "What's with the gloves and Streetman? Everything okay?"

"No, it's not. Shirley and Lucinda each got cryptic messages in the form of a doll with a note. My mother may have one, too. She's going to check out front once the dog does his business."

I gave Marshall the lowdown on the notes, but before he could say anything, the phone rang. My mother again.

"It's here! The maniac killer sent me a death doll, too. I always thought those things were supposed to be ugly and scary, but this one's really pretty. Looks like a homemade Cabbage Patch Doll. Cute little violet dress with matching socks and ribbons in her hair."

"Forget the doll's clothing for a minute. Does it have a note?"

"Pinned to her chest as if she was being stabbed. It says, 'Mouth.' What kind of message is that?"

"One that makes perfect sense if all three dolls are put together."

"Three? You mean to tell me there are more than the ones Shirley and I got?"

"Yeah. Lucinda called me a few minutes before you did. Hers says 'Keep.' Look, it doesn't take a rocket scientist to figure out the gist of the message. 'Keep Your Mouth Shut.' I bet Myrna got the one that says 'Your.'"

A loud, pounding sound interrupted me.

"Someone's at the door, Phee. I'm putting the phone on Speaker in case it's the killer."

"Don't open the door if you don't know who it is!"

The next voice I heard was one I recognized, only he wasn't talking about trout fishing.

"Is this your idea of a joke, Harriet? Because if it is, it's not very funny."

"Don't be absurd! Shirley, Lucinda, and I all got those dolls. Oh, yours is really pretty, too. I like the pink and mauve dress with the little strawberries."

"The hell with the dress! What does this mean? All it says is 'Big.' Big what?"

Keep Your Big Mouth Shut! Duh!

"My daughter's on the phone. Hold on. I'd let you inside, but it would upset the dog."

"Mom!" I yelled loud enough, hoping she'd hear me.

"I'm here. It's Paul Schmidt from the radio station. He got one of those death dolls, too."

"I know. You have the phone on Speaker. Ask him to take his doll to the posse station. That's what I told Lucinda. Call Myrna. I guarantee she's got a doll waiting for her, too. Same deal. Posse station. Got it? Oh, and tell Shirley to do the same thing."

"I'm not daft, Phee. I'll talk to you later. *If* I'm still alive."

"Stop being so dramatic." Then I paused. "But, uh, just in case, take that Screamer thing, will you? I don't care if it does go off and the dog pees. Better safe than sorry."

My mother agreed to put the ear-piercing Screamer device Myrna had gotten her a while back in her bag. When I got off the phone I felt as if I had just done battle with the Trojan army.

CHAPTER 25

Marshall stopped by the posse station on his way into the office and had a look-see at the dolls. The book club ladies couldn't get them into the hands of the Maricopa County Sheriff's Office fast enough, according to Marshall, when he finally showed up at Williams Investigations.

"Shirley and Lucinda were on their way out of the place when I got there. Shirley told me she wanted to get a closer look at the exquisite hemstitching, but she was afraid to touch the doll again. Also told me she and Lucinda washed their hands with antibacterial soap and used hand sanitizer as well."

"I seriously doubt those handmade dolls are carrying any toxins."

"Me too. In fact, the posse volunteer said the same thing. One of the deputies is on his way over there and will take all five dolls to the lab for testing. Maybe we'll get lucky this time and find viable prints."

"When yesterday's fiasco hit the airwaves it must have struck a nerve with the killer. Whoever it is, they don't want the book club ladies snooping around. And now Paul Schmidt is in the middle of it, too. He couldn't keep his large mouth shut either."

Marshall laughed. "Yeah, like one of those bass. Maybe that will be his next program–*Big Mouth Bass Fishing in Arizona*."

"Ugh. As long as it doesn't conflict with the murder mystery show. What a mess! That forensics team better find something or our last-ditch hope is the memorial service. With food and drink, people will talk. I think there's a good chance the killer will be there, and maybe he or she will inadvertently let something slip."

"That's the plan at this point. Nothing else is working. By the way, do you know how the arrangements are going?"

"Oh yeah. Got an earful the other day from my mother. The radio station is paying for a good chunk of the food and drink. Putters Paradise is going to cater it. Plus the ladies agreed to bring desserts. Herb and his pinochle crew will set up the tables and chairs. The Rec Center maintenance department will drop them off earlier in the day. Anything for a free meal, according to my mom."

"Too bad George Fowler nixed the eulogies."

"No kidding. If I wasn't so sure Sylvia was the murderess, I'd ask her to do it. She knew Howard best. And she knew Bucky, too." Then I paused. The strangest thought came to mind and I shook Marshall's wrist. "I *am* going to ask her. If she's our murderess, she might lose it altogether and give herself away. This could work."

"Or it could be a complete disaster. Isn't there anyone else you could try?"

I let go of his wrist and gave him a thumbs-down. "Nope. No one."

"There's always Paul Schmidt."

"Not on your life. Hearing him yesterday was enough. I'll figure something out."

"Hey, I forgot to ask you at breakfast: Are you sure you'll be okay tonight while Nate and I catch up on some target practice downtown? This time of year, we really need to use the indoor shooting range."

"Of course. It's not as if I received one of those dolls. Besides, I already made arrangements to meet Lyndy for burgers at Texas Roadhouse after work."

"Great, because Nate's been hankering for a deep-dish pizza at a place near the shooting range. If it's any good, we can go there sometime."

Nate and Marshall were in and out most of the day, leaving me less than five minutes to give him a peck on the cheek when all of us left the office for the day. Augusta was in a surefire hurry because it was her canasta night. Needless to say, at five on the nose she scurried us out of the place and locked the door.

I got to Texas Roadhouse before Lyndy and grabbed a table near the grill. The place was filling up quickly, and I thanked my lucky stars I wasn't stuck waiting in one of those uncomfortable chairs by the entrance. Winter was the worst time for dining out after four. The abundance of snowbirds made it impossible to get a seat without waiting. And not just in the retirement communities—everywhere! I couldn't believe myself, but after living in the West Valley for two years, I was grumbling as much about the snowbirds as my mother. Yeesh.

Lyndy sat down just as the waiter showed up to take our drink orders. "Sorry I'm late," she said after we simultaneously said "Coke" and the waiter trotted off. "I meant to call you. I'm dying to know how the investigation is going. Did you sic the hounds on Sylvia Strattlemeyer?"

"Not exactly. Circumstantial evidence. Everything is circumstantial evidence. No wonder the investigators can't get anywhere. Meanwhile, there was a radio show mix-up and, as a result, my mother and her friends, along with another guy, talked about the investigation on the air. On the air! I'm holding my breath they don't get carted off."

The drinks arrived, and I took a sip, and finished telling Lyndy exactly what happened. Almost verbatim.

At one point she laughed and Coke spewed from her nose. "That's hilarious, Phee. You have to admit, it was hilarious. Too bad I was at work and missed it."

"Yeah, well, what happened next wasn't so hilarious. Everyone on that show got these weird death threats delivered to their doors."

"Letters?"

"Dolls."

I then explained about the pinned, one-word notes on the cloth dolls.

The waiter returned and we put in our orders for burgers. I was all but salivating from the aroma emanating from the grill. "Anyway, those dolls weren't all that menacing. In fact, they were kind of like Cabbage Patch dolls, from what my mother described."

"Cabbage Patch dolls?"

"Uh-huh. Why?"

"When we were scouting for Howard Buell's information in those yearbooks a week ago, I saw a photo of what I thought were Cabbage Patch dolls in a showcase, but the caption said it was a sewing project."

"Yeah, and I bet I know which teacher it was. Hmm, seems the ghost of Ursula Grendleson hasn't wasted any time. First, the scissors and now her homemade cloth dolls. For all any of us know, that hatpin might've been hers as well. Until it wound up with Sylvia . . ."

"Uh, you don't know that for a fact, do you?"

"No. A theory. I think Sylvia murdered Howard out of revenge and somehow Bucky found out, so she had to kill him as well."

"Okay, suppose that's true, but how do you think she got her hands on those dolls and the scissors?"

"The scissors part is easy. She probably used the pair from her prize and replaced them. All sorts of craft places can frame and reframe things. And as for the dolls . . . well, maybe Ursula gave them to her, or maybe Sylvia helped with one of those school cleanup days and took them with her. All sorts of stuff gets tossed out. Believe me, I know. My daughter, Kalese, once came home with a box of snakeskins, a bird's nest, and a rather large owl pellet her science teacher had discarded."

"Lucky you. So now what?"

"Unless some new and relevant information emerges, we're back to old school. Poking. Prying. Snooping. Eavesdropping. And we'll be doing it at the memorial service."

"That's this coming weekend, isn't it?"

"Yeah, Sunday at the Meditation Garden. The program begins at two. Be thankful you don't have to attend."

"Don't I wish! My aunt insisted I join her. She was very fond of Bucky's radio shows. If you want to know the real reason she's going, it's for the free food. Can you believe it?"

"I can believe anything. I've seen those women at half-price night at Bagels 'N More, not to mention my mother's neighbor Herb and his buddies."

The waiter was back with our burgers and fries and we dove in.

"If there's one thing I've learned since I moved out here," I said, "it's that no one can keep their mouths shut. I'm counting on it."

"Even the killer?"

"Especially the killer."

I reached for ketchup and gave my fries an extra dose. "Speaking of the killer, I intend to ask Sylvia to deliver the eulogies. Unless she's as practiced as Angela Lansbury or Meryl Streep, she might fall apart in front of the crowd and give herself away."

"And when exactly did you plan on asking her? The memorial is only three days away, if you don't count the day itself."

"Aargh. If you don't mind, I'll do it right now. My mother made me a list of all pertinent phone numbers relating to the murder investigation. I've got Sylvia's in my bag. Give me a second."

Lyndy sipped her Coke and watched while I thumbed through my bag, pulled out the paper with Sylvia's number, and tapped my iPhone like nobody's business.

"It's ringing," I said. "Hang on."

Putting it bluntly, the only pleasant part of the conversation was when Sylvia said, "Hello, this is Sylvia." It all went downhill from there. Well, not all of it. She *did* say she enjoyed making my acquaintance at the Creative Stitchers Club, but when I asked if she would consider giving the eulogy for Howard Buell, she said she'd rather jump into an active volcano. All the while, Lyndy kept her face locked on mine, while simultaneously giving me the thumbs-up and -down.

I, in return, gave her a dramatic thumbs-down as I continued to listen to Sylvia.

"You expect me to give his eulogy? That lowdown, no-good snake played around behind my back while we were dating. If anyone should deliver that eulogy, it should be Betty Hazelton. I had a hunch Howard was getting it on the side, if you know what I mean, and one night, after spending an entire day at a casino, he shows up at my house, makes some lame excuse, and leaves. Naturally I followed him. And guess where he went?"

"Um, to Betty Hazelton's house?"

Lyndy mouthed *Who's Betty? What did I miss?* but all I could do was motion for her to hold still.

"Got that right," Sylvia said. "I didn't know it was Betty's house until later that night, when I did a little internet searching. But here's the best part—just as Howard got out of his car, another guy came out the front door. Too dark to get a good look at his face, but he was taller than Howard. And more muscular. I got a bird's-eye view of everything from my parking spot two houses down. Howard waited for the guy to leave and then headed around the back of the house. The back of the house! What the heck was that woman running? A bordello? Separate entrances for different Johns? I wasn't born yesterday."

"Gee, I, uh, really don't know what to say. I don't suppose you'd be willing to say a few words about Bucky?"

"It would be a few words. 'Nice guy. Good DJ.' Not

much of a eulogy. Sorry, but you'll have to ask someone else."

I thanked her and ended the call. "So much for that plan."

Lyndy patted my hand. "You'll find another way to root her out."

"I'm not worried about that part. I'm worried about who's going to give those eulogies. My God, Lyndy! I think all we're left with is Paul Schmidt, and if *he* were a fish, I'd toss him back in the lake."

CHAPTER 26

The moment I got in the door the first words out of my mouth were "Why would Betty Hazelton lie to Nate about not knowing Howard?"

"Um, good seeing you, too, hon," Marshall said. "I must have missed the first act. What's going on?"

I gave him a hug, asked how his evening went, and then immediately told him about my conversation with Sylvia.

"And you know what the worst part is? We have no one to give the eulogies and no way to trap Sylvia into a confession. Heck, I don't even know if she'll show up at the memorial."

"She'll show up all right. If I've got a good handle on Sun City West, nothing brings the crowds in like free food. Besides, if she didn't show up, it would look like she had something to hide. I think you can relax as far as that goes."

"And the eulogies?"

Marshall grimaced. "You've still got a few days."

"Ugh. You know, I really should call Nate and tell him about Betty. If he talks with her again, maybe he'll get the truth this time. He can always hold Bowman and Ranston over her head. I mean, even on my best day those are the last two people I'd want to speak with."

"Yeah. This is scary, but we're beginning to think alike. I'll send him a text. Now, how about we forget about business and enjoy the rest of our evening?"

"Say no more."

When I got in to work the next day Augusta said, "What did you do, Phee? Scare our investigators away? Marshall was in and out of here like a fox in a henhouse, and Nate said he 'didn't want the wrath of Phee to come down on him.' What gives?"

I moseyed to the coffee maker, put in a K-Cup, and grinned. "Marshall had to meet with a client in Buckeye, and I caught Betty in one great big fib. She does know Howard. Maybe intimately."

Augusta, who was holding her own cup of coffee, put it down and motioned me over to the desk. "Tell me more."

I hadn't gossiped like that since I was in junior high and it felt like a guilty pleasure. For at least three or four uninterrupted minutes Augusta and I conjured up more X-rated and ill-fated scenarios than a Hollywood screen-writer.

"Sylvia's still numero uno in my book," I said. "The revenge thing and all that. Plus, she had Ursula's scissors."

"She had *a pair* of Ursula's scissors. That Grendleson woman probably had an entire arsenal."

Just then the phone rang, and Augusta picked it up. "Phee, it's for you. It's Shirley Johnson."

My first thought was that some God-awful catastrophe had befallen my mother or, worse yet, Streetman. I reached across the desk and took the receiver from Augusta's hand.

"Shirley. Hi! Is everything all right?"

"Put her on Speaker," Augusta whispered.

Apparently not soft enough because Shirley answered, "You can put me on speaker phone. It's good news. Well, good and bad, but not *that* bad. Not pleasant, but not life-threatening."

"What? What happened?" I pushed the Speaker button and Augusta leaned back.

"I was going to call you at home last night, but it was late when I got back from the Rip 'n' Sew meeting. You won't believe this, but Deputy Ranston found my scissors. The Gingher sewing scissors. That's the good news."

"Um, er, and the bad?"

"Someone must have seen them at our last meeting and borrowed them while they were sitting in one of the large, overstuffed chairs. The best I can figure, whoever used them got up in a hurry and left the scissors in the chair. The scissors slipped between the cushion and the side of the chair. Pointed side up."

"And?"

"Oh Lordy! When Deputy Ranston sat his not-so-delicate bottom in that chair, the pointed end of the scissors stabbed him right in the patootie. That man yowled like a cat in heat before announcing he was on his way over to the Sun City West Urgent Care for a tetanus shot. I found out this morning that he had to have two stitches in his rump. I called the posse station to see if they heard anything and the dispatcher on duty, who happens to be in the Creative Stitchers Club, told me. I feel terrible about it. Even though it wasn't my fault."

Augusta put her hand over her mouth and shook her head. At first I wasn't sure if she felt genuinely sorry for Deputy Ranston or if she was holding back a laugh. It turned out to be the latter.

"I'm glad you found your scissors and I'm sure Deputy Ranston understands."

"I soaked the scissors in rubbing alcohol when I got home. Then I sat down and sewed a lovely travel cushion that he can use until that fleshy skin heals."

"That's very nice of you."

"The Rip 'n' Sew president sent us an email first thing this morning. Deputy Bowman will now be interviewing the club members regarding Ursula. Probably sometime next week, after the memorial service."

"Thanks for calling me about the scissors. I knew you were worried, even though you were off the hook."

"Your mother hasn't said anything, so all of us are figuring the killer is still on the loose."

The way she said "loose" made me think of some zoo animal that had escaped from its habitat. "Most likely the killer or killers knew their victims. From what I understand, it was deliberate, not some crazed maniac, as my mother would like everyone to believe."

"Crazed or composed, a killer's a killer, and none of us are going to sleep well until he or she or . . . even they, are apprehended."

"We're working on it. Every single minute."

"If I hear anything at all, I'll call you."

"Thanks again, Shirley, and have a good day."

Once the receiver was safely in its cradle Augusta and I burst out laughing. It wasn't funny to make jokes out of people who met with misfortunes, but, in the case of Deputy Ranston getting pinched in the butt by the sharp end of a Gingher, it was absolutely hilarious.

"Holy cow!" I said. "I really need to go back to my office and work before Nate returns. He'll think all I do is loll around and gossip."

"And drink coffee . . ."

I gave Augusta a scowl and walked directly into my office. I didn't emerge until two and a half hours later, when Nate came back from Sun City West. He leaned into the doorframe. "Betty's sticking to her story, and I tend to believe her."

"What? I need another cup of coffee to hear this. And by the way, I think Ranston will be out of commission for a day or so."

"Ranston? How'd you find out?"

"Shirley Johnson."

"I see. Those scissors of hers, huh?"

"She feels terrible. She's even making Ranston a travel cushion for his rear end."

Nate opened his mouth, then closed it for a second. "Okay, then. Coffee. I won't hold you up."

"Wait! You can't just announce Betty is off the radar without telling me why. Sylvia was adamant Howard snuck around Betty's house. And there was another man who came out the front door."

"For all we know, Phee, the other man might have been a neighbor, or maybe her petsitter or her pastor. And as for why Howard might have snuck around the house is anyone's guess. But I can tell you one thing with absolute clarity—it wasn't for a piece of action."

"How do you know?"

"Because Betty told me she prefers a different team."

"Huh?"

Just then, Augusta shouted, "It means she's not interested in men. Want me to explain it to you?"

As if on cue, Nate and I both shouted "*No!*"

By now the two of us were in the outer office and inches from the coffee maker.

Nate motioned for me to go first. "Sorry, kiddo. Sometimes we hit a dead end. And a relationship between Betty and Howard is as dead as they get."

"Fine. Then what *was* he doing behind her house?"

"Snooping? Stalking? We did get that anonymous phone call from one of the pickleball players informing us Howard ogled Betty at the pool. Maybe he was unaware of her preferences. In any case, she was unaware of him."

"Give it up, Phee," Augusta called out. "Plenty of other suspects splashing around in this murky pond. We can sift through the mire and dredge them up."

Nate looked at me and then at Augusta. "If anyone's doing the dredging, it'll be Bowman, Ranston, Marshall, or me. Which reminds me: The forensics team sent us a complete report from their search of Howard's house. No different from what they told us originally, but now we have it on paper. Nothing like reading a report that doesn't say much. Aargh. No motive for his death. And other than a few buffet receipts from casinos dating back six months or more, it was pretty clean. Same deal for Bucky's residence."

"What about their bank accounts?" I asked. "Was the sheriff's office able to look into their finances?"

"Bucky was like a Boy Scout when it came to his finances. Everything on the up and up."

I put my coffee cup on the edge of Augusta's desk and went back to the counter for another packet of sugar. Augusta caught my eye, but before she could say anything, I announced, "Only sixteen calories." Then I turned to Nate. "What about Howard?"

"On the verge of bankruptcy. A year ago his savings account was like a roller coaster, but in the past few months it resembled the downhill ski slope at the Olympics. I imagine that's pretty typical of a seasoned gambler. The deputies think maybe some loan shark got tired of dealing with him and put an end to it, but Marshall and I disagree."

I opened the sugar packet and poured it into my coffee. "Not that I'm all that familiar with loan sharks, but honestly, who would choose a pair of scissors as the weapon?"

"That, and the fact it makes absolutely no sense to murder someone who owes you money."

"And what about Bucky? Does the sheriff's office have any theories about his death?"

"They do, but I don't think you'll want to hear them."

I froze. "Why?"

"Because they believe you and your mother were the last people to see him alive."

"*What*? And they think we killed him?"

"Don't get your blood pressure up, but Bowman has concocted some bizarre scenario about your mother holding Streetman in front of Bucky while you snuck behind to do the deed."

"Is he insane?"

"No, I just don't think he likes Streetman."

"Tell him to take a number and stand in line, but that theory is ludicrous."

"Relax. Even with timeline and opportunity, there's no motive."

"Now what?"

"More digging."

Apparently, my boss and my boyfriend weren't the only ones who took the task of digging seriously.

Shortly after lunch my mother called. "Phee! Stop what you're doing and listen."

"Um, I've already stopped and I'm listening. What's going on?"

"Forget Lassie and Rin Tin Tin. Remember when Streetman curled up in that lost-and-found box?"

"Hard to forget, Mom."

"Well, before he got situated in that pile of old clothing, he poked and nuzzled everything in the box. And before that, he sniffed under the shelves. Took his time, as a matter of fact."

Big surprise there. "And?"

"And I'm positive he found something and brought it home with him. I know, because it wasn't there before."

"What wasn't there? Where?"

"Under my bed. You know how he likes to find little treasures and hide them in his mouth until he gets home."

"The last 'little treasure' your dog found was in the Stardust Theater, and that discovery still gives me nightmares. What was it this time?"

"A five-dollar casino chip for Desert Diamond West. And before you say anything, I called Herb and the book club ladies, and it doesn't belong to any of them. That casino is right here in Glendale. Most likely Howard was gambling there and forgot he had a chip tucked away. It must have fallen out of his pocket when he got into the radio station the next day. You know how men are; they never clean out their pockets. And they wear the same pants day after day."

"Forget about men's pants. You said it was a five-dollar chip?"

"That's right, why?"

"Um, you may be on to something. Desert Diamond West had to be the last casino Howard frequented the day before he was found dead."

"What makes you say that?"

"He was desperate for money. He wouldn't knowingly leave the casino with a five-dollar chip."

"How do you know?"

"Uncle Louis. His motto was 'Never leave a casino if you're still holding a chip.' And that included fifty-cent chips. The one you found was five bucks. Five dollars can be parlayed into twenty-five. And twenty-five into a hundred. Howard would have bet it."

Suddenly my mother shouted, "Good little Streetman. You're mommy's little private eye."

I felt like gagging. "Mom, hold on to that chip. The investigators have been trying to find out which casino Howard was at. This could be major. I'll let them know and I'll talk to you later."

"Do you want to thank Streetman? He can hear your voice, you know."

"Uh, just give him a message."

CHAPTER 27

Augusta informed me that while I was on the phone with my mother Nate left the office and Marshall returned.

"Is Marshall with anyone?" I asked.

"No. Feel free to barge right in."

His door was partially ajar and I called out, "We may have to add Streetman to the payroll."

"Pull up a chair. This is sounding good."

Five minutes later I had explained about the dog's recent acquisition. Marshall got on the phone with Deputy Bowman, and after what seemed like ages, the call ended.

"Lucky my schedule's free this afternoon because I'm on my way over to Desert Diamond West. It hasn't been a month yet so they'll still have the security footage from that day. Now that the casino is narrowed down, we can broaden the search."

"Don't you need to stop by my mother's house and get the chip?"

He gave me a wide grin. "Nah. I don't intend to gamble."

"That's a relief."

"Seriously, we've got the info we need. Bowman's sending a posse volunteer to your mother's house to pick up the chip and I plan to sift through security footage to see what I can turn up regarding any contacts Howard might have had at the casino."

"Do you want me to pick up something for dinner?"

"More like a late-night snack, but sure." He gave my hand a squeeze and sighed. "I have a feeling it will be a long night. A long, boring night. Make sure you eat something; don't starve yourself waiting for me. Believe it or not, that little Chiweenie may have saved us a hell of a lot of time. If Howard's on that footage, we'll know exactly where he was twenty-four hours before his murder. And what might have led up to it."

"Have you talked to Nate about Betty?"

"He sent me a text that read 'No XY for Hazelton. Only XX.' I didn't know he was up on his chromosomes."

"Surprising the stuff that guy knows."

"Speaking of texts, I've got to let him know what I'm up to."

"Don't be surprised if you run into any of the book club ladies at that casino. Lucinda's hooked on the king crab legs, according to my mother."

"Those ladies gamble?"

"Are you kidding? They eat at the buffet. The closest any of them come to gambling is buying a two-dollar lottery ticket when the prize is close to a billion."

I buried myself in accounts for the remainder of the afternoon. Mainly a check-off list of sorts for the office, which only took me an hour, and another in-depth look at the Home Products Plus spreadsheets. I knew I was right. It was a slow leak, but it resulted in a loss of inventory that was bound to impact profits. The time at the bottom of my monitor said 4:51 and I closed the program for the day.

Seconds later I heard Nate's voice. Loud and clear, even with the door closed. "Can you believe it? Can anyone believe it?"

I didn't think it was a rhetorical question, so I stepped into the outer office just as Augusta responded, "Believe what, Mr. Williams? I think the entire street heard you. Even the people who need Miracle-Ear."

Nate grumbled and plopped himself in the chair next to Augusta's desk. "I got a call from the Phoenix manager of Home Products Plus shortly after lunch. Said there was something I needed to see. That's where I've been. Someone took a BB gun to their new, outdoor, wide-angle surveillance system. It's kaput. He notified the police, but all they did was file a report and refer him to his insurance company."

At that moment I knew my hunch about how those products were being moved was right. "What about the Glendale store?"

Nate rubbed the nape of his neck and leaned back. His arms were stretched out in front and it looked as if every muscle was taut. "Aargh. While I was in Phoenix, *that* manager called my cell. Same exact deal. BB gun to their system as well."

"Didn't think there were that many sharpshooters in this area," Augusta said.

Nate gave her a look. "Only need one."

"Maybe I'm looking at this wrong, but I think it could actually be good news."

Like a well-rehearsed scene for a movie, Nate and Augusta opened their mouths, but neither of them spoke.

"Whoever it was didn't waste any time getting rid of the only piece of equipment that could put them in jeopardy. That means they've got another one of those garage sale operations ready to go."

Nate shook his head. "They may be ready, but we're not. Those places can't afford twenty-four-hour stake-outs, and besides, if the perpetrators notice anything different, they won't make a move."

I smiled. "They won't, but I guarantee the Sun City West gossip crew is already aware of their next not-to-be-missed garage sale. Give me thirty seconds."

Having two conversations with my mother in the same day wasn't exactly up my alley, but this was a major deal. I walked closer to Augusta's desk, and without even asking, she handed me the phone.

"Hi, Mom! I need to—"

"Tell me they caught the lunatic killer? It was Sylvia, wasn't it? And Bucky found out, so she had to do him in. Where did they arrest her? Hold on. I need to turn on the TV. The news is about to come on."

"Stop! Slow down! No arrests. No Sylvia. I have a question for you, that's all."

"Oh." Then a few sighs and silence. "Okay. What question?"

"It's about the home products you got from those garage sales."

"Are you calling to tell me it's all right to use them?

Myrna wants to try out her new Krups waffle maker. She's getting impatient."

"Tell her to wait a little while longer." *Just don't tell her she may be giving it up for evidence.* "She's lived without a waffle maker up until now. A few more days *or weeks* isn't going to make a difference."

Augusta motioned for me to hurry up and pointed at the wall clock. I shrugged and kept talking. "Do you remember that first garage sale a few weeks ago? The one where you got us all those linens?"

"Of course, Phee. If this is one of those question-and-answer things to find out if I'm cognitively impaired, you can forget it. There's nothing wrong with my memory."

"Good. Because I need you to find out where the sale *before* that one took place and what they were selling. It's urgent. I need you to get on the horn and track it down."

"What on earth for? Those products have already been sold."

"I know. I know. But I need to see if those products match up to an inventory loss I'm doing."

"Fine. I'll make some calls."

"That's not all. I need you to find out where and when the next garage sale will be taking place. It's really, really important. Oh, and whatever you do, do *not* go there."

"Are those sheriff's deputies setting up a sting?"

"Not unless they have a time and a place."

"So it *is* a sting."

"I didn't say that."

"I'm not about to argue with you. I'll see what I can do. It's not like we get a lot of advance notice on these pop-up sales. Never mind. One of the girls is bound to know something. I've got to go. It's Streetman's dinner-time. I like to feed him a half hour before I eat so he won't beg."

"That works?"

"In theory, yes."

I rolled my eyes and grimaced. It was a good thing we weren't on FaceTime. "Don't forget. Call me as soon as you find out."

"Oh goodness. It almost slipped my mind. Were you able to find someone to deliver those eulogies?"

"Um, uh, well, sort of."

"Good. Because the last thing we need is one of those painful moments when the audience is asked to come up front and say a few words. I've been to memorials where no one makes a move. Let me tell you, it's very embarrassing. Good thing the person they're memorializing is dead, that's all I can say."

"Uh, yeah."

"I have to go, Phee. The dog needs to eat."

Before I could say goodbye the call ended, and I felt as if I had competed in a marathon. "You owe me," I said to Nate.

He gave me a nod. "Well, no sense all of us sitting around here. Let's lock up the place and get going."

"If my mom calls with any info, I'll call or text you. I've got a few things to finish up in my office, so I'll make sure everything's zipped up for the night."

"You sure?" Augusta asked. "I can stick around. No card games tonight."

Card games. It was as if those two words lit a spark under me. "Maybe for a few minutes. Sure. Thanks."

Nate stood, stretched, and walked to the door. "All right, ladies. I leave Williams Investigations in your capable hands. Don't burn the midnight oil."

"He really is dating himself," Augusta said once Nate had left. "Burning the midnight oil. He really needs to get with today's jargon if he ever expects to attract a woman."

"I don't think he has any trouble with that."

"Speaking of trouble, I saw the look on your face a few seconds ago. It was when I said, 'card game.' What's going on?"

"I need to check something out tonight, but I have to do my homework first. Do you know where we put the phone directory for Sun City West? I've got to find Betty's address."

"Good thing Sun City West has its own directory. Much easier than poking around the internet. Of course the directory is a big dinosaur of a thing, but it's still faster. Hold on. I'll get it."

Augusta opened one of the file cabinets next to the copy machine, pulled out the directory, and handed it to me. "Don't tell me you're going to pay her a visit?"

"Betty? No. But I need her address."

"Let me get this straight: You're not going to stop by her house, yet you need her address?"

"Uh-huh." I thumbed through the pages.

"I knew it would come to this. You've been hanging around those book club ladies way too long."

"Ha-ha. I *need* her address so I can put it into Zillow and pull up an area map of the street directly behind hers."

"Okay, then. Now I'm officially lost."

"It's easy. I just didn't figure it out until you mentioned playing cards. Sylvia was convinced Howard was having an affair with Betty, and, in fact, Sylvia saw Howard slipping behind Betty's house one night. A night when he got home from gambling."

"Go on. This part I can understand."

"Nate is convinced there's no love interest between Betty and Howard. So, how do you explain what he was doing behind her house?" I didn't give Augusta a chance to speak. "I can. Or at least I think I can. I'll know more later tonight."

"Oh no. This isn't sounding good."

"Relax. It's only a paper search at the moment. Until you said, 'card game,' I had completely forgotten Howard's major interest. So major, in fact, that, according to Nate, Howard's finances were a stone's throw from rock bottom."

"And?"

"I'm no gambler, but I'll wager it wasn't Betty's house he was going to, it was a house behind hers. One of those houses that are always listed for illegal gambling activities in the police beat section of the newspaper. Oh look! Here's her address: One five three five seven West Domingo Lane. Hang on. I'll punch it into Zillow and pull it up on my computer."

"I'm sitting right here at my desk. Give me those numbers again. I'll do it."

Thirty seconds later Augusta and I were staring at a street map that showed West Arzon Way as the block directly behind Betty's and, more importantly, the house right behind hers. Unlike the multigenerational housing in Surprise and Vistancia, most Sun City West and Sun City houses didn't have block walls to separate the residences. People could mosey from one house to the next without any barriers.

"Google 'crime reports Sun City West' and see what happens."

Augusta's fingers barely tapped her keyboard. "Got it. I can filter it by date."

"Go back a month."

"Bingo! One five three six two West Arzon Way was listed as a location for fraud, gambling, and illicit card games."

"Too bad they didn't take roll call."

Augusta shook her head. "I don't get it. Everyone in those communities plays cards. Bridge, euchre, pinochle . . ."

"Yeah, but I think these types of games have really, really high stakes. If I'm right, Sylvia and Betty were both telling the truth about Howard. Sylvia *did* see him going behind Betty's house, but he was really headed to a house on West Arzon Way. Sneaking in their back door."

"All that proves is what you already know—the guy was a compulsive gambler."

"True, but who was he gambling with?"

CHAPTER 28

"Leave it for Nate and Marshall," Augusta said. "You've got enough on your plate with that memorial service."

"But I've got a free night tonight. Marshall won't be home until late. All I plan to do is drive by that address and get the name from the mailbox. Believe me, my mother's sources will be able to fill in the rest."

"Write quickly. For all you know that person could be Howard's killer."

"Now you're sounding like my mother."

"God help me."

When I left the office I felt energized and focused. Until my mind wandered to Bucky. How on earth did he fit into this picture? Howard I could understand. A jealous woman, a gambling problem, programming issues with advertisers . . . but Bucky? Whose feathers did he ruffle, or was he merely at the wrong place at the wrong time?

I was more than miffed that Deputy Bowman would even think my mother and I had anything to do with Bucky's death. Granted, I'd seen Streetman lunge at things, but they were usually inanimate objects like cameras or packages. Still, it was concerning.

Bucky's killer resorted to something subtle—a hatpin or a reasonable facsimile. And I was pretty sure whoever did it snuck up on him while he was napping in front of the broadcast equipment. A fast stab and an even faster death. I cringed. The method was one thing. It was the motive that puzzled me. Unlike Howard, Bucky was a regular Eagle Scout.

The GPS system in my car took me directly to West Arzon Way. It wasn't too far from my mother's house and close to St. Stephen's Church, where I had my first and only experience playing Bingo in Sun City West. It was still daylight, but not for long. I made a right turn on West Arzon and eyeballed the street numbers. One five three six two came up fast, and I immediately pulled over to the mailbox.

Of all things to forget! Unlike the mailboxes where I lived, these were tandem boxes, separated by a metal rod. And in this case both of them had the vacation mailbox feature. In addition, the names were written on the interior of the boxes. That meant I had to get out of my car, violate the tampering with the US mail thing, and open the box. I looked around as if I was about to abscond with a national treasure and then made a beeline for the mailbox.

It was only eight or nine feet to reach it, but given the trepidation I felt, it might as well have been a mile. I turned my head once and nothing. Then I grabbed the small pull tab and read the lettering inside the box. The name all but screamed at me: Vernadeen Stibbens. It couldn't be. She was in Iowa on that state fair committee.

I looked at the house. The plantation shutters were closed tight and there was no sign of activity. Vernadeen Stibbens. Could I have been wrong about the address? I went back to the car and did another quick search on my phone. The address was right. On a hunch, I did something that, under normal circumstances, would definitely fit the ew factor in any investigation. I walked over to the ground-level garbage receptacle and lifted up the lid. I knew with absolute certainty garbage pickup day was scheduled for tomorrow. My mother had that information plastered on her refrigerator, along with the phone numbers for all the major utilities, her hairdresser, and Streetman's vet. If Vernadeen was indeed back from her home state, she'd have trash.

Sure enough, Vernadeen's silver garbage can was full, but not with the usual garbage. Shredded paper filled at least three clear plastic bags. Maybe she was concealing evidence. Iowa my you know what. Vernadeen had to be back in town. Back in town and running an illegal gambling operation. Howard was probably one of her regulars. After all, they knew each other from the radio station, and he definitely supported her live broadcast sewing program. Whatever the heck it was called.

Sewing! The scissors! Vernadeen must have gotten hold of Ursula's scissors. And maybe she and Howard had a falling out over some gambling debt. My newest theory was now making perfect sense.

No sooner had I let the lid fall back on the garbage when I heard a man's voice. "You can't put your own trash in someone else's bin! We pay for this service. It's not a public dumping area! Are you throwing away dog poop? Too lazy to go back to your own house?"

Suddenly I stood face-to-face with someone I thought I recognized. The Hawaiian shirt guy from the Rec Center meeting last fall. What was his name? Russell something?

"Um, er, I'm not throwing away trash or doggy bags."

"Ah-ha! I know what you're up to and you won't get away with it. Identity theft is a crime. I've read about people like you. Sifting through other folks' garbage to steal information."

This is the last thing I need. "I'm not stealing anything. If you must know, I thought Vernadeen was home, but she's not answering any of my calls, so I figured I'd see if she had any trash in her bin. That would mean she's back from Iowa."

It was amazing how fast and smooth I could lie without even breaking into a sweat. "Have you seen her?"

"Vernadeen's still in Iowa. And after the fiasco last month, I don't blame her if she stays in Davenport indefinitely."

"Fiasco?"

"That's a nice way of putting it. While my wife and I were visiting our daughter in Florence, Vernadeen's house became a floating gambling casino. If it wasn't for the two old maids living across from us, the sheriff's deputies wouldn't have busted the party."

"Floating gambling casino? I'm not sure I understand any of this."

"What's to understand? Happens all the time. Usually in the summer, when the snowbirds are gone. It doesn't take a rocket scientist to get into a vacant house and use it as a temporary location for a high-stakes card game. Heck, half the people around here have keys under their doormats or inside those idiotic fake rocks. In Vernadeen's case she gave so many spare copies to her friends, who knows which one of them might have passed it along?"

For a moment I was stunned. "What happened to the people who broke into her house?"

"Far as I know all they got were desk appearance tickets for court. Whoopee."

"Did they trash the house or anything?"

"No. These are old men and women playing cards. Not teenage hooligans. In fact, from what I heard, they even wiped her counters and swept up the place. It's just the idea of the thing. Unauthorized people using someone's house for nefarious purposes."

I thought back to the holidays and that little bordello scheme in my mother's backyard. That involved teenagers, but gambling was the last thing on their minds. "Do you have any idea who the card players were?" *Other than the late Howard Buell . . .*

"Not a clue. But I will tell you this much: a desk appearance ticket isn't going to put a stop to this kind of activity."

But a pair of scissors in the gut might. "No, I suppose not. Anyway, I should be going. I'll keep trying to call Vernadeen."

"Yeah. Good idea. She's probably up to her elbows with that state fair stuff. Hey, sorry I yelled at you."

"No problem. Have a nice night."

I got back in the car, and once I left Vernadeen's neighborhood, I pulled over and dialed Nate. With Marshall glued to security footage at Desert Diamond, he'd be too occupied to deal with my latest finding.

Nate answered on the first ring. "Hey, kiddo! What's up? Don't tell me you're still in the office."

"I'm in Sun City West and Howard wasn't snooping around Betty's house. Don't ask me how I figured this out because it sort of popped into my head when Augusta mentioned card games."

Nate's response was all but monotonic. "Remind me to thank Augusta."

"You can thank both of us. Listen, Howard cut through Betty's yard to inconspicuously sneak into an illegal card game at the house behind hers. I know because Augusta and I checked the police beat. Get this: The house belongs to Vernadeen Stibbens. That's the woman from the radio program who went to Iowa and, thanks to her departure, my mother and Myrna got her slot for their murder mystery show."

"Whoa. Slow down. I'm still processing illegal card game. And Augusta's impersonation of Sam Spade."

I took a breath. Slowly and succinctly, I explained what I had discovered. "Maybe Howard got into it with whoever ratted him out. Or maybe with someone who cheated. Oh my gosh. What if Howard cheated? Maybe that person was a friend of Sylvia's and knew about her precious scissors."

"I think you're reaching at straws, but you did manage to accomplish one thing."

"What?"

"Give us more suspects. I'll put a call in to Bowman to find out who the illicit card players are, but only if you promise me to go home and quit snooping around for the night."

"So you're not upset?"

"How can I be? I'm the one who encouraged you, but honestly, rooting through garbage cans?"

"I looked. I didn't root."

I stopped by Salad and Go on my way home and bought two Cobb salads. Usually one was enough for Marshall and me, but I figured he might be really famished and I didn't want to take any chances.

The blinking light on my landline caught my eye as I walked into the kitchen. My gut instinct told me it was my mother because she hates to call me on my cell phone. I put the salads in the fridge and played the message. No surprise there.

"Okay, Phee. I found out about that sale. The first one. Window treatments. Sheers. Scarves. Valances. No wonder no one mentioned it. We all have plantation shutters or blinds. It was in Sun City on Conestoga Drive off Union Hills. That's the best Lucinda's neighbor can remember. Call me if that killer's been caught."

Sheers. Valances. This was no coincidence. Those items were one of the first to mysteriously dwindle from the Home Products Plus inventories. I was absolutely certain I had uncovered that scheme, but the second half of the puzzle was still missing. I needed to find out where the next hoo-ha was going to take place. Maybe Lucinda's neighbor would have an epiphany, but I wasn't counting on it.

Too hungry to wait for Marshall, I ate my salad, took a hot shower, and settled in front of the TV. I dozed off sometime between the nightly news and Jimmy Fallon and had it not been for the phone ringing, I would have remained in blissful sleep. Still groggy, I picked up the landline and mumbled.

Marshall's voice, unlike mine, was clear and chipper. "Phee? Did I wake you? I'm so sorry. I left you a text message about an hour ago and thought you'd text or call back."

"Aargh. I was in the shower. Is everything okay at the casino?"

"Better than okay. I owe your mother's dog a steak. If it wasn't for him finding that casino chip, it would have taken us months to figure out which casino Howard was in the night before his death."

"Did you find anything from the security footage?"

"Oh yeah. I put calls into Bowman and Ranston. One or both of them should be here any minute."

"I hope the casino has padded seats."

Marshall laughed. "I think Ranston will forget about the pain in his butt when he takes a look at the tape. Casino security is making a copy for the deputies."

"What was it? What did you see?"

"Bucky seated next to Howard at the slot machines, and it gets better. Bucky up and left, but not before he gave Howard a punch in the shoulder. Playful, not threatening. Then I was positive Herb approached and got in Howard's face. After three rounds of double-checking I knew it wasn't Herb, but talk about a doppelgänger."

"Balding head and potbelly?"

"Balding head, potbelly, and a gesture I still don't understand."

"What?"

"He took a greenback from his wallet and threw it at Howard."

"I doubt it was a charitable contribution."

CHAPTER 29

Marshall went on to explain that he and the deputies would be reviewing the tapes to see if they could track the man in question.

"Malcolm Porter fits that description," I said. "In fact, when I was in his store and saw him at first I thought it was Herb, too. And Malcolm was at odds with Howard over the live programming."

"Interesting. Sadly, the image on the tape wasn't clear enough to run it through facial recognition. Of course that only works if the person has a record, so it was iffy to begin with. That's why we'll be looking at more footage. Figure at least another hour or two. There's one thing, though, and it may help."

"What's that?"

"The surveillance caught a woman walking toward him and linking her arm under his. Again, not clear."

"A sexy, escort type?"

"More like a matronly, motherly type with love handles and one of those tight, bouffant hairdos."

"Had to be the wife."

No sooner did I say that when I realized there was one surefire way to find out if it was Malcolm. "I'll call you right back. I might be able to find out."

Before Marshall could utter a word I hung up and went into the garage to our recycling bin. I had made it a habit to toss all the ads and flyers into the recycling before they made it inside the house. Now, at a little past one, I was flinging magazines, ads, flyers, and newspapers all over the place. Thankfully, we had a separate bin for bottles and plastic.

Laxative ads, makeup ads, cat food ads . . . I was up to my elbows with discounts, not to mention the numerous offers for hearing aids. Fifteen minutes had gone by and nothing. I tried a more organized tactic. I moved the papers, one giant scoop at a time, onto our washer and dryer. Less stress on my back.

Finally I found a six-page flyer for Malcolm's Variety Store. It was a Valentine's flyer featuring all sorts of cutesy items like flowers with faces on them and candies that could be personalized. But the feature I knew I had seen was the photo of Malcolm and his wife posing in front of a large display of artificial flowers. The sign said, "Give the love of your life roses without the thorns."

I immediately snapped a photo and emailed it to Marshall. Then I called him. "Have Bowman and Ranston arrived?"

"Bowman's walking in the room now."

"Check your incoming mail. I sent you a photo of Malcolm and his wife."

"You're amazing, hon. Absolutely amazing. Guess I'll owe you a steak, too."

"A steak and shrimp to go with it. Listen, if you get lucky, maybe the photo will match a clearer image of them somewhere else in the casino."

"If I get lucky, I'll get out of this place while I can still focus. Everything's beginning to blur. I don't know how those security guys manage to do this. Anyway, Bowman will be looking at the tapes with a fresh pair of eyes. That should help."

"Drive safe. I'll keep the bed warm."

"Sleep on my side, then."

I heard Bowman's voice in the background and ended the call quickly. I was too wired to turn in for the night and too jittery to read or watch TV. Instead, I did what every amateur sleuth did. I went over my list of suspects, ranking them as if I was posting a review on Yelp. Another thought crossed my mind, but I brushed it aside. That casino chip Streetman found might have belonged to Bucky. Still, it netted the same results. Random thoughts came and went, each one more bizarre than its predecessor. Finally I gave up. I wasn't getting any closer to figuring out who sent Howard and Bucky to the proverbial cabin in the sky, and if I didn't want to look like I'd been washed ashore by a tsunami, I should at least make an effort to get some sleep.

Sometime before dawn, Marshall's leg lay on top of mine, and even though it was heavy, it was a comforting and soothing feeling. I rolled over and whispered, "I'm glad you're home safe."

He, in turn, snored.

"Any luck matching the photo with the surveillance tape?" I asked as soon as he was conscious.

"The potbellied Mr. Porter not so much, but a real clear shot of Mrs. Porter leaving the buffet table with enough king crab legs to start her own restaurant."

"Wow. Now what?"

"Bowman and Ranston plan to have a little chitchat with the Porters. And that's not the best part. Mrs. Porter had some sort of wacky, feathery thing attached to that teased-up hairdo of hers."

"A fascinator?"

Marshall looked as if I had named an alien species. "Hmm, I suppose that's a good word for it. Anyhow, they were able to zoom in the camera, and guess what held that thing together?"

Before I could answer, he did. "A large hatpin. Looked exactly like the one you and your mother found. Do they sell those in sets?"

"Sometimes. But with different-colored stones or ornaments. Why? Are you thinking Malcolm's wife might have been responsible for Bucky's murder?"

"I'm not thinking anything. I'm too damn tired."

In spite of doubling up on coffee before we left the house, both of us were totally whipped. Marshall needed to stop by the posse station in Sun City West before making his way to the office. I, on the other hand, stopped at Dunkin' Donuts for another caffeine fix and some assorted donuts for Augusta and Nate.

"What did you do? Pull an all-nighter?" Augusta asked the moment she saw me.

I waved the donuts under her nose and put the box on her desk. "Marshall pulled the all-nighter. I pulled some strings from my laptop."

"And some jelly donuts. My favorite. Thanks. Keep it

up and they'll need to add your name to the sign on the door.

"For the donuts or for my detective work?"

"Take your pick. FYI, Mr. Williams is in his office and busy as all get-up-and-go. He must've gotten to work with the roosters. The sheriff's office faxed him the names of the card players cited for that illegal game behind Betty What's-her-name's house."

"Hazelton."

"Yeah, her."

"Do you have the names? Who are they? Who?"

"And they say the apple doesn't fall far from the tree. Hold on. I've got the list." Augusta reached for a piece of paper next to the stapler and handed it to me. "Recognize anyone?"

"Not offhand, but it doesn't mean the voice of Sun City West won't. I suppose there are worse ways of starting my work day."

"What? No coffee?"

"I'm three cups in already. At this rate I should be bouncing off the walls. I suppose Nate's doing background checks, huh?"

Augusta nodded. "They should change the name gumshoe to finger tapper."

I laughed and walked into my office. If anyone could get the dirty details on those card-playing gamblers, it would be my mother. Unfortunately, I knew the minute I got her on the phone she'd ambush me with questions regarding who was doing those eulogies. To avoid the drama, I placed another call instead.

"Aunt Ina? I hope I didn't wake you."

"Oh no. Did something happen to your mother? Did that dog finally go berserk and attack her? I read about three Maltese mixes that turned on their owner. Poor woman was nearly ripped to shreds."

"Uh, no. Nothing at all like that."

"The radio station killer. Did he strike again? I wish Louis would get off the national news and turn to something local."

"No, no. The investigation is ongoing, but no new murders."

"That's a relief, I suppose. Not for those two men, but still . . ."

"Um, yeah, about those two men . . . We need someone to deliver their eulogies on Sunday at the memorial, and I immediately thought of you."

"That's so sweet of you, dear, but I didn't know them."

Even more reason. "It doesn't matter. You have a certain stage presence that's indescribable." *Understatement of the year.* "With your poise and elocution, those two men will be remembered indefinitely." *My God, I cannot believe the crap emanating from my mouth.* "I can email you all their information and leave it to you to compose an eloquent and touching memorial. Oh, and brief." *So no one starts snoring.* "We really need someone with your, your . . ." *What the heck can I say?* "Distinction."

"Well, if you put it that way, I most certainly can't say no. Of course I'll do it."

"Aunt Ina, I can't thank you enough. I'll get that information to you today. Send my love to Louis."

The moment I got off the phone I let out a long and heavy sigh. I wasn't sure if Howard and Bucky would be remembered indefinitely, but knowing my aunt's penchant for drama, her performance stood a good chance of being remembered well into the next century.

With that onerous task off my plate, I picked up the

phone and dialed my mother. I was itching to know if she knew any of the people who had been arrested. Not convicted, mind you, but arrested and ticketed.

Thank goodness for foresight, because the moment she heard my voice, the first thing she asked was if I'd taken care of the eulogies.

"Of course I did. No problem."

"You were able to talk George into it?"

"Um, not George."

"Don't tell me you asked Sylvia?"

"No. I did not."

"You found a pickleball player?"

"I asked Aunt Ina, if you must know."

The shriek that followed was deafening. "You did *what*? Aunt Ina? That sister of mine will read those eulogies as if she's delivering the Gettysburg Address. Phee, how could you?"

"It's not like I had any choice. No one wanted to do it, and I'm certainly not a public speaker."

"Mark my words, this is going to be a disaster."

Little did I know at the time how prophetic my mother's words were going to be.

"Listen, I called because I need to ask you something. The sheriff's deputies cracked down on an illegal card game that Howard took part in. I've got the names of the participants."

"You mean the *gamblers*?"

"Yes. Fine. The gamblers. Do you know any of them?" I recited the names without stopping to catch my breath.

"Offhand, no. Speak slowly. I need to write them down. I'll run them by the book club ladies. Only five names? I thought there would be more."

"Maybe some people left before the game got busted. Say, this is funny. I just realized Howard's name isn't listed. Must be an oversight. Anyway, call me if you find out something."

"Fine. And next time you decide to involve your aunt in anything, call me first."

CHAPTER 30

It couldn't have been an oversight. If Howard Buell was gambling at Vernadeen Stibbens's house, his name would have been on that list. After all, it was a fax from the sheriff's office and they tended to be pretty thorough when it came to names, dates, and places.

I didn't waste a second charging over to Nate's office and knocking on the door.

"It's open. Come in." Nate looked up from his computer and motioned me over. "What gives, kiddo? You look as if you've seen a corpse."

"I have. But not where I thought."

"Huh?"

"Howard. His name isn't on the list of gamblers who commandeered Vernadeen's place. Does that mean he wasn't there when the place got raided? If so, he either snuck off before the sheriff's deputies arrived or he was never there to begin with. Please tell me he snuck off, making him persona non grata with those card players. Because if he wasn't there to begin with, I've wasted everyone's time."

"You can relax. Ranston did his homework while Bowman caught up on his zees from last night. Turns out Howard was there, and that's not all. So was Cornelia. But both of them left before the neighbors from across the street notified the posse."

"How did you find that out?"

"From the other players who couldn't wait to tell Ranston how Cornelia was at Howard's throat all night."

"Her lost job? Her lost income?"

"According to Ranston—and this is the diluted, second-hand version from the gamblers—they were arguing about something else. But they did hear Cornelia say, 'We're done with the payoffs.'"

"Hmm, that's odd. 'Payoff' isn't usually a term for a gambling debt, if that's what it was. Gee, I wonder what she meant."

"You and the rest of the sheriff's office. That woman is harder to find than D. B. Cooper."

"Especially if she's sitting on some money. And speaking of which, I'm keeping my fingers crossed someone in my mother's coffee klatch will find out where and when the next super-duper garage sale is going to take place. I hate all these loose ends. I know with absolute clarity how that nefarious little operation at Home Products Plus is organized, but until we have a point-of-sale, we might as well throw our hands in the air."

"Whoa! I've never seen you so fired up about investigations before. If I didn't know you better, I'd think you were after my job."

"Not on your life. But the Home Products Plus thefts are right up my alley because the investigation involved bookkeeping and not, well, you know. Frankly, I'd much rather concentrate on who's going to rip off the next Crock-Pot as opposed to who might decide to pick up a pair of pinking shears and aim it at someone's chest."

"Good, because I've got to track down the Lynch woman and look for any connections she might have had with the other suspects."

"My money's still on Sylvia. It's the most tangible evidence we have: those scissors she got as an award. I hate to say it. I really do. But this time I think my mother's go-to theory about the jilted ex-girlfriend may really be true."

Nate ran both hands through his hair, pausing to massage his scalp every few seconds. "It's downright frightening, but Harriet may be sitting on the only reasonable explanation we have. Of course who the hell knows how Bucky fits in to any of this."

I walked back to my office more frustrated than when I left. Midafternoon, Marshall returned to the office, having spent the past six hours reviewing the information that the forensics team was able to glean from Howard's laptop and Bucky's ancient relic of a computer. Other than finding out about Howard's online poker sites and Bucky's video downloads of cat antics, there was nothing whatsoever that would indicate why anyone would murder them. Especially with such bizarre weapons.

"Lucky me," Marshall muttered. "Ranston's now suffering from gluteus maximus fatigue and Bowman's too damn sleep-deprived to tackle dealing with the public. The little chitchat they planned to have with the Porters is now sitting in my lap. No sense putting this off. I'm head-

ing over to that variety store before it closes. At least I'll
be able to have a few words with Malcolm. Of course, by
the time I get to speak with the feathery-topped Mrs.
Porter, he will have given her the party line to recite.
Aargh. Hey, don't cook anything. I'll pick up steaks for
the grill. Butcher Bob's isn't too far from the variety
store. Besides, grilling always clears my head."

I wished something would clear mine. I went back to
my spreadsheets and relished in the normalcy of accounts
receivable. It was a short respite.

Augusta rapped on my doorjamb. "Shirley Johnson is
on the phone for you. Something about tot lots and grandparents' afternoon."

Whatever it was, I knew it couldn't be good. But tot
lots? And grandparents? This was a first. I cringed and
picked up the phone. "Hi, Shirley! I hope you're—"

"Oh Lordy, Phee, I figured you should hear about this
before anyone else does. I was scrolling through the
weekly events bulletin when I saw it. Now it's too late to
do anything."

"Do what? What did you see?"

"Grandparents' afternoon at the Beardsley tot lot.
Some service club will be doling out hot dogs and chips,
and all Sun City West grandparents are invited. It's a free
event. You know what that means. Even the grandparents
whose grandkids are in Wisconsin will still attend for the
free meal."

"Um, I'm not sure what the problem is."

"Pardon my vernacular, but that tot lot is spitting distance from the Meditation Garden where our memorial is
going to take place. Spitting distance. Who puts a meditation garden next to a playground in the first place? Whatever was that planning board thinking? And now this.

How can we have a quiet and reflective service with all that yelling and screaming?"

"Maybe we can ask the grandparents to monitor the children."

"The children? I'm talking about the grandparents! They'll be the ones yelling and screaming. 'Don't swing from that rope.' 'Don't stick your head between those bars.' 'Don't eat something that's been on the ground.' Have you ever seen a tot lot in a senior community? It's a nightmare. And with free food? It'll be like Armageddon."

"Are you sure the events are taking place at the same time?"

"Two o'clock. When your mother finds out she'll be beside herself."

Beside herself and lamenting in my ear. "I don't suppose we can keep it from her and act as surprised as anything when we arrive for the memorial service, do you?"

"Maybe. If you can keep the recreation center news away from her until Sunday. If she hasn't read the online bulletin yet, she might not do so. But it will be in the *Saturday News*, and that gets delivered to all the residents in Sun City West. It's a free paper."

"What time? What time do they make the deliveries?"

"They start tossing those papers from the cars at five thirty and usually finish up in an hour. There are at least eight drivers riding around. But she'll see you if you park by her house. Or anywhere on her street."

Wonderful. It's either chase down her driver and offer a tip for not delivering a paper or offer to take Streetman to the dog park and then chase down the driver before he gets to her house.

"Maybe we can post a sign by the tot lot that says 'Tick infestation. Play at own risk.'"

"I've got some mortarboard in my garage and lots of markers. Lucinda and I can do it."

Yikes. I wasn't serious. "Um, well . . ."

"Back to the original plan, I suppose. I'll call the ladies to tell them not to tell Harriet. Good thinking, Phee. I'm relieved I called you."

And while Shirley might have been relieved, I was all but twitching. The first thing I needed to do was get back on the phone with my mother to tell her I decided to take her dog to the park at the crack of dawn because I had totally lost my mind.

"I was going to suggest Cindy Dolton in the first place," she said when I called. "She might know who those gamblers are." I was about to say something when her next sentence was directed at the dog. "Lucky little man! Your sister's going to take you to the park tomorrow morning." Then, to me, "What time?"

"Early. Real early. Five thirty."

"Five thirty in the winter? I didn't think Cindy got there until later. Of course the new lighting does make a difference. Okay, Streetman will be ready. By the way, George called a few minutes ago. I still can't believe what he told me."

"I'm sorry, Mom. I know that radio show meant a lot to you and Myrna, but after that disaster when Paul showed up, I can understand why the station decided to cancel it."

"Cancel it? They're not canceling it. George called to tell me the station got more phone calls and emails about that show than they had in the station's entire history. Can you imagine? People thought it was a hoot. Now they want us to do some combined shows with Paul starting this summer. I honestly don't know what that's going to be like, because all that man wants to talk about is fish, but meanwhile our murder mystery show is still set for its regular slot this Tuesday morning."

"Oh good. Glad to hear that."

"And you'll also be glad to hear all the arrangements are set for the memorial service on Sunday. It will be a dignified and lovely affair. I know Nate and Marshall plan to do some snooping around, but tell them not to muck it up."

Nate and Marshall are not the ones you need to worry about. "Uh-huh."

"The book club ladies will have their ears to the ground, and Cecilia said she'll discreetly use the short-hand she learned in high school to take notes if she hears anything that points to the killer."

"Terrific. As long as she leaves the holy water where it belongs—in her church."

The remainder of the day flew by with no one getting any closer to solving anything. Not the product thefts and certainly not the murders.

"Maybe we'll get lucky on Sunday," Nate said "And pick up the one piece of information that will lead us to the killers. I've been so busy I haven't even looked at my calendar. Are you and Augusta coming in tomorrow?"

"I am," Augusta said. "Until noon. Phee's off."

"I can come in if you need me," I quickly added.

"Nah. Trust me, you'll be working Sunday, even if it's not on our payroll."

I didn't know it at the time, but truer words were never spoken.

CHAPTER 31

The hazy glow from the two overhead lights in the dog park's canopy gave the place an eerie, unsettling feeling as Streetman and I entered the gate. Other than a tall, thin man with a cane and a Boston terrier, we were the only ones in the park. I intended to make it a short visit, having accomplished my goal of removing the Saturday paper from my mother's driveway prior to knocking on her door. Aurora Teagarden would have been proud.

"You can take him off the leash," the man said. "I already scoped out the place. No sign of coyotes. And it's winter, so you don't have to worry about those damn Sonoran desert toads."

"Thanks." I unleashed the dog and grabbed a plastic poop bag from the dispenser. "I guess not too many people show up at this hour, huh?"

"Give it another minute or two and they'll start arriving. The five thirty bunch is a spunky crowd. Mostly boomers who plan to hit the fitness center by six or retirees who have part-time jobs at those fast-food places."

I smiled. "Which one are you?"

He winked. "I'm the cranky seventy-plus guy who plans to get on the casino bus by seven. Have a good day!"

With that, he and the little terrier left the park. Streetman moseyed around and finally did his business near the fence. I was about to get him back on the leash when two women in heavy parkas and scarves wrapped around their necks came in with small white dogs. Granted, I needed to wear a sweatshirt, but Siberia it wasn't.

Streetman ambled over to the little dogs, sniffed them, and turned away. I let out the breath I had been holding.

Just then, one of the women shouted, "Hurry up, Queenie. We can't stay long this morning."

I was only a few yards from her and her friend, and in the quiet morning air, their voices carried.

"What time does it start?"

"Seven, but you know they'll be lined up already." Then, to the dog, "Come on, Queenie. Quit sniffing. Do something."

The other woman chimed in, "You, too, Freddie."

I moved a few steps in their direction, trying to be inconspicuous. "Good boy, Streetman." Fortunately, neither of the women seemed to be acquainted with my mother's dog and continued their banter as if he wasn't there.

"Talk about last minute. At least it's off Tom Ryan and not across town. I heard they'll be unloading the van with the merchandise before six and then open up for sale at seven."

The words "van" and "merchandise" shot through me.

No one said "merchandise" when referring to ordinary garage-sale items. And Tom Ryan. That was a major street in the north end of Sun City West. I pretended to look at my phone while they continued speaking.

"What did you say they've got this time?"

"Nellie said Crock-Pots, comforters, and kitchenware. Said to buy our holiday gifts now because this may be the last sale in the area for a long time."

"That figures. Just when a good garage sale comes along. And new items in their original boxes."

Garage sale. New items. Original boxes. That cinched it. It *had* to be the latest inventory from Home Products Plus. And who the heck was Nellie? Probably one of their gossipy friends. I was about to figure out a way to break into the conversation when all of a sudden the women grabbed their dogs and headed for the gate. Streetman was under a tree using one of his paws to scratch at the bark.

"Come on, boy," I shouted. "We've got to go!"

He looked at me and continued scratching. By now the women had reached the only Lexus SUV in the parking lot and were getting in. I bent down, scooped up the dog, fastened the leash to his collar, and made a mad dash to my car. Seconds later, with Streetman settling into the passenger seat, I followed the Lexus out of the parking lot and down Meeker Boulevard, turning left on 135th Street and again on Deer Valley. I fumbled for my cell phone at a red light and dialed my mother.

Talking without a hands-free device in a car is against Arizona law, so I'd better not get caught. "I'm taking Streetman to a garage sale. It's very last minute. Talk to you later."

"The mega sale? You found it! Don't tell me this is one

of those SWAT situations with the sheriff's office. Where is it?"

"I'm not sure. Off Tom Ryan. Two ladies talked about it at the park and headed over. I'm following them. Oops. The light changed. Talk to you later."

The Lexus made so many side-street turns once it got on Tom Ryan that I lost count. The women were right about one thing, though: Parked cars lined the street on both sides, many of them with their headlights still on.

"I should have asked for your ThunderShirt." I maneuvered the car into a parking space meant for a golf cart. "Guess you'll have to manage without it."

Not daring to let him out of my arms, I carried him across the street and followed what looked like a processional leading to the only house whose lights were on in the front. With one hand clutching the dog and the other holding my phone, I called Marshall.

His voice was soft and groggy. "What time is it? It's still dark out. Everything okay with the dog?"

"The dog's fine. I'm fine. Long story short, I think I found the next illegal garage sale for Home Products Plus. Call Nate and send him to this address. Call the sheriff's deputies, too."

"Hold on. I'm getting a pencil."

Thirty seconds later I'd given Marshall the address. "Use your GPS. I'm not even sure how I got here."

"Be careful."

"So far it's just a garage sale, not Walmart on Black Friday. I'll snoop around and see what I can find. Holy moly! I hope we nail it."

"Take a breath, hon. I'm heading over. No sense waking up Nate. Besides, the only thing he and the sheriff's deputies can do is ask questions. They don't have search warrants, so unless something out of the ordinary happens, it's an investigation as usual. I'll fill him in once I get there."

"Good. We can match up products to the most recent inventory lists, but that will take time. And a computer. And my notes at the office. Geez, I need to be in two places at once."

"Slow down. Best thing you can do right now is mill around. Act nonchalant."

"Easy for you to say. I've got Streetman tucked under my arm without his ThunderShirt."

"Yeesh."

Whoever this Nellie was, she was right on the money about the van drivers unloading merchandise into a garage. What she neglected to mention was that it was a huge cargo van, and from what I could see, there were boxes everywhere in every size and dimension. Unlike most of the garages that belonged to my mother's friends and to Herb Garrett, this one wasn't piled high and deep with its own collection of must-store-and-save items.

I couldn't get a good look at the drivers because it was still dark, but, given their physiques and fast-paced movements, my guess was that they didn't hail from Sun City West. They had backed the van into the driveway and were hustling with all sorts of boxes as the crowd approached. Inside the garage a stocky woman in jeans and a heavy sweater pointed to different tables, where the drivers were to stack the boxes.

A smaller table was set up near the garage door. In lieu of a tablecloth, it had a sign in front that read, "All Sales Final. Cash, check, or credit cards."

At one time I would have thought only legitimate businesses could take credit cards, but now everyone was able to do so with their iPhone, thanks to Square, Intuit, and a myriad of other similar credit companies. Entrepreneurship certainly had taken on a whole new meaning.

I was elbow-to-elbow with more women than I'd seen from the footage of the Women's March on Washington. Only these women were after bargains, not human rights. I extricated the phone from my bag, having plunked it in there as soon as my call to Marshall ended. I checked the time. A quarter past six. Even if Marshall moved at breakneck speed, it would still take him at least thirty more minutes to arrive. I crossed my fingers the MCSO deputies who were housed in Surprise would be quicker.

Then I remembered something my mother told me: The posse began its day at five thirty. Maybe the deputies had given them a shout-out and they'd be here sooner. Streetman started to wiggle and squirm in my arms, so I put him down for a moment. He watered the gravel rocks on the next-door neighbor's yard and then began to root around, spraying the rocks all over the place. I immediately snatched the dog back into my arms and kicked the rocks off the sidewalk and back into the yard.

"Last thing I need is for you to mess up someone's lawn. You're already on notice at the dog park again," I whispered.

Like everyone else on the block, I found myself watching the endless treks back and forth that the drivers made as they unloaded the goods. Behind me, a few women chatted about lightweight comforters. I rolled my eyes and held my breath. I was literally watching a crime scene with absolutely no way to do anything about it. Even Marshall had said as much.

The most the deputies could do would be to question the homeowner, but sometimes that was all it took.

Suddenly I heard someone shout, "Nellie! I didn't expect you here!"

A petite woman exited from the garage and zipped up her windbreaker. "I'm only here to make sure everything gets set up all right. I hate these last-minute changes. We were supposed to be at Mountain Vista, but that fell through."

Just then, one of the drivers approached the woman and motioned that he needed to speak with her privately.

"Excuse me," she said. "Enjoy the sale."

The two of them walked to the van while I edged closer to the garage. The nameless delivery guy and Nellie were now inside the vehicle. Nellie. Suddenly that name was familiar, and I struggled to remember where I had heard it. Then it hit me. That jogger who'd thought my mother's brunch was an estate sale in progress had mentioned Betty and Nellie's Bargains. Was this the same woman? And if so, she was Betty Hazelton's cousin. I all but did backflips. This couldn't be a coincidence. The jogger had said something about Betty taking on a different job. I guessed reselling stolen merchandise would qualify.

By now the crowd was growing and the street was jam-packed. Even if Marshall made record time, it would be slow going on foot. At least the posse and the sheriff's deputies could double-park with their flashers on. I looked around, but that wasn't happening either.

Without warning, the van drove off. Had Nellie gotten out? I wasn't paying attention. In fact, I wasn't thinking. I needed to get the license plate number. With the dog under one arm and my handbag in the other, I pulled a maneuver that I quickly regretted: reaching into my bag with one hand to dig for a pen and a scrap of paper. Why

I didn't think to snap a photo with my phone was beyond me. Too many old habits. The only thing I did manage to do—and I didn't realize it at the time—was click on my phone and push the record button. Something I hadn't been able to master when not holding a crazed dog in my arms.

In a flash, the dog's nose went up in the air and he squirmed. Not one of those I'm-uncomfortable-so-I'll-move-around squirms, but more like an I'm-getting-the-hell-out-of-here ones.

Before I could tighten my grip, Streetman sniffed again and charged toward someone. I did a double take. It was Nellie, and her arms were loaded with all sorts of blanket throws. The dog let out a bark that made the hairs on the back of my neck stand at attention.

"Streetman! Stop that!" I yelled, but it was too late. It was surprising how high a six- or seven-pound, overfed Chiweenie could jump. With one fast move, the dog latched on to one of the blanket throws and yanked it out of Nellie's arms, causing her to lose her balance. The remaining blankets and throws fell to the ground, much to the dog's delight. Without wasting a second, he pounced on the pile and dug his paws into anything and everything that had landed within a three-foot radius.

"He's destroying this shipment of blankets," Nellie shouted, "Home Pro—I mean, *we* won't be able to get another batch like this for who knows how long."

She said it. I heard her. "Home Pro." She never finished the full word, but it was enough for me. I reached down and snatched the dog, who had by now torn off a small piece of a fleece blanket and refused to let it out of his mouth. Wasn't that something my mother had told me? About the dog being territorial over his fleece blanket? It didn't matter. I yelled at the top of my lungs, "These are stolen goods. The sheriff's deputies are on their way!"

I expected the crowd to dissipate, but my words had the opposite effect. A sea of humanity poured into the garage and everyone spoke at once.

"I want five of these Crock-Pots. Are there any more?"

"Do you have the Keurig single shot in teal?"

"Can I put the self-closing, stainless-steel garbage can on hold? I need to call my husband."

"Stolen goods!" I all but shrieked. "These are stolen goods."

"Get a grip, lady," a male voice shouted back. "We've heard that ploy before."

It was useless. I would have had better luck separating Streetman from one of his chewy toys than these bargain hunters from their treasures. I did the only sensible thing. I stepped aside and watched the melee unfold. Surprisingly, the stocky woman with the heavy sweater and jeans appeared to be unfazed. She handled the transactions as if she was stamping Metro tickets.

I looked around for Nellie but couldn't spot her. My accusation must have spooked her, or she would have insisted I pay for the products Streetman destroyed. I figured she was probably in the house calling her travel agent for a flight out of the country.

At that moment red and blue lights illuminated the street. The cavalry had come at last. I raced to the curb, expecting the MCSO deputies, but instead it was a citizen's posse patrol car. Still, the light show was all the effect needed to ensure a stampede. Only, in this case, the crowd didn't leave the premises, they rushed into it.

CHAPTER 32

Streetman was in his glory. He shook the swatch of fleece material frantically while I tried to hold him still. Around me, the growing crowd of bargain hunters moved in on the boxes like ants at a picnic. So much for my bellowing. Even the woman with the heavy sweater and jeans paid no attention and processed the transactions like clockwork.

I tried a different tack. I wrestled my way to the makeshift cash register line and shouted, "Has anyone seen Nellie?"

In that instant one of the women I recognized from the dog park earlier thrust a throw pillow at me. "Hold this for a minute, please. I've got to get my hands on one of those soda dispensers."

The pillow had barely grazed my chest when Streetman decided to bump it with his head. Of course he was still holding that ridiculous piece of fleece material, making it impossible for me to hang on to everything.

Just as the pillow tumbled to the ground, a gray-haired posse volunteer announced, "I'm looking for a Sophie Kimball. Anyone by that name around here?"

Two thoughts crossed my mind, and not in any particular order. Number one, Marshall had informed the posse of the situation and they needed to speak with me. And number two, my mother couldn't get through on my cell phone and called the posse to contact me because, God forbid, she should miss a good bargain at the sale.

"I'm Sophie Kimball," I shouted back.

He motioned for me to leave the garage and follow him to the street. The once-pristine throw pillow was now covered in dog hair. I plopped it on the nearest table and made my way to the front of the house, where the posse volunteer was now standing.

Again he motioned to me, but this time to his car. The flashers were still on and it was double-parked. If he thought the lights were a deterrent, he was sadly wrong. If anything, they served as a neon display sign, beckoning all would-be bargain hunters to a sale in progress.

"Miss Kimball?" he asked.

We both stood against the passenger side door and watched the sea of humanity in front of us.

"Yes." My voice was surprisingly loud.

"We got a call from dispatch. Someone phoned in and mentioned your name. The MCSO deputies should be here any minute. Something about a robbery in progress? All I see is a sale."

"The robbery already took place." *And the someone is a detective.* "These are the stolen goods. From Home Products Plus stores in Phoenix and Glendale."

"I hope you have evidence. Doesn't look as if that crowd's about to part with anything."

I turned away from his car and I could have sworn the crowd had quadrupled in the last five minutes. Meanwhile, Streetman clutched his new chewy fleece and growled at the posse volunteer.

"Does he bite?" the man asked.

I shrugged. "I think he snaps, but according to my mother, whose dog it is, he's never actually made contact with anyone's flesh." *But no sense putting it to the test.*

The man stepped back. "Good to know."

"Listen, it's a long story, but I work for Williams Investigations in Glendale and we've been tracking a major inventory loss at those stores. The products at this sale match up to the ones that were siphoned from their stock."

Before he could press me further another official vehicle pulled up, this time one that was clearly marked MCSO and not Citizens Posse. It was still dark outside, but the combination of streetlights, houselights, and flashing car lights showered Deputy Ranston's car with enough illumination to ensure no one could mistake it, or him for that matter. He strode toward us like one of those cowboys from an old Western, only the cowboys didn't pause occasionally to catch their breath.

"Miss Kimball," the deputy announced, "this had better be worth losing a good hour and a half of sleep." Then he noticed Streetman. "Keep that little tyrant at bay. I heard he bites."

Bites. Snaps. Growls. The dog's a national treasure.

The three of us moved from the side of the posse car to the side of Deputy Ranston's car.

I made sure my grip on the dog was steadfast. "If I've

got this right, someone named Nellie is running this illegal operation. She's a cousin of Betty Hazelton, a Sun City West resident, and together the two of them ran Betty and Nellie's Bargains. Estate sales."

I went on to explain about the thefts and how the inventory at these floating sales matched the missing Home Products Plus items. "It's all documented on the spreadsheets, but that will take time, and judging from the voracity of the crowd, everything's going to be cleared out before it's even daylight. My God! These people are like the seventeen-year locusts!"

"I'm afraid we're going to need more evidence than that," Ranston said. "Best we can do is question the sellers. Where did you say this Nellie woman is?"

"She *was* here, but I don't know where she went."

"What about the van you saw? Did you get a license?"

"Um, no. Not exactly. But it was white. A white cargo van."

Ranston groaned and ran his hand through his thinning hair. "Splendid. A white cargo van." Then he groaned again. Louder this time. "Don't leave the premises. I'll have a word with that lady over there who's collecting all the money." Then he turned to the posse volunteer. "See if you can find anyone else working the sale."

The man nodded and disappeared into the crowd. I figured it would be a good time for me to take out my phone and see where Marshall was. I leaned against the deputy's car and pulled my iPhone from my bag. By now I had gotten better with that maneuver.

I started to push Speed Dial when I noticed something. The Voice Memos app, something I'd never used and never bothered to delete, displayed a message. Curious, I played it. "He's destroying this shipment of blankets. Home Pro—I mean *we* won't be able to get another batch like this for who knows how long."

Oh my God! It was Nellie. On my phone, with a full-fledged confession. Okay, so maybe it wasn't exactly a *full-fledged* confession, but it was a slip of the lip that certainly implicated her. I raced over to Deputy Ranston, who was in the middle of a conversation with the petite cashier, and interrupted him.

"I've got evidence these are stolen goods! I didn't know it until I took out my phone, but Nellie pretty much said the goods came from Home Products Plus. Here! Listen for yourself."

I tapped the app, tapped again for the message, and handed the phone to Ranston.

His expression never changed during all three times he replayed it. "Doubt it will stand up in court, but coupled with the documentation you say you have on the inventory depletion, it may be enough for a search warrant. I need to make a few calls."

"But these people are all leaving with the evidence. Shouldn't you do something?"

"I *am* doing something, if you'd let me."

Ranston bolted for his car, leaving Streetman and me face-to-face with the cashier. I had to act quickly because I knew that even if Deputy Ranston was able to secure a search warrant in record time, there would be nothing left to find.

Suddenly I had become a madwoman. Worse than Jean Shepard's Ralphie when he pummeled the red-haired bully in the snow. Maybe it was because I had worked so hard to untangle the accounting mess and I wasn't about to see my results slip away. But truth be known, it was more than that. I was tired. I was frustrated. And, most of all, I hadn't had my morning cup of coffee.

I leaned over the small table. "He's the best behaved of all my dogs. That's why the others are still in my car. Unless you stop this sale immediately, I'm going to let them out. I can't guarantee the shape your garage will be in afterward. Do you know how expensive it is to replace Sheetrock?"

The woman gasped. "You're crazy and I'm calling nine-one-one."

"Go ahead. In case you didn't notice, those two county cars out front aren't here to manage the street traffic. You're dealing in stolen goods. When they return, it will be with a search warrant and you'll need to find a good lawyer."

"Lawyer? Stolen goods? Was that you making all that commotion? I figured you wanted the other buyers out of the way so you could snatch up more merchandise. What makes you so sure these things are hot?"

I gave her the abbreviated version while Streetman amused himself with the ragged end of the fleece. *At least he isn't dressed like a Christmas tree for the outing.*

When I finished talking she stood up and held her hands in the air. "Listen up, everyone! We've got a slight issue with regulations. The sale is now closed and will be rescheduled. I must ask you to leave. So sorry for your inconvenience."

"Damn homeowners' associations!" A man's voice. "Have to stick their bloody noses into everything. Can't even fart in your own backyard without getting permission from your HOA."

Then another voice. "I'd like to tell the HOA where to go!"

I wasn't so sure this particular street was part of a homeowners' association; that varied throughout Sun City West. Still, if that was what the crowd thought, so be it. I stepped aside and watched as small cadres of grumbling shoppers exited the garage. When I looked at the street, Deputy Ranston's car was gone. I figured he was off to secure that search warrant. Only the posse car remained, but the volunteer was nowhere in sight.

"I had no idea these were stolen goods," the petite woman said. "All I did was provide a location for the sale. You can ask anyone."

"How about Nellie? She's the organizer, right?"

"She and a cousin of hers. I heard from someone in the pickleball club that Nellie was looking for a one-day venue, so I offered up my house. Up until this morning I hadn't even met her face-to-face. I did hear she used to be quite the pickleball player until she fell and fractured her elbow. From what I understand these sales are run strictly through the internet as far as the setup goes, but this one turned out to be last minute."

"Did she pay you with cash or a check?"

"No. In fact, I still had to go through some wacky internet site and provide my bank routing number. The payment was deposited to my account the same day."

"You wouldn't happen to know who the cousin is?" *Like I'm not already 100 percent sure.*

The woman shook her head, but before she could answer, I heard another voice.

"Looks like I missed all the fun." It was Marshall, and he gave me a wave as he and the posse volunteer walked toward us.

Without wasting a second, Marshall introduced himself to the woman and told her he had received a text from one of the deputies that a team of MCSO officers would be arriving any minute with a search warrant. At that moment she broke into tears, which morphed into uncontrollable sobs.

I fumbled for a tissue from my purse, which was no easy feat given Streetman's squirming. Then, without warning, sirens sounded from everywhere. I turned to face the street, but the only thing I saw were the blinding flashers from the Sun City West's Posse Patrol. There were more official vehicles lined up in front of me than the ones you saw at military parades. Next thing I knew, the stocky woman let out a wail that could be heard in Montana. Naturally I froze.

CHAPTER 33

What followed was an endless blur of sheriff's deputies traipsing all over the place, Ranston muttering and groaning, and Bowman arriving on scene in case Ranston didn't mutter enough expletives. Both of them used the words "Search Warrant" so often I was beginning to think it was someone's name.

The deputies must have instilled the fear of God into the woman whose house we were in, because with the exception of wringing her hands, she sat motionless at the small table in the garage.

Marshall pulled me aside and glanced back at the woman. "She'll be all right. Once it's determined she was duped she'll get off the hook. Nate owes you. Big-time. Think you can drop off the dog, copy the info from your spreadsheets onto a flash drive, and get back here as soon as you're done?"

"Anything to return Streetman to my mother. By the way, what have you heard from Nate?"

"He's been bouncing back and forth between the deputies and Rolo Barnes. They've got the banks identified. That was the easy part. But get this: they can't nail down the payer. Not yet anyway. Too many layers of bogus companies."

"It's Betty Hazelton. Betty and Nellie's Bargains. It *has* to be."

Marshall arched his back and stretched. "It might as well be Mary Poppins as far as the sheriff's office is concerned."

"Can't they just haul in Betty Hazelton?"

"Not without a valid reason she was behind the operation. And by reason, I mean proof."

"Aargh. So we're back to where we started?"

"Not exactly. I should have mentioned this first. Bowman told me they were able to locate the white cargo van. A vehicle fitting that description blew a tire a few miles from Sun City West and caused a major traffic jam. Get this: The van had enough empty Keurig boxes in it to raise suspicions. The drivers were taken in for questioning."

"Oh my gosh. That could be the break we need. See you in a bit."

"Use Bell Road, not Grand. No sense in you getting caught up in that traffic mess."

I darted out of the garage and hightailed it to my car, stopping once to let Streetman water some more gravel in front of one of the houses. Five minutes later I delivered him to my mother.

"My precious little man," she cooed as I handed him off to her in front of her house. "You must be starving."

I could chew off my arm, too, you know. I'm famished.

Then she turned to me, "You were gone forever. Tell me, what happened? Who was at the sale? Anyone I know? No, first tell me what they were selling."

"It doesn't matter. It was all stolen goods. A zillion deputies are at that house right now, and I'm on my way to the office to get some vital information they need. Accounting information, if you want to know."

"Call me later and tell me what you find out."

I nodded and started to leave when I thought of something. "Um, this may be a long shot, but do you happen to know anyone by the name of Nellie, as in Betty and Nellie's Bargains?"

"Betty and Nellie's Bargains. That was eons ago. They were running estate sales when your father and I first moved here twenty years ago. Quite the energetic crew from what I heard. Of course when you're in your forties, your energy is boundless."

Hmm. Seems I didn't get that memo. "What else can you tell me?"

"Not much. I never got to go to those sales. You know how your father was about buying other people's stuff. Said we had enough of our own junk to last us well into the next century."

I laughed. "Yeah, sounds like Dad. Listen, I think those two women might be the ones running this illegal operation. Any chance you can do a little prying?"

"I'll call Shirley. If she doesn't know, I'll try Myrna. Worst-case scenario, I'll give Herb a call. Why? Is this Nellie woman the kingpin in the garage sale scheme?"

"I think so, along with Betty Hazelton, but we don't have any evidence."

"Relax. We have the book club ladies. One of them is bound to know something."

"You're the best. Talk to you later."

With the exception of a quick detour at the nearest Starbucks drive-through, I headed directly for the office and those spreadsheets.

Augusta looked up from her computer screen and winced. "I thought you were off today."

"Off and on. Long story. We busted that illegal garage sale with the stolen goods."

"Who do you mean by 'we'? I know Mr. Williams has been on the phone with Rolo Barnes and a few of the Maricopa County sheriff's deputies, but that's all I know. He raced out of here as if his trousers were on fire."

"Okay. Listen. I'll talk fast, but you have to follow me into my office while I explain. I've got to make a copy of those accounting spreadsheets onto a flash drive and deliver it ASAP to Marshall, who's still at the scene of that sale."

Augusta threw back her chair and was at my heels in record time. If I could get an award for multitasking, that would've been the moment. I booted up my computer and downloaded the information onto a thumb drive, all the while providing Augusta with the salient details of my morning's experience, beginning with the removal of the daily newspaper from my mother's driveway.

"I don't know what's more hilarious: you threatening to unleash drywall-eating dogs in some woman's garage or Streetman toppling over those blankets."

"It was a tie. Look, I've got to get back to Sun City West with this info. I'll give you a call later. Are you leaving at noon?"

"Not sure. Mr. Williams said to hold tight in case something else cropped up."

"Good deal."

The something else really didn't require Augusta's attention, but it made for one hell of a moment. No sooner had I gotten back to the residence in question when Marshall took the flash drive from me and handed it to Deputy Ranston. The deputy was still sputtering and muttering as he walked off with the drive.

Meanwhile, Marshall gave my wrist a squeeze. "You will never, in a zillion years, guess who that cargo van is registered to."

I shrugged. "Anyone I know? And I think I can safely rule out my mother's friends."

"Malcolm Porter."

"What? Malcolm Porter, as in Malcolm's Variety? He was behind this?"

"That's what we're about to find out. Nate's on his way over to the variety store as we speak. We may not have solved those murders, but who says we can't track down pilfering and theft?"

"Now what?"

"Now the sheriff's office examines your spreadsheets and, if Mr. Porter confesses, make an arrest."

"Holy cow! And all because I took Streetman to the park. Hey, if you don't need me, I'm going to head home and catch up on some work around the house. But not before I stop somewhere and get a bite to eat. I'm way past ravenous. Want me to get you anything?"

"Believe it or not, two of the posse volunteers are bringing us breakfast sandwiches and coffee from Putters Paradise."

"Lucky you."

I was so wired up from the recent revelation that I had to spill the beans to someone, and who better than my friend Lyndy? She agreed to meet me in a half hour at the Wildflower Bread Company in Peoria.

With a vegetable frittata in front of me and a large Sumatra coffee within arm's reach, I told her everything that had happened, beginning with Malcolm's cargo van and my suspicions about Sylvia.

"Maybe you should have ordered an herbal tea instead of that coffee. You're jumping all over the place."

"I am, aren't I? It's just that I never expected the circumstances to work in my favor. I mean, about uncovering that garage sale location as a result of something I overheard at the dog park this morning. And as far as Sylvia is concerned—"

Just then my phone rang, and I recognized Nate's number. "It's my boss. I've got to take the call."

Lyndy took a bite of her brie and leek omelet as I listened to Nate.

"Are you sure?" I asked him. "Absolutely sure?"

What? Lyndy mouthed and I grimaced.

The call seemed endless. Finally Nate stopped talking.

"Okay, at least it's a start," I said to him. "Thanks for letting me know."

Lyndy was all but done with her omelet. "What? What's a start?"

"More like a roadblock, but I was being diplomatic. Turns out Malcolm Porter had nothing to do with the Home Products Plus thefts. Nate's at Malcolm's Variety Store right now. Seems Malcolm loaned the van to his wife's nephew so the kid could transport his band's instruments to some gig they had."

"Guess that's a new meaning for 'gig,' huh?"

"It wasn't the first time Malcolm loaned his van to that kid. Something about placating the wife. Nate said Malcolm showed him the calendar dates of when the van was borrowed, and they matched up to the timeframe for the thefts. Nate had a record of the dates."

"That should cinch it, then. The nephew will have to confess about his role, as well as identify who's in charge."

"Oh, he confessed his role all right, once those deputies put the pressure on him, but he has no idea who is behind the operation. Said he got paid directly into his bank account via a money transfer."

"What about this Nellie you mentioned? Didn't you say you saw her talking to one of the drivers?"

"According to Nate the deputies asked the nephew about that. He said he and the other driver thought the woman was one of the sale workers. Had no idea who she was. And the conversation they had was her telling him to stop by the house later in the day to pick up any leftover products."

Lyndy put her elbows on the table, cupped her hands, and put down her head. Her gaze never left me. "And then what?"

"Here's where it gets good. Nellie gave him an address for the unsold products. Nate didn't say as much, but I'm figuring those deputies are going to get that kid to deliver the boxes to that address and then arrest the head honcho."

"Sounds like a good plan. Think they can pull it off?"

I crinkled my nose. "It's Bowman and Ranston we're talking about. Plus, I'm not sure they'll actually *do* that. I only figured it would be the logical thing to do. I'll let you know."

"You'll know where to find me tomorrow. At that memorial service with my hard-of-hearing aunt who refuses to get a hearing aid. She'll be nudging me the entire time, asking which dead person they're talking about. Should be exasperating as all get-up-and-go."

I laughed. "The Howard Buell and Bucky Zebbler memorial service. Why do I have the feeling it has disaster written all over it?"

"Past experience?"

"Foresight."

CHAPTER 34

Normally I was happy when it turned out I was right about something, but in this case I wasn't so sure. Although I had to admit, I doubled over with gales of laughter when Marshall told me about it later that day. He was exhausted from the garage sale debacle, but not too tired to join me in laughing as well.

Bowman and Ranston did send the cargo van to the address like I figured they would, but instead of having Malcolm's nephew do the driving, Ranston did. And when he arrived at the address there was no one in sight. Apparently, the nephew had forgotten to tell Ranston the place would be vacant. The nephew had been told to use the keypad on the side of the garage door for entry. Once in, he was to unload the merchandise and leave it there.

When Ranston showed up with the cargo van and pulled into the driveway, the neighbor thought a heist was about to take place and called the posse. Three citizen patrol cars blocked the van and, because Ranston was dressed in plain clothes, refused to believe he was a deputy sheriff, even when he showed them his ID.

As if that wasn't bad enough, the neighbor who made the call to the posse turned out to be none other than the guy who accosted me at the mailbox. And the house in question? Vernadeen Stibbens's place. The woman left more keys floating around than peanut shells after the circus left town, not to mention giving away her garage like penny candy.

"Yeesh," I said to Marshall. "Ranston must have pitched a fit."

Marshall's grin got wider. "Wish I could have seen it firsthand. Bad news is Vernadeen's house was a decoy. Still no idea who's running that show. Maybe Rolo will have some better luck tracking down the final destination for those bank routing numbers."

"And that Nellie woman from the garage sale? What about tracking her down?"

"Believe me, the sheriff's office is trying. Which brings me to tomorrow's 'plan.'"

He used air quotes when he said plan and I bit my lip. "The snooping around at the memorial?" I asked.

"Uh-huh. *That* plan. Nate and I figured why not kill two birds with one stone. Or, in this case, get one of those henhouse chickens to spill the beans about the murders and the thefts. Those crowds are virtually petri dishes of untapped information. All we need to do is open the lid."

"Whoa. Where'd all those clichés come from?"

"Augusta. You can blame Augusta. Ever listen to one of her stories? Garrison Keillor could take notes."

"He won't be there tomorrow."

"No, but most of Sun City West will be. Free food. Remember? If that doesn't draw in the crowds, nothing will."

"It had better draw in Sylvia and Betty. Good grief. I'm beginning to think of them as if they are Disney villainesses. Betty, not as bad, but still . . . Oh my gosh!"

"What?"

"Remember when I originally thought Howard might have been having a dalliance with her? And then he drove to her house, but skirted around back to that card game?"

"Yeah. So?"

"So maybe something *was* going on with Betty. Maybe he needed a spot to check out her house, and what better place than Vernadeen's? After all, no one would suspect anything. And remember? He left early after arguing with Cornelia. She lost her job over the lack of advertising, and that was because of his insistence on live programming. But that's not what's plaguing me. I've got a hunch and I need Rolo's help. He's up at all hours. Please grab the phone and call him."

"Okay. Okay. Slow down and tell me what you're thinking."

"Betty and her cousin were estate sale mavens. I think they continued their business. Only instead of acquiring inventory from customers, they found a way to steal it from Home Products Plus. If you don't have to pay for inventory, you stand to make a whole lot of money. I'll wager Howard found out about it and either wanted to be cut in on the deal or was blackmailing them, and that's what got him killed. I think I can prove it. The deal part. Not the murder. Not yet."

"What do you need from Rolo?"

"Access into Howard's bank accounts. Not so much

the money, but the timing. From what we understand, Howard had gambling debts. But he also needed a source of income that was more than his social security and retirement money. If deposits into his bank accounts match up to the time of those thefts and sales, I'm pretty certain that's what got him killed."

"Hang on. Got Rolo on speed dial. Pray he hasn't started a new diet or this will cost us."

As it turned out, Rolo was more than happy to look into Howard's transactions, and even happier to expound upon the benefits of his newest diet: kelp cleansing.

"I should have something for you late tonight," he said. "If not, first thing in the morning. I'm meeting some friends for a potluck dinner. I'll be in touch."

"Did you hear that?" Marshall asked. "He's meeting friends for a potluck dinner."

I shuddered. "Ugh. I picture the stuff looking worse than what they make you eat on *Survivor* or *The Amazing Race.*"

"At least you'll get your answer. Hold tight."

At a little past eleven I got an answer, but not from Rolo. It was my mother. "You can thank me later."

"For what? Waking me up?"

"I thought you said this couldn't wait. Betty and Nellie's Bargains. I called Shirley. She didn't know anything, but thought Louise might. Anyway, it was Louise who cut to the chase and called Herb. Not that he knew anything either. Said he only went to garage sales that had tools."

"Um, you're calling to tell me you didn't find out anything?"

"No, I did. That's the point. Herb went on about his pinochle crew and told Louise that Kenny spent half the time playing cards and the other half complaining about his wife at all of these garage sales. Then you'll never guess what happened."

"It's late. Just tell me."

"Louise got Kenny's phone number from Herb and called the wife. Turns out she knew all about Betty Hazelton and Cornelia Lynch."

For a second I thought I hadn't heard her correctly. "Did you say Cornelia Lynch?"

"Yes. That's her full name, but Betty and Cornelia's Bargains didn't sound as good as Betty and Nellie's Bargains, so she took that moniker. Phee, are you still on the line? Say something."

"I think I know why Howard was murdered. And Bucky too. Thanks, Mom. See you tomorrow."

"Don't you get off this phone so fast without telling me what's going on. Do I have to worry about a homicidal maniac showing up at tomorrow's memorial service?"

"Uh, no. No. You shouldn't worry about *that.*"

"Ah-ha! I don't like the way you said *that.* It implies there is something I have to worry about. What is it?"

"Nothing. Really. Get some sleep. We're simply closer to solving those murders, that's all."

"You can thank Louise when you see her tomorrow."

Marshall rolled over and gave my shoulder a shake. "Was I dreaming or did I hear you say we're closer to solving those murders?"

I reached my hand across the nightstand and turned on the light. "That was my mother. Nellie is Cornelia Lynch. And I'll wager anything it wasn't the radio station politics that got Howard and Bucky killed. Let's hope no one at Rolo's dinner party gets food poisoning from that raw fish and seaweed. At this point he's the only one who can give us the answer we need."

"Hon, he may give you the information you need, but it won't be enough without a confession. I seriously doubt Betty or Nellie are going to come forth. Still, it certainly gives Bowman and Ranston all the ammo they need for a serious interrogation. Too bad Cornelia hasn't been seen around her house. Or anywhere, for that matter, other than her brief sojourn in that garage today."

"All that matters is she'll be seen tomorrow, and I have a strong feeling she will."

By now Marshall had propped himself up with an elbow and was leaning his head on his palm. "What makes you so sure?"

"Her little business venture was busted this morning. She'll want to know what the sheriff's office *has* on her. She'll be snooping around the memorial service to pick up her own intel. She has no idea Williams Investigations is going to be there."

"Hmm, your detective skills are putting me to shame."

"Never."

"Keep your fingers crossed Rolo comes through in the morning." He gave my back a rub and I flipped off the light.

In seconds I was out cold.

CHAPTER 35

Putters Paradise planned on serving finger foods and assorted canapes at the memorial service. My mother insisted it be a reflective and dignified affair. The book club ladies had agreed on the desserts they were bringing and arranged for the outdoor tables and chairs to be delivered to the Beardsley Meditation Garden by the Rec Center maintenance crew. The restaurant even agreed to supply the tablecloths and the table service. In theory it should have gone off without a hitch. In theory . . . but that was before we got the news from Rolo.

The phone rang a few minutes past seven in the morning, and I all but knocked the receiver from the cradle. "The deposits to your guy's bank accounts were as regular as the colon on a flaxseed diet. Three bank accounts. And get this: one of them has two parties on it."

"Two parties? Who's the other person?"

"Name's listed as Bertrand Zebbler. Ring any bells?"

"Bucky? Bucky Zebbler?"

"If you say so. Hey, before I forget, tell Marshall I'm emailing him an article about a kelp cleanse that will lengthen your lives. I'd send it to your boss, but there isn't enough kelp to combat all the starch he's got in his system. Listen, I'm not done checking those banks yet. Still could be more Klingons."

Klingons. Rolo's way of saying connections to other financial institutions . . . or worse. "Thanks, Rolo. I really appreciate it."

"I'm in to bento boxes now. Part of my new diet."

"Uh-huh. I'll let Marshall know." *Bento boxes. Can't wait to see the price tag.*

Rolo's wakeup call at seven was a worse jolt to my system than drinking Mountain Dew. I felt as if every nerve was on high alert.

"Let Marshall know what?" came a raspy voice a few inches from my neck.

"I was right about the deposits into Howard's bank accounts. And get this: One of those accounts had Bucky as the other party. Those two must have been in cahoots. No wonder they were knocked off. They had to be blackmailing Betty and Cornelia. Darn it. I can't believe we were so dense as not to realize Nellie was a natural nickname for Cornelia."

"I guess this means Sylvia is off your list as the temptress who beguiled Howard and later sought revenge?"

"She's been moved to second string. Seriously, I'm not removing anyone from my suspect list, but I'm pretty certain those murders were over money, not love. Then again, I'm stymied by the murder weapon. Sylvia was the logical person to be in possession of Ursula's scissors. I hate it when my mind bounces all over the place."

"Get used to it if you plan to pry into murders."

"Right now I plan to pry open that box of Entenmanns donuts someone stashed in the pantry. How many can I put you down for?"

"At least two with my coffee. I'll hit the fitness center for an hour before we take off for the memorial service."

"Have fun. I've got a few things to do around here. The service starts at two, but I figure we should be there by one at the latest in case my mother or the ladies need any help. I hope she doesn't lose it when she realizes it's grandparents' afternoon at the tot lot. So far, everyone's managed to keep that info from her."

"From what I've seen of your mother, she's not too keen on surprises."

You think?

We arrived at the Beardsley Recreation Center Meditation Garden a few minutes before one. A full hour ahead of time. I heard Kenny's voice all the way across the parking lot. Something about wobbly table legs. I squinted and took a better look.

He was speaking with the maintenance guys from the Rec Center and couldn't have been any louder if he had a megaphone. "The chairs are all set up in a widening circle like the diagram shows, but you'd better move that table over to the Contemplation Corner."

"The Contemplation Corner?" Marshall gave me a jab with his elbow.

"Don't ask. Looks like a bench surrounded by oleanders."

Suddenly my eyes were blinded by a balloon-carrying

troop of men, presumably from that service club sponsoring the grandparents' afternoon at the tot lot. Bright red, yellow, and blue balloons were everywhere, and if that wasn't enough, a few of the men carried a large banner that read, "Welcome, Grandparents!" The Entenmann's donuts I ate were no longer settled in my stomach.

Marshall stopped dead in his tracks and watched the procession. "What moron puts a meditation garden a few yards away from a playground?"

"The same one who put up the park schedule for today. See for yourself. The sign is posted by the walkway. Oh my gosh. It says, 'Grandparents Romp and Play on the right, Final Goodbye Memorial on the left.'"

Marshall burst out laughing. "It might as well read, 'Play and Die in the Same Day.'"

"Oh no. That may just happen. Look over to your far left. That's my mother, and she's got her hands on her hips. Not a good sign. Not at all. Let's go the other way and see if Herb's pinochle crew needs any help."

We did a quick turnaround, but not quick enough.

"Phee! Is that you?" My mother's voice could be heard all the way into the aquatics building. "Some nincompoop scheduled a party for grandparents today!"

"Might as well calm her down." Marshall guided me in her direction.

"Um, I don't think that's going to happen any time soon. Look who just walked in. Or should I say, *cascaded* in."

When my aunt Ina agreed to give the eulogies, I'd had a sneaky feeling she'd overdo it as far as her attire was concerned. She epitomized the term "a flair for the dramatic," but even I had to admit she went overboard this afternoon.

"Ina!" my mother shrieked. "You look like Queen Victoria in mourning!"

An understatement as far as I was concerned. Lacy black dress with layers of black veils and some sort of crinoline sash draped across her chest. And while Queen Victoria's hair was modestly parted down the middle and pulled into a bun, my aunt's hair was woven into two long braids she had wrapped on either side of her head à la Princess Leia.

I kicked Marshall in the ankle and whispered, "Don't mention clothing, whatever you do."

"For goodness' sake, Harriet," my aunt said, "this *is* a memorial, not a hootenanny. And why are there so many children running around? And balloons? And what's that over to the right? Looks like a giant barbeque pit. I can see the smoke from here."

Before my mother could answer, Marshall broke in. "Good to see you both. And yeah, it's a barbeque pit for the grandparents' afternoon. Guess the folks in scheduling didn't look too closely at the event venues. I don't think you have to worry, though. We'll stay on our side by the memorial garden, and I'm sure the kiddies and their grandparents won't be venturing too far from the play area."

Talk about wishful thinking . . .

Behind us, I heard Herb's voice as well as Kenny's. I glanced their way and saw that the Putters Paradise catering truck had arrived, along with Herb's cronies from pinochle: Bill, Wayne, and Kevin.

"Isn't that Myrna over there?" Marshall asked. "She's heading in the wrong direction."

"No, she's going in the right direction as far as she's

concerned. I can smell the first batch of hot dogs coming from the barbeque pit. Our tasteful finger foods and assorted teas are going to have some tough competition."

In the fifteen or so minutes we spent perusing the garden, the memorial crowd had grown from the five or six people we originally spotted to a full-blown swell of friends, coworkers, mourners, curiosity seekers, yentas, and food opportunists. Nate must have slipped in at some point because he was face-to-face with Sylvia, and from my vantage point it seemed as if she was fawning all over him. Today she sported a blue-and-white scarf draped over a long, white sweater.

The book club ladies arranged the desserts they'd brought and repositioned the Putters Paradise canapes at least a half dozen times. I took out my iPhone and checked the time. It was 1:37.

"We'd better make the most of this," Marshall said, "and snoop around. Sure, there'll be plenty of time after the program, but why waste the few minutes we have?"

I nodded. "Agreed. I'll mosey over to that group of talkers over there. Wait a minute. I think I recognize some of them from that day when Howard's body was found. It's got to be the pickleball players. I'll do my best to eavesdrop."

"And I'll do mine with those guys who breezed past here sans grandchildren. I'll wager it's the euchre club on their way to grab a hot dog before the program begins."

If nothing else, the Meditation Garden boasted tall oleanders and Mexican bird-of-paradise bushes. I was able to discreetly hang back from the pickleball crowd and catch tidbits of conversation.

"Are you sure it was her? She hasn't been on the play list for weeks. Too busy or something."

Who? What her? I listened some more.

"I'm telling you, she showed up, then darted off into the Men's Club building."

"You don't suppose—"

"Oh, I suppose all right. After the fracas they got into. But if you ask me, she could drive any man over the edge."

I bit my lip and took a breath. Whoever was talking had to be the anonymous caller who got Williams Investigations into the case when all the pickleball players had to be interviewed. But why not disclose who she thought the person was? Especially if that person could be the killer.

Come on. Come on. Spit out a name.

I had no choice but to make a subtle move to find out whose voice it was. Unfortunately, someone else made a move and there was nothing subtle about it. Thanks to Herb, I'd never find out who could identify the mystery woman and possible killer who snuck into the Men's Club building.

"Hey, cutie! Is that you? What'd you do? Take a short-cut here? Come on, lots of seats down front. By the way, where's that detective boyfriend of yours?"

"Um, talking with some people, I think. I was on my way over to the seating area."

"Well, it's this way. Follow me. Oh, and don't tell anyone I told you, but the hot dogs from that tot lot shindig are really good. Someone sprang for a brand name. And they've got all the fixings, too."

I shrugged and followed Herb. "Do you hear that?

Sounds like church music. Dear Lord. Did Cecilia bring her boom box?"

Suddenly "Ave Maria" was squelched by an explosive version of "Sunshine, Lollipops, and Rainbows." The music came from the tot lot and Lesley Gore's recording could be heard all the way to Milwaukee. In that second I knew we were all in trouble.

CHAPTER 36

Thanks to Kenny, the seating arrangements resembled a small amphitheater that had been sliced in half. Someone remembered to place a podium in front, complete with two vases that held an assortment of supermarket flowers.

It was anyone's guess who was going to conduct the memorial because the station manager, George, had outright refused, along with delivering the eulogies. And while my aunt was poised to send Howard and Bucky off to the netherworld with her final words, she wasn't prepared to run the entire program.

Without warning, a dizzying sense of nausea engulfed me. *My God! I'm going to get stuck with this, aren't I?* The expression "fight or flight" sprang to mind, and I scanned the area for a quick escape. At that moment Herb said something to me and I realized I hadn't been paying attention.

"What? Come again. Sorry, Herb. I didn't catch what you said."

"I said, 'I've got to get to the podium.' I'm the MC for this farewell party. Your mother stuck me with it a few days ago. You know me, I'm always there to come to the rescue."

My racing pulse slowed and I gave him a smile. "We're all grateful." *Some of us more than others.* "I'd better find a seat."

With that, I left Herb and scouted around for Marshall. No luck. It didn't matter. It was probably best if we were in different parts of the garden in order to pick up more gossip. I knew if I seated myself with my mother's friends, it would be the same gossip she reiterated to me on a daily basis. And if I seated myself near Herb's pinochle buddies, it wouldn't be gossip, it would be X-rated. Needless to say, when I saw an empty chair at the end of the fourth row, I grabbed it.

Seconds later Herb arrived at the podium. "The memorial service will begin in three minutes. Please turn off your cell phones."

And then, out of nowhere, the loudest boom possible. I could have sworn we were under enemy attack. And, in a way, we were.

An equally loud voice followed the boom. "The three-legged piggy race behind the seesaw and slide area is now underway!"

Shrieks, bellows, and screams followed. It was impossible not to hear that ruckus. I craned my neck to see beyond the bushes, but they were too dense. Just then, I felt a hand on my shoulder and I jumped.

"Lyndy! My gosh."

"Didn't mean to scare you. Someone vacated these seats so we're snagging them. You remember my aunt, don't you?"

I recognized the small woman with wire-rimmed glasses and short, graying-blond hair. "Of course. Good to see you again."

No sooner did I shake her hand than Herb introduced himself to the crowd. He made a point of sucking in his stomach, and I wondered how long that would last.

"Ladies and gentlemen," he said, "we are here to remember two of our community members who were taken from us much too soon, Howard Buell and Bucky Zebbler. To offer a poem about life's passing, please welcome—What?"

Shirley and Louise all but knocked him off the podium as they placed a small boom box on top of it and whispered something.

Then Herb spoke. "Not a poem. A song. Shirley Johnson and Louise Munson will be singing 'Swing Low, Sweet Chariot.'"

Shirley pushed a button on the box, the music came up, and she and Louise began to sing. They had gotten past the part about looking over Jordan when another blast from the tot lot shook the area.

This time it was followed by, "And now, the fun-filled potato sack race around the sandlots will begin!"

More screams and shrieks from behind the bushes as Shirley and Louise moved on with the song. Something about friends getting there first, but I wasn't sure. At any rate Shirley snatched the boom box from the podium and flashed a nasty look at the tot lot beyond the oleanders off to her right.

"Thank you, ladies, for that lovely rendering. And now, Mr. Paul Schmidt will read a poem he wrote about our dear departed friends."

Paul thundered to the podium and glared at Herb. "I already told you, it's not a poem. It's an analogy."

"Fine," Herb said, loud enough for the audience to hear. "I stand corrected. Mr. Schmidt will be reading an analogy."

Paul threw back his shoulders and lifted his head. "Death is a fishing trip, and you won't know if your pond is stocked until you cast that first line. But what choice do you have? Knowing Howard and Bucky, they brought along lots of bait."

With that, Paul walked away from the podium, and Lyndy poked me in the back. "What the hell was that?"

"I think it was a metaphor, but what do I know? I was a business major."

"Uh-oh. Look over there. That's your aunt, isn't it?"

"Uh-huh." Sure enough, Aunt Ina made her way down the middle aisle of the Meditation Garden turned amphitheater and strode to the podium with a solemn dignity usually reserved for state funerals.

I turned back to Lyndy. "God help us."

My aunt folded her hands and placed them on the podium. I'd only witnessed that move on two occasions: once during Passover, when she decided to reenact the crossing of the Red Sea, and once during a family dinner, when she decided my cousin Kirk and I should be privy to Lady Macbeth's sleepwalking scene. I think Kirk still has nightmares.

"Thank you, friends, for coming together to reflect on the lives of two gentlemen who gave our community—"

"*Hot dogs*! Get 'em now! And we've got a new batch of sauerkraut, too!"

Lyndy poked me again. "Isn't there some way we can get them to rein it in over there?"

I shook my head. "Impossible. Besides, my aunt will just get louder."

". . . a sense of pride in our own accomplishments and an appreciation for—"

"*The urinals aren't meant for hide and seek*. Please ask your grandkids to use them appropriately."

"Let me begin with Howard Buell, who was known for his—"

"*Porta-potties are not toys*. I repeat, they are not toys."

I don't know how my aunt Ina managed to stay focused amid the boisterous announcements from the playground party next door, but somehow she eulogized Howard and Bucky to the point where either of them could be nominated for sainthood. Then she asked everyone to close their eyes for a full minute and envision the two men "spinning songs into the great eternity." I figured she hadn't realized radio stations were now digital. I also realized now was a good time for me to stand and peruse the crowd.

I immediately recognized Betty from her brief visit to our office. She was seated in the last row next to George, and neither of their eyes were closed. At least not from the body language I witnessed. I swung my head around, pretending to be looking for someone so they wouldn't get suspicious. Two rows in front of them were Malcolm and a heavyset woman with her head bent down. I couldn't get a good look, but I presumed she was his wife, Penelope, the one in the Valentine's Day ad. In any case, both sat motionless, in meditational splendor. *That* or they had fallen asleep participating in my aunt's contemplative moment.

Off to the far left was Cindy Dolton, who looked as if she had fallen asleep during Herb's welcome. Not too far different from the book club ladies, who were also trying to stay awake.

Then, in a blink, George and Betty got up from their seats and continued their conversation by the benches at the edge of the Meditation Garden. It would be too obvious for me to leave the area, skirt around to the tot lot side, and listen in behind the clump of decorative bushes, but my options were running out. Instead I made my way to the podium, all but shoved my aunt aside, and shouted, "That was splendid. Simply splendid. Thank you, Ina Melinsky. And now, everyone, please take hands and join Shirley Johnson as she leads you in one of her favorite songs."

A dazed Shirley stood and approached the podium. "I only know gospel songs by heart," she whispered.

"Good," I whispered back. "Pick one. One with lots of verses. And keep going."

"You found the killer?" she mouthed.

"Maybe."

All of a sudden my aunt Ina turned to Shirley and said, "Let's sing 'This Little Light of Mine.' It's the only gospel song I know."

"Me too," Louise shouted as she made her way to the podium. "I love singing gospel songs." Next thing I knew, the three of them linked hands and began to sing.

And while Louise may have loved the music, she was as tone deaf as they come. And frankly, my aunt wasn't much better. Only Shirley could carry a tune.

Half the audience tried to sing along while the other half sat wide-mouthed and motionless. It was the perfect moment for me to make my move. I figured with all the distraction I could maneuver my way to that clandestine chat Betty and George were having. I was halfway to the backside of the oleanders when I heard Marshall's voice.

"What's going on?"

"Shh," I whispered. "I need to record a conversation."

The two of us slipped past the amphitheater and ducked behind a thick clump of lantanas that desperately needed trimming. Two voices, a male and a female, were clearly audible from the other side. I reached into my bag for my phone, having finally figured out how to record something, when I heard another voice. One I was all too familiar with.

"Phee! Marshall! What are you up to?"

In a voice barely audible, Marshall said, "Reconnaissance." Then, before my mother could say a word, he took her by the arm and leaned his head close to hers. "Best thing you can do to help is go back to your seat and act as if nothing's happening."

"Should I get Nate? Should I call for those bumbling deputies?"

I envisioned my one opportunity to secure viable evidence disappearing with every question my mother asked. "No, no. Go back and act natural. And don't say anything to anyone or it might cause a commotion. Okay?"

"You know me. My actions are the epitome of decorum."

Delirium, maybe, but not decorum. "Fine. Fine. We'll catch you later."

She gave us a quick hand wave and started back to the memorial service. In the background I could still hear the crowd singing.

"By the way," Marshall said, "Nice move getting Shirley to sing."

"It was either that or have my aunt Ina give her rendition of Blanche in *A Streetcar Named Desire*."

"Yeesh."

CHAPTER 37

Thankfully we could still hear the two voices coming from the other side of the bushes, only now they were joined by a third voice. Another woman.

"I'm betting money that third voice is Cornelia's," I muttered under my breath. I fumbled for my phone, found the fast app shortcut for recordings, and activated it. "Let's hope this works."

The first voice was a man's. It had to be George. "So far, so good. No one's made any connections and no one's about to. I want to keep my nose clean."

"Too late for that," the third voice said. "Look in the mirror. You're the one who elbowed himself into the operation. The money could only be split so many ways before anyone would make a profit. Too bad some people got greedier than others."

George's voice was gruff and raspy. "Give it up, Nellie. I'd hardly call that kickback a profit. More like hush money."

I gave Marshall a jab in the elbow and kept my voice well below a whisper. "Got my answer. He said 'Nellie.' The third voice is Cornelia's."

Cornelia continued and I held still. "Well, it certainly hushed up Bucky, didn't it? He was fine with his share of the moola, but what a Boy Scout when it came to protecting our assets."

"Protecting our assets?" Is that what they call murder these days?

I jabbed Marshall. This time he put up his hand in mock self-defense and pressed his mouth against my ear. "Seems we've got a boatload of nebulous confessions. One of us needs to get into the conversation so we'll have a witness to this baring of souls or whatever you call it."

"One of us as in *me*?"

"I'd just scare them away, hon. You've got a knack for making people trust you."

"But what if they—"

"Don't worry. I'm carrying a gun. And my permit. One shout from you and I'll be over there in record time."

"I have absolutely no acting skills."

"Even better."

I was about to cut through the bushes on some ridiculous pretense I hadn't yet worked out when I heard the words, "Scavenger hunt." Heard? I was practically deafened. Whoever made that announcement on the megaphone from the tot lot all but screamed out his lungs.

"SCAVENGER HUNT! WE'VE GOT PRIZES HIDDEN EVERYWHERE. PICK UP YOUR PLAY SHEET AND START LOOKING!"

I had barely processed the information when I was surrounded by screams and shouts.

"It's now or never," Marshall said. "Go for it."

I took a long breath, handed him my iPhone, which was still recording, and made my move. Just in time to witness four or five kiddies descending on the spot where George, Betty, and Cornelia were talking. Something wasn't right. Cornelia, aka Nellie from the garage sale, was a petite woman, but the Nellie talking to Betty and George was anything but. I was all wrong about the identity of the woman standing with George and Betty. I stayed back by the shrubbery and squinted my eyes to get a better look.

"There's nothing here, kids," George yelled. "Go the other way."

Like speed demons, the children left the area, only to be replaced by a few more. This time one of them raced over to George and, as loud as could be, said, "You're Grandma's neighbor! The one with all the sheets in the garage! She calls you the garage sale junkie. Is that 'cause you have so much junk?" The kid ran off before George could respond.

I laughed when I heard the word "sheets" and then it was as if all the puzzle pieces were coming together at once. This time I was certain I had an answer and not another theory. I raced to where George and the two women were standing and, before I lost my nerve, blurted out, "You're the one who killed Howard Buell. With Ursula Grendleson's scissors. The ones you bought from Betty years ago, when she ran Betty and Nellie's Bargains and bought out Ursula's estate."

To emphasize my accusation, I actually pulled a Harriet Plunkett move and pointed a finger at Betty. "That's why Ursula's fingerprints were still on them."

Betty didn't say a word, but George stepped forward.

"You're nuts," he said. "Why would I do something like that?"

"Because Howard and Bucky, along with Betty and Cornelia, wherever the heck *she* may be, had a nifty little scam going and you wanted in." Next I turned to the woman who I originally thought was Cornelia. "Why did George call you Nellie? Even with the noise from the playground, I heard him."

Silence.

"Never mind," I said. "Theft is one thing. Murder is another. Am I right, George?"

"What? Are you accusing me of killing Howard and Bucky?"

"Not intentionally, no. The way I see it, you wanted in so bad you threatened to blackmail Howard. What better time to have a private talk than at the crack of dawn, when you knew he'd be at the radio station. Unfortunately things got out of hand that morning. You knew those Gingher scissors were within easy reach because you'd been through those boxes and had stashed them in the storeroom." *And please don't tell me you've got another pair in one of your pockets.*

"That's insane. I got there around the same time you did. I was at Dunkin' Donuts, and they can vouch for it. The only thing you got right was that I stashed some of my stuff in the storeroom, including that box with the scissors. Those vintage scissors are worth something. *Were* worth something. The box was right on a front shelf, along with other boxes, marked 'Betty and Nellie's Bargains.'"

Then George glared at the two women. "I kept my mouth shut about the pilfering, but murder? Both of you knew I was storing those boxes at the station. So tell me, which one of you witches did it? I'm not about to hang for this."

I opened my mouth to say something when all of a sudden, Malcolm appeared out of nowhere. "Penelope! The damn thing's over. Where'd you disappear to? They're serving the refreshments, and for once they look pretty decent. Come on. You can chitchat later. Hurry up. I'm going back. They have stuffed mushrooms."

Penelope.

A million thoughts crossed my mind, but none of them made any sense. *Penelope?* My throat felt as if a frog had nested in it and wasn't prepared to vacate any time soon. I took a step toward the woman I originally thought was Cornelia Lynch. "You're Penelope Porter? You're Nellie?"

Oh my gosh. The apostrophe wasn't a mistake after all. There are three of them—Betty, Cornelia, and Penelope.

She didn't say a word, but that didn't prevent me from opening my mouth. "That must have been convenient for you, having your nephew handle the deliveries."

And most likely the actual product thefts, with some inside help at the stores.

Betty, who had been silent up until this point, finally spoke. "Don't say anything, Nellie. For all we know, she's recording everything we say."

I held both of my hands in the air and shook my head. "I don't have a recording device on me, but it's already too late as far as your Home Products Plus deal is concerned. Wonder why Cornelia isn't here? That's because she already confessed to it. And that's not all. She told them who killed Howard and Bucky. And if you want to know how I know, it's because I work for Williams Investigations and we're really tight with the local deputies."

Just don't tell Bowman and Ranston I said that. And while you're at it, pray to the gods Cornelia doesn't make an appearance.

"That witch!" Betty said. "I knew we couldn't trust her. She even panicked at the last minute and left that hatpin of hers somewhere in the radio station. Said she had everything under control. Under control, my you know what. She'll sell us out."

"Shh!" Penelope hissed. "You're making this worse."

As if things could possibly get worse, the next sound I heard was a screech that made chalk on a blackboard sound like a soothing lullaby. It was coming from the memorial service, and it was followed by a loud crash.

George, Betty, and Penelope charged toward the fracas, and I took off after them as fast as I could. As I ran, I heard the scavenger-hunting kids shouting, "Food fight! Food fight!"

Sure enough food was flying, but the correct words would have been "cat," not "food." Two women had knocked over one of the canapé tables and were at each others' throats. They were on the ground pulling hair, clothing, and anything that wasn't permanently attached. At one point a hair extension flew off and landed in a cup of herbal tea. I half-expected to see a set of dentures joining it.

In the middle of the melee Nate was frantically trying to separate the two lightweight contenders. Marshall thundered past me and, along with Paul Schmidt and Herb Garrett, the four men managed to pull the two women apart. And while the ladies could no longer throw jabs at each other or rip clothing to shreds, it didn't stop them from bellowing.

"You stinking harlot! You used him and killed him."

"Stop lying, you festering maggot. Howard would still be alive if it wasn't for you."

My mother, Myrna, and Shirley crowded in front of where I was standing. I imagined they wanted to get a better look.

"Which one is the maggot and which one is the harlot?" My mother poked me in the elbow.

"How should I know? That's Sylvia with the ripped boucle sweater and—Oh my gosh! I recognize the other one. She was managing yesterday's illegal garage sale. She's got to be Cornelia!"

I had barely made that connection when Betty and Penelope broke through the crowd. Betty's hands were flailing all over the place, but it was Penelope who made a mad dive for Cornelia.

She knocked her backward into Paul and screamed, "You miserable turncoat! How could you rat us out? Well, I've got news for you: I'm not about to rot in a prison cell for murder! I'll deny it. I'll get a damn good lawyer. And the next pair of scissors I get my hands on will be for you!"

Cornelia gasped and started to hyperventilate.

"The phone! The phone!" I shouted to Marshall. "Is it still recording?"

He shook his head and kept his grip on Cornelia.

"It doesn't matter, kiddo," Nate said. "The entire city heard that confession."

With one hand still firmly clamped on Sylvia, Nate

used the other to extricate his own phone from his pocket and make a call. No doubt to Bowman and Ranston. We were so engrossed in the murder confession playing out in front of us that no one noticed the rampage on the tasteful food table behind us.

Scads of children stuffed themselves with minimeat-balls, cheese puffs, assorted wraps, fried mushrooms, and pepperoni rolls. It was only when they dashed toward the dessert table that Shirley Johnson bellowed, "Make one move toward those pies and it will be your last."

CHAPTER 38

"Shoo! Shoo!" she said. "Go back to your own hot dogs and soda pop!"

Her directive came just seconds before the final megaphone blast for the day. "IT'S ROOT BEER FLOAT TIME! BRING YOUR SCAVENGER HUNT SHEETS TO THE ROOT BEER FLOAT BOOTH!"

The kids held their ground in front of the dessert table. I figured homemade pies and chocolate layered cakes probably looked a whole lot more appealing than ordinary root beer floats. In the distance I heard sirens. Lots of them.

Shirley didn't waste any time. "Hear that? Those are the county sheriffs and they're headed our way. If you don't want to get arrested for taking food that's not yours, leave now and go get one of those root beer floats."

She didn't have to say it twice. The kids raced off amid shrieks and bellows, but the screams weren't theirs. It was Cornelia, Betty, and Penelope spewing expletives at one another.

"Lordy, this is going to be one very long afternoon," Shirley said.

What happened next was one of those scenes I doubted my mind would ever erase. I couldn't tell how many sheriff and posse cars came screeching into the parking lot behind the Meditation Garden, but it had to be at least a half dozen, given the blue-and-red-light show.

Not a single person remained seated in the Meditation Garden. A few of them were gathered around the four women, who were still sputtering and swearing, but most of the attendees charged the dessert table with breakneck speed. Comments like, "Hurry up before they move us out of here" could be heard from every direction.

Sure enough, these folks must have been familiar with scenes like this because they were right. In a matter of seconds uniformed deputies, along with Bowman and Ranston, lit on the area like flies at a picnic.

"Everyone clear the area!" Bowman announced.

I witnessed women stuffing food into their bags and men stuffing it into their mouths. Lyndy and her aunt made their way to me and stood there, absolutely shell-shocked. I wasn't sure if it was because they were witnessing the now-verbal catfight my boyfriend, my boss, my mother's neighbor, and the local fishing aficionado were trying to contain, or the complete and utter chaos that engulfed us.

"Remind me never to move to a senior community," Lyndy said.

At that moment Ranston and a uniformed deputy marched over to where Cornelia, Penelope, Betty, and Sylvia were being restrained.

"We'll take it from here!" Ranston shouted. Then he looked around. "On second thought everyone remain in place. Remain in place." He motioned for more deputies, and within seconds uniformed deputies and posse volunteers surrounded the area.

Out of nowhere, George burst on the scene. "I was at Dunkin' Donuts. You can ask anyone."

No one paid much attention because Malcolm Porter was louder. "Penelope! What's this I hear about you wielding a pair of scissors? I thought I took care of any gambling debts you had with Howard when we were at the casino."

Penelope never got to answer. At least not right there and then. It took five uniformed deputies, plus Bowman and Ranston, to bring all three suspects and one admitted killer to the Maricopa County Sheriff's Station in Surprise.

Marshall, Nate, and I got to take part in that miserable process because our firsthand knowledge was paramount. I gave my statement and watched from the sidelines as Marshall and Nate conferred with the deputies.

I later learned—from my mother, who else?—that more deputies were called to the scene at Beardsley Recreation Center's park so they could take written statements from the attendees at the memorial and any grandparents from the tot lot who might have witnessed anything. According to what she observed, deputies were called in from as far away as Avondale and Buckeye.

It was past six and I felt as if I had been dragged

through a marsh. One of the posse volunteers offered me a cup of coffee, but I declined. My stomach was in knots and the pounding in my head wouldn't stop. Finally, at twenty minutes to nine, Marshall and I got into his car and he drove us home.

The light on our landline was blinking, and when I reviewed the machine there were three messages. I skipped over the other two and played the most innocuous one first—Lyndy's. She told me it was a regular fiasco at the park, but once the deputies left the scene, the book club ladies and a few very boisterous men, most likely Herb's crew, stayed around to clean up the Meditation Garden area.

The next call was from my aunt Ina, who informed me that she was going to take a spa vacation at the JW Marriott in Scottsdale because her nerves were shot from that "hellish nightmare."

"It's not your fault, Phee," she said. "How could you possibly have known we'd be surrounded by murderers and little hooligans?"

Finally the call I expected. My mother wasted no time filling in all the details and congratulating me for catching the killer. "Join us this coming Saturday at Bagels 'N More for brunch. If it's one of your workday Saturdays, tell your boss he owes you one."

"Did we catch the killer?" I asked Marshall. "I mean, Penelope admitted to doing Howard in, but what about Bucky? Betty said it was Cornelia. Not in so many words, but something about panicking and leaving the hatpin at the station."

"Trust me, hon, It's getting sorted out right now.

Meanwhile the only thing I want to do is take a warm shower and crawl into bed."

"Sounds like a good plan to me. Keep the water running."

We got our answers the next morning. Marshall via Nate and me via Augusta. That was what happened when you took separate vehicles and arrived at different times.

Augusta all but accosted me when I stepped in the office. "Good morning, Phee. Mr. Williams was in early. Early. It just so happened I came in early, too, in order to catch up on some paperwork, and he told me all about yesterday's takedown at the park. Remind me to stay away from those retirement places."

"Um, it wasn't exactly a takedown, but yeah, it was a debacle all right. I still don't know who got charged for what."

"I think I've got it straight. By the way, both men left for Sun City West to meet with those deputies, in case you were wondering."

"I wasn't. Let me get a cup of coffee. I'm dying to hear this."

Augusta was in her glory, expounding on all the sordid details. The kicker was that it all came down to an apostrophe as far as Betty and Nellies' Bargains were concerned. And poor Sylvia. She really didn't have a gosh darn thing to do with the murders. Cornelia apparently made that accusation to get herself off the hook.

Turned out it was purely coincidence that Sylvia was Ursula's star pupil and wound up with a pair of those Ginghers. And none of those deaths had anything at all to do with the live broadcasting versus the canned commercial shows that reaped in the advertising money. But money *was* the motivator.

"Here's the deal," Augusta said. "Straight from the horse's mouth. I mean, Mr. Williams."

"Tell me!"

"All six of them were in that Home Products Plus scheme together: Betty, Cornelia, Penelope, George, Howard, and Bucky. Not to mention Malcolm's nephew and some paid workers."

Wow. Right all along.

Augusta fluffed her bouffant hairdo. "Howard demanded a bigger share of the money and threatened to turn the women in if they didn't agree to his new terms. Penelope went to the radio station that morning to talk him out of it, but instead wound up killing him. They were arguing in the storeroom and she noticed the open box of goodies with the scissors in it. And get this! Her fingerprints weren't on the scissors because she still had on her gloves for pickleball. Ursula was probably the only person to have ever used those scissors until, of course, Penelope picked them up."

"So that anonymous caller was right about seeing a woman leave the pickleball courts that morning. But that still doesn't explain why Bucky was murdered. Or who did it."

"According to what Mr. Williams said, Bucky was in the radio station the morning Penelope killed Howard. He was in the room behind the storeroom and witnessed everything from an open space that linked them both. Penelope caught sight of him and told Cornelia and Betty."

"Wow. Those women must have been sitting on eggshells waiting for Bucky to blackmail them, huh?"

"Uh-huh. That's what Mr. Williams said. Imagine that!

The three of them drew straws to see who would pull off the dirty deed and ax Bucky."

"Let me guess. It really was Cornelia?"

"Yep. Mr. Williams thinks those women didn't tell George because they were planning on setting him up to take the fall. Of course that can't be proved one way or the other."

"How did Sylvia find out?"

"Oh, you're going to love this one. The murder weapon belonged to Sylvia. It was a hatpin she lost at some Victorian tea fundraiser. She posted reward information for that hatpin on her Facebook page and a bunch of other sites."

I was so engrossed in Augusta's exposé I hadn't realized I had finished my coffee. I immediately popped in another K-Cup. "Shirley Johnson was right. She said she saw Sylvia with that exact pin. Still, it doesn't explain how Sylvia knew it was Cornelia."

"Sylvia isn't the only one who posted on Facebook. Cornelia took a selfie and that hatpin was on the beret she wore. Sylvia immediately went to the sheriff's office."

"Holy cow! What a mess!"

"That's not all. Malcolm went into cardiac arrest when he found out his wife killed Howard. They had to rush the poor guy to the hospital. Want to know what Penelope needed the money for?"

"Um, her gambling debts?"

"Face-lifts. Body-lifts. Body sculpting. You name it. Mr. Williams couldn't keep a straight face when he told me."

Frankly, I couldn't keep a straight face either.

CHAPTER 39

Every news station from Sun City West to Mesa carried the story. It played out during the entire week with more and more salient details every night. It was as if we had our own version of Telemundo, only instead of seasoned actors, we had greedy retirees.

In spite of catching the perpetrators, I was furious at myself for targeting the wrong person. George might have been guilty of commercial theft, but not murder. No wonder I handled the accounts and not the investigations.

When Saturday morning finally rolled around I braced myself for the conversations that would take place at Bagels 'N More.

Marshall gave me a pat on the back, a quick kiss, and a grin. "I'll be thinking of you, hon, during my workout today. Got to admit I'm really enjoying the tai cheng class at the fitness center."

"The only exercise I'll be privy to is the moving of mouths, but I'm used to it."

The usual crowd was seated at the large rectangular table in the center of Bagels 'N More. A few of the snow-birds had joined my mother, Shirley, Lucinda, Cecilia, Louise, and Myrna. Across from them, Herb's rowdy crew was commiserating.

"Hell of a show, huh?" he said when I made my way to my mother's table.

I smiled. "Yeah, I guess you could say that."

"Hurry up, Phee," my mother said. "Your coffee will get cold. I had the waitress pour a cup for you. Drink it fast. You're not going to believe this."

"What?"

"Remember those hideous dolls with that threatening message?"

"Um, yeah, but in retrospect it wasn't all *that* threatening. It said to keep your mouths shut." *Always a bit of good advice.* "Why? Did someone admit to it?"

"Maybe part of a plea deal. Who knows? But it was Betty. Deputy Bowman called this morning to let me know. Betty Hazelton. Of all people. I never thought she could sew. Anyway, she must've found out we were kind of snooping around."

"Kind of? We were. We absolutely were snooping around. Was she the one responsible for that talcum powder?"

"The talcum powder came from Ursula's stuff. That forensic lab was right. The stuff was ancient. Ancient and harmless. But it was George who sent it. Can you imagine? What a self-serving shyster. He must have thought we'd find out about that scam of theirs. Tsk-tsk."

I took a huge gulp of my coffee and sat back. The next

ten minutes were spent listening to the ladies talk about the radio station murders, as well as anything else that came to mind, including recent restaurant reviews, allergic reactions to medications, and the grandest topic of all: the Greater Phoenix Broadcast Dinner.

"Myrna and I just got our tickets this morning. They arrived in the mail," my mother said. "It lists our table, but I'm not sure who we'll be seated with. I'm hoping it will be with the anchors from 99.9 KEZ."

Just then Paul Schmidt walked in and headed right to our table. "Good morning, ladies." Then he turned to my mother and Myrna. "Did you get your tickets for the broadcast dinner? I'm seated at table eleven."

Myrna nudged my mother. "That's our table."

"Wonderful," Paul said. "We can talk about the new show KSCW wants us to do. Guess our last little bout together was a success, huh? Just imagine what the next one will be like."

I did five mental eye rolls and clamped my mouth shut as Paul continued, "Are you planning on discussing any books about fish?"

My mother dropped the bagel she was holding. "The only book about fish any of us have read is *The Old Man and the Sea*. And it's not on our murder mystery list."

"No worries. Got lots of books you can read. Angling, fly-fishing, choosing bait—"

"We're not about to read or discuss books about fish, fishing, fish recipes, or, God forbid, bait."

"I have a wonderful recipe for a creamed lox spread," Cecilia said. "First you take—"

Myrna shushed her. "Paul can talk fish and Harriet and I can just talk."

My mother nodded in agreement. "Fine." Then she

turned to Paul. "Just don't bring any fishhooks or fileting knives to the radio station."

"Don't worry. For your information, I still can't look at a pair of scissors. I had to use a toenail clipper to cut off some tags on my new fishing vest. By the way, guess who's up for one of the awards at the banquet? Vernadeen Stibbens! I've got an in with the guy who's printing the programs. That's how I found out."

"Vernadeen Stibbens?" my mother shouted. "Why, she'll have to fly all the way in from Iowa."

"Good," I said. "Maybe she can collect all those house keys of hers that are floating all around. Her place had more turnovers than most winter rentals."

Herb moved closer to our table and leaned forward. "Vernadeen must be getting the award for putting the most people to sleep in the least amount of time. But enough about Vernadeen and fish. No offense, Paul. I've got some really important news. Bruce Bennings is going to be the new station manager now that George resigned. Bruce is on loan from Sun City, but here's the best part. I'm going to be DJing until they can hire new staff. Kenny and Kevin are joining me."

My mother looked at Herb and picked up her cup of coffee. "Too bad this is a family restaurant. I think all of us could use something stronger."

Later that afternoon when I told Marshall about the brunch conversation, he smiled and shook his head. "We're not getting roped into attending that broadcast dinner, are we?"

"Oh, heavens no! It's bad enough my mother wants us to help select Streetman's costume for the Christmas in July event. It's down to that bizarre hoop-skirt Christmas tree or some sort of green, Grinch-type thing. We are definitely not attending the broadcast dinner. If we have to drive to Las Vegas for the weekend in order to get away, we will."

"Um, uh, speaking of which, I don't know quite how to put this, so I might as well blurt it out now. I love our life together, Phee. It's everything I've wanted. But something's missing."

Oh no. He wants a dog. I never should have mentioned Streetman's costumes. "Do we really have the time and the commitment?"

"Not sure what you mean about the time, but we have the commitment. Besides, I'm not interested in a big shindig wedding. The only person I want to impress is you. I want a marriage, *our* marriage, not a Broadway production. So, um, will you—"

I know he finished the last two words, but my mind was reeling so fast I didn't think I heard them. It didn't matter. I was positive the look on my face was enough to give him an answer.

END NOTES

All of the cozy mysteries mentioned in *Broadcast 4 Murder* are real books, as is the non-fiction book, *The Art of Pickelball,* by author Gale H. Leach. That book is now in its fourth edition. However, do not try to find *Murder in the Family Crypt,* by Prussian author Hostalena von Honigsburg, because it exists only in the minds of the authors. And Aunt Ina.

The holiday season has arrived and bookkeeper/amateur sleuth, Sophie "Phee" Kimball, would love nothing more than to enjoy the comforts of her new home with her detective boyfriend near Arizona's Sun City West. Instead, her mother, Harriet, wants to showcase her chiweenie-chihuahua-dachshund, Streetman, in the Precious Pooches Holiday Extravaganza costume event. The festivities begin in October and end on St. Patrick's Day—with the winner starring in the St. Pat's Day parade. But things quickly turn an awful shade of green when Streetman uncovers a dead body under a tarp-covered grill in the neighbor's yard.

The victim is Cameron Tully, a seafood distributor working out of Phoenix, who died from ingesting a toxic sago palm leaf. Before the police can even find a motive and suspect, another Precious Pooch owner nearly dies from the same poison. With Harriet believing someone's targeting her and Streetman because of the costume contests, Phee will need a potful of Irish luck to sniff out a killer . . .

CHAPTER 1

Harriet Plunkett's House
Sun City West, Arizona

"Doesn't he look like the most adorable little dog you've ever seen?" my mother asked when I walked into her house on a late Wednesday afternoon in October. Signs of autumn were everywhere in Sun City West, including pumpkins on front patios, leaf wreaths on doorways, and someone's large ceramic pig dressed like a witch. Of course, it was still over ninety degrees, but that wasn't stopping anyone from welcoming the fall and winter holidays.

My mother had begged me to stop by on my way home from work to look at Streetman's costume for the Precious Pooches Holiday Extravaganza for dogs of all ages and breeds. And since her dog was a Chiweenie, part Chihuahua, part Dachshund, he certainly qualified. The contest made no mention of neuroses.

I tried to be objective, but it was impossible. "He looks like an overstuffed grape or something, if you ask me. And what's he doing? He's scratching at your patio door. Does he need to go out?"

"He's not a grape. He's going as an acorn. He'll look better once I get the hat on him. When he stops biting. And no, he doesn't need to go out. We were just out a half hour ago."

"Maybe he's trying to escape because you're about to put the hat on him."

"Very funny. It's not easy, you know. There are three separate category contests, and I've registered him for all of them—Halloween, Thanksgiving, and Hanukkah/Christmas. And just wait until it comes time for the St. Patrick's Day Doggie Contest in March. The prize for that one is almost as good as a pot of gold."

St. Patrick's Day? That's months away. And what's next, dressing him up as "Yankee Doodle Dandy" for the Fourth of July?

"Like I was saying, Phee, Shirley Johnson is making the costumes. You're looking at the Thanksgiving one. I can't make up my mind if I want Streetman to go as a pumpkin for Halloween or a ghost. Goodness. I haven't even given any thought to the winter costume. Maybe a snowflake . . ."

"Right now, I think he wants to go. Period. Look. He's frantically pawing at your patio door."

"He only wants to sniff around the Galbraiths' grill. A coyote or something must've marked the tarp, because, ever since yesterday, the dog has been beside himself to check it out. I certainly don't need him peeing on their grill. They won't be back until early November. I spoke to Janet a few days ago. She really appreciates Streetman and me checking out her place while they're up in Alberta. You know how it is with the Canadian snowbirds. They can only stay here for five months or they lose their health insurance. Something like that."

"Uh-huh."

"Anyway, how are you and Marshall managing with your move? That's coming up sometime soon, isn't it?"

"Not soon enough. I feel as if I'm living out of cardboard boxes, and Marshall's place is no different. We won't be able to get into the new rental until November first. That's three weeks away and three weeks too long."

Marshall and I had worked for the same Mankato, Minnesota, police department for years before I moved out west to become the bookkeeper for retired Mankato detective Nate Williams. Nate opened his own investigation firm and insisted I join him. A year later, and in dire need of a good investigator, he talked Marshall into making the move as well. I was ecstatic, considering I'd had a crush on the guy for years. Turned out it was reciprocal.

"Do you need any help with the move?" my mother asked. "Lucinda and Shirley offered to help you pack."

Oh dear God. We'd never finish. They'd be arguing over everything.

Shirley Johnson and Lucinda Espinoza were two of my mother's book club friends and as opposite as any two people could possibly be. Shirley was an elegant black woman and a former milliner while Lucinda, a retired housewife, looked as if she had recently escaped a windstorm.

"No, I'll be fine. The hard part's done. I can't believe I actually sold my house in Mankato. Other than autumn strolls around Sibley Park, I really won't miss Minnesota."

"What about my granddaughter? Did she get all nostalgic?"

"Um, not really. In fact, she had me donate most of the stuff she had in storage to charity. She's sharing a small apartment in St. Cloud with another teacher and they don't have much room. Besides, Kalese was never the packrat type."

My mother had turned away for a second and walked to the patio door. "Maybe you're right. Maybe he does need to go out again. Hold on. I'll grab his leash. We can both go out back." With the exception of the people living next door to my mother and busybody Herb Garrett across the street, the other neighbors were all snowbirds. Michigan. South Dakota. Canada.

"Dear God. You're not going to take him outside in that outfit, are you?" I asked.

"Fine. I'll unsnap the Velcro. Shirley's using Velcro for everything."

At the instant in which the sliding glass door opened, Streetman yanked my mother across the patio and straight toward the Galbraiths' backyard barbeque grill.

"I should never have taken the retractable leash!" she shouted. "He's already yards ahead of me."

"Can't you push a button or something on that leash?"

"I haven't learned how to use it yet. It's new."

I was a few feet behind her, running as fast as I could in wedge heels.

Her voice bellowed across the adjoining yards as she approached the Galbraiths' grill. "Streetman, stop that! Stop that this instant!"

The dog zeroed in on the tarp and gripped the edge of it with his teeth. My mother stood directly behind him and fiddled with the retractable leash.

"Now see what you've done," she said to the dog. "You've gone ahead and uncovered the bottom of the grill. I'll just shove those black boxes back a bit and put the tarp back down."

"Don't move, Mom!" I screamed. "Take a good look. They're not boxes. They're shoes."

"What?" My mother flashed me a look. "Who puts shoes under a grill where snakes and scorpions can climb in them?"

I bent down to take a closer look and froze. Streetman was still tugging to get under the tarp and my mother seemed oblivious to what was really there.

"Um, it's not shoes. I mean, yeah, those are shoes, all right, but they're kind of attached to someone's legs."

"What??"

If I thought my mother's voice was loud when she was yelling at the dog, it was a veritable explosion at that point. "A body? There's a body under there? You're telling me there's a body under that tarp? Oh my God. Poor Streetman. This could really set him back."

Yes, above all, the dog's emotional state was the first thing that came to my mind, too. "Mom, step back."

At that moment, she scooped Streetman into her arms and ran for the house. "I'm calling the sheriff. No! Wait. We have to find out who it is first. Once those deputy sheriffs get here, they'll never let us near the body."

"Good. I don't want to be near a dead body. Do you?"

"Of course not. But I need to know who it is. My God, Phee, it could be one of the neighbors. Can't you just pull the tarp back and take a look?"

Streetman was putting up a major fuss, squirming in my mother's arms and trying to get down.

"Okay, Mom. Go back to the house. Put the dog inside

and come back here. I won't move until you do. Oh, and bring your cell phone."

My mother didn't say a word. She walked as quickly as she could and returned a few minutes later, cell phone in hand. "Here. Take this plastic doggie bag and use it as you pull the tarp away. Don't get your fingerprints on the tarp."

"I'll pull the tarp back and take a look, but I won't have the slightest idea if it's one of your neighbors. I don't know all of them."

"Fine. Fine. Oh, and look for cause of death while you're at it."

"Cause of death? I'm not a medical examiner." I bent down, put my hand in the plastic bag, and gingerly lifted the tarp. I tried not to look at what, or in this case who, was underneath it, but it was useless. I got a bird's-eye view. Male. Fully clothed, thank God, and faceup. Middle aged. Dark hair. Jaundiced coloring. Small trickle of blood from his nose to shirt. No puddles of blood behind the head or around the body.

My mother let out a piercing scream. "Oh my God. Oh my God in heaven!"

"Who? Who is it? Is it someone you know?"

I immediately let go of the tarp and let it drape over the body.

"No, no one I know."

"Then why were you screaming bloody murder?"

"Because there's a dead man directly across from my patio. A well-dressed dead man. Here, you call the sheriff's office. I'm too upset. And when you're done, give me the phone. I need to call Herb Garrett."

"Herb Garrett? Why on earth would you need to call Herb?"

"Once those emergency vehicles show up, he'll be pounding at my door. Might as well save us some time."

I started to dial 911 when my mother grabbed my arm and stopped me. "Whatever you do, don't tell them it was Streetman who discovered the body."

"Why? What difference does that make?"

"Next thing you know, they'll want to use him for one of those cadaver dogs. He's got an excellent sense of smell. Don't say a word."

"You're kidding, right? First of all, the law enforcement agencies have their own trained dogs. *Trained* being the key word. No one's going to put up with all his shenanigans. And second of all, how else are you and I going to explain how we happened to come across a dead body under the neighbors' tarp?"

My mother pursed her lips and stood still for a second. "Okay. Fine. Go ahead and call."

The dispatch operator asked me three times if I was positively certain we had uncovered a dead body. I had reached my apex the third time.

"Unless they're starting to make store mannequins in various stages of decomposition, then what we've discovered is indeed a dead body. Not a doll. Not a lifelike toy. And certainly not someone's Halloween decoration!"

Finally, I gave her my mother's address and told her we were behind the house. Then I handed my mother the phone. "Go ahead. Make Herb's day. Sorry, Mom, I couldn't resist the Clint Eastwood reference."

My mother took the phone and pushed a button. "I have him on speed dial in case of an emergency."

All I could hear was her end of the conversation, but it was enough.

"I'm telling you, I had no idea there'd be a body under

that tarp. Sure, it was a huge tarp, but I thought it was covering up one of those gigantic grills. . . . Uh-huh. . . . Really? A griddle feature? . . . No, all I have is a small Weber. . . . Uh-huh. Behind the house. . . . Fine. See you in a minute."

"I take it Herb is on his way."

My mother nodded. "Do you think I should call Shirley and Lucinda?"

"This isn't an afternoon social, for crying out loud; it's a crime scene. No, don't call them. It's bad enough Herb's going to be here any second. Maybe we should go wait on your patio. We can see everything from there."

Just then I heard the distant sound of sirens. "Never mind. We might as well stay put."

My mother thrust the phone at me. "Quick. While there's time, call your office. Get Nate or Marshall over here."

"Much as I'd like to accommodate you by having my boss and my boyfriend show up, I can't. Marshall's on a case up in Payson and won't be back until the weekend. I think he took the case so he wouldn't have to be stepping over cartons. And as for my boss, Nate's so tied up with his other cases, he certainly doesn't have time to interfere with a Maricopa County Sheriff's Office investigation."

"Humph. You know as well as I do those deputies will be bumbling around until they finally cave and bring in Williams Investigations to consult."

Much as I hated to admit it, my mother was right. Not because the deputy sheriffs were "nincompoops," as she liked to put it, but because the department was so inundated with drug-related crimes, kidnappings, and now a highway serial killer in the valley that they relied on my boss's office to assist.

"Look, if and when that happens, I'll let you know."

The sirens were getting louder and I turned to face my mother's patio.

From the left of the garage, Herb Garrett stormed across the gravel yard. "Where's the stiff? I want to take a look before the place is plastered in yellow crime tape."

"Under the tarp." I failed to mention the need for a plastic bag.

Herb made a beeline for the Galbraiths' grill and lifted the tarp. "Nope. Don't know him. Damn it. I forgot my phone."

"Don't tell me you were going to snap a photo. And do what? Post it on the internet?"

Herb let the tarp drop and positioned himself next to my mother. "How else is poor Harriet going to sleep at night knowing some depraved killer is depositing bodies in the neighborhood? If I post it, maybe someone will know something."

My mother gasped. "Depraved killer? Bodies?"

"Herb's exaggerating," I said. "Aren't you?"

Suddenly it seemed as if the sirens were inches away from us. Then they stopped completely.

"Oh no," I said. "This can't be happening. Not again."

My mother grabbed my wrist. "What? What's happening?"

I took a deep breath. "Remember the two deputy sheriffs who were called in to investigate the murder at the Stardust Theater?"

"Uh-huh."

"Looks like they're back for a repeat performance. Deputies Ranston and Bowman. I don't know which one dislikes me more."

Well, maybe "dislike" wasn't quite the word to describe how they felt about me. "Annoyed" might have summed it up better. Over a year ago, when my mother and her book club ladies were taking part in Agatha Christie's *The Mousetrap* at the Stardust Theater, someone was found dead on the catwalk. And even though I wasn't a detective, only the accountant at Williams Investigations, I sort of did a bit of sleuthing on my own and might have stepped on their toes. What the hell. They're big men. They needed to get over it.

"Miss Kimball." Deputy Ranston's feet crunched on the yard gravel as he approached us from the side of my mother's house. "I should have taken a closer look at the name when I read the nine-one-one report. Seems you're the one who placed the call."

"Nice seeing you again, Deputy Ranston." I turned to his counterpart and mumbled something similar before reintroducing my mother and Herb.

"So, was it you who found the body?" Ranston asked.

I honestly don't know why, but for some reason, the man reminded me of a Sonoran Desert Toad. I kept expecting his tongue to roll out a full foot as he spoke.

"Um, actually it was my mother's dog. Streetman. He found the body."

Deputy Bowman cut in. "Just like that? Out of the blue?"

My mother took a few steps forward until she was almost nose to nose with Bowman. "For your information, Streetman and I cut across the Galbraiths' yard every day while they're still in Canada. We keep an eye on the house for them. Usually the dog is more concerned with the quail and the rabbits that hide under the bushes. He never as much as made a move toward the grill. Until yesterday afternoon. That's when he started whining to go over there. I thought a coyote might have marked it or left a deposit there."

"So you lifted the tarp up to check?" Bowman asked.

"Of course not. The dog was on a retractable leash and got to the grill before I did. He nuzzled the tarp aside, and that's when we saw the body."

Bowman gave his partner a sideways glance. "How big a dog is this Streetman that he could lift an entire tarp off of a body?"

"He's less than ten pounds," I said, "but very strong."

Bowman wasn't buying it. "Look, Miss Kimball, I know you have a penchant for unsolved crimes and I'm more likely to believe it was you who lifted the tarp."

My mother responded before I could utter a word. "Only for a split second and only because she happened to see someone's legs attached to the shoes that were beneath it. And she used a plastic bag so she wouldn't get fingerprints on the material."

Then the deputies turned to Herb and Ranston spoke. "Were you here as well when the ladies discovered the body, Mr. Garrett?"

"No. Harriet called me after dialing nine-one-one."

"I see."

Ranston wrote something on a small notepad and looked up. "The nine-one-one dispatcher gave us the Plunkett address. Would any of you happen to know the Galbraiths' address?"

"Of course," my mother said. "Something West Sentinel Drive. It's the small cul-de-sac behind us."

I could hear both deputies groan as Bowman placed a call.

"In a few minutes," he said, "a forensic team will be arriving as well as the coroner. I suggest you all return to your houses and stay clear of this property until further notice."

"Will you at least tell us who it is?" Herb asked. "For all we know, it could be one of our neighbors. Or a cartel drug lord who was dropped off here."

"Here? In Sun City West? That's what we have the desert for," my mother said.

Deputy Bowman forced a smile and repeated what he had told us a second ago. "Please go back to your houses. This is an official investigation."

"Will you be contacting the Galbraiths?" I asked.

Bowman gave a nod. "Yes."

I tapped my mother on the elbow and pointed to her house. "He's right." Then I whispered, "If you hurry, you can call the Galbraiths first."

Connect with Us

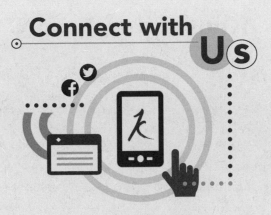

Visit us online at
KensingtonBooks.com
to read more from your favorite authors, see books
by series, view reading group guides, and more.

Join us on social media

for sneak peeks, chances to win books and prize packs,
and to share your thoughts with other readers.

facebook.com/kensingtonpublishing
twitter.com/kensingtonbooks

Tell us what you think!

To share your thoughts, submit a review,
or sign up for our eNewsletters, please visit:
KensingtonBooks.com/TellUs.

Grab These Cozy Mysteries
from
Kensington Books